THE HOUSE
THAT
SUGAR BUILT

DONNA BREWSTER

Second edition published by:
Second Sands Publications
18 North Main Street
Wigtown
DG8 9HL

ISBN 9780992657659

First edition published in 1999 by GC Books

The cover features an original drawing of the house by Toby Gough and is reproduced with his kind permission.

PREFACE

There was always something of a mystery about our house. We moved into 'Dunure' in 1971 and from that time local people told us little snippets of information about the property. Their stories never completely explained its history. We learned that the house had been built in 1833 and that we were only the fourth owners in almost 140 years. We were told that the man who had built the house, John McGuffie, had retired to Wigtown from the West Indies where he had made his money in tea, or in sugar, or in slave trading. It was whispered in the town among children of earlier times that the man had kept slaves in his cellar. The house had previously been called 'Barbados Villa' until the turn of the century when its second owners had renamed it.

These fragments of knowledge did not add up to a proper account of the place in a town where so much is known about houses and people for many generations into the past. Even the nineteenth century writings about the town containing descriptions of all its major properties seemed to avoid mentioning this particular house in detail, or at all. More than once, while puzzling over such omissions, I remarked to my husband that our John McGuffie must have been greatly disliked to have been thus ignored.

In the late 1980s, while I was involved in compiling local historical material for the primary schools of the area, an elderly lady in a nearby village concluded an arranged interview with the information, 'A black lady once lived in your house.' I was absolutely staggered by this statement, for no one had ever suggested the presence of a person of colour in the history of the house's occupants.

I began to ask the older people of Wigtown if they had heard of 'the black lady', and none of them had. Some of them had been born in the town and their parents would have been young adults when this woman was still alive. As I began to search local records in earnest, I found her easily enough. Her name had been present on every census entry of the household from 1841 to 1891 except the year 1851, the one entry I had previously seen. I finally found her name carved on a tombstone in Mochrum parish churchyard. The granite obelisk there named her as Margaret McGuffie, the daughter of Provost John McGuffie of Wigtown. She had died at Barbados Villa in 1896.

For ten years I have researched the life and times of this forgotten person. She was born in Barbados, the daughter of a 'free mulatto'. She came to live in Scotland with her father who eventually became the provost of this Scottish burgh. Margaret McGuffie lived in this house, my family home, for approximately sixty-five years, mostly during the fascinating years of the reign of Queen Victoria. After her father's death, she lived alone except for her servants, and after her death no one cared to remember for very long that she had ever existed.

My search to find and to understand her took me back into earlier centuries, slave-trading centuries, and it plunged me into unfamiliar cultures. It took my heart into Africa and my feet to Barbados. It led me to the streets and docks of Liverpool, to London and Edinburgh, and along the lanes around Penrith. It opened another world to my eyes, and at times it broke my heart. It has challenged my understanding of many aspects of life and, I hope and pray, has given me clearer vision and deeper compassion. I know that it has made me angry in the face of evidence of hypocrisy, intolerance and cruelty.

I gathered as faithfully as I could all the scraps of information that I could find relating to Margaret McGuffie, the people she knew, the places with which she was familiar and the fascinating period in which she lived. I studied local, national and international events that were part of her time. I inevitably developed impressions and formed opinions about people and places involved in the weaving together of this tale, and for that I make no apology. I only hope that these events as I have attempted to recreate them, and these people as I have portrayed them, bear strong resemblance to actual events and the very real people who lived through them.

Throughout history, enterprising people were lured to faraway places where riches were promised as a reward for the successful pursuit of silk, spices, gold and, as in this story, 'King Sugar'. That sweet commodity, so much prized, gave birth to ambitions and dreams: that people of humble origins could, with sugar's wealth, rise to positions of power and lives of luxury. Many such dreams were realised, but the sad truth is that the appalling misery brought by the slave trade, an integral part of economic sugar production, stole much of the sweetness from any of the stories connected with those times. This is one such story.

Donna Brewster, Wigtown, 1999

It is 24 years since 'The House that Sugar Built' was first published, and I truly gladly note that there is now much more public awareness and sensitivity about the subjects dealt with in this book than there was then. In acknowledgment of this, one word in the first edition has been 'starred' in the second. With all my heart, I hope that we keep learning, and changing, so that the past sorrows of inhumanity do not return and that present ones will one day be ended. 'Dunure' is no longer my home. The beautiful 'Barbados Villa', again a much-loved private family home, is not open to the public.

Donna Brewster, Wigtown, 2023

PART ONE

AFRICA

CHAPTER ONE

The hut of Amina, the Fulani woman, sat squat on the bank high above the dark river, a bank so high that when the river flooded during the times of the rains the waters did not reach the hut. The hut was safe from the river, but, for Amina, safe also because of the nearness of the water. If times of danger came, she could escape on the current down the river in her carefully hidden canoe, just as she had escaped to this safe place from further up the river with her baby son five rainy seasons before.

Amina's two children slept in the hut. Amina was watching over their peaceful slumber with quietness in her heart and love in her eyes. She was watching the long-limbed boy child with copper skin and the plump black baby girl.

Amina felt the heat of the day's beginning, the heavy, wet heat of a day when storms would blacken the sky, roar into the silence, shoot screaming blue flames of fire along the earth, smash the greatest of trees to the ground, and tear with angry fingers at the brush of the roof of the hut that was her safe refuge.

★

Abubakar, a nomad of the Fulani tribe, had been known for his great courage and disregard of pain during the Sharo, his initiation into manhood. He was the bravest, it was said, of a whole generation. The daughter of the powerful chief of the town Fulani people desired the tall fine herdsman, the proud, brave Abubakar, for her husband. She wheedled and she threatened, she bribed and she connived, until enough cattle joined the herd of the young nomad to make her father believe that Abubakar was wealthy enough to deserve the daughter of a chief.

A marriage was celebrated, but, after their union, the town bride would not consent to leave the comforts of her family's large compound for the sparser, rootless existence of her nomadic husband. Abubakar visited her when he passed near the town with the grazing migration of his herd, and in time four daughters were born to the couple.

One season, several groups of nomads met at the grasses close to Minna town, and there Abubakar shared his fire and nighttime tales with them under the open sky. One herdsman of the group had a very beautiful daughter who followed the herds with him. She was Amina. Amina loved the great expanse of sky that stretched over the wide grasslands on this north side of the dark river, and she loved also the gently rolling countryside south of the river where trees made soft and shady places, places for the camping. She loved her varied life in her varied world as she travelled with her father to serve his food, make comfortable his shelters and help with the cattle. Amina of youth, of softness, and of strange, light-coloured eyes, captured the heart of brave Abubakar. He took her to be his second wife and she left the tent of her father to follow and serve her husband as he moved eastwards with the grazing pattern of his large herd.

He knew without asking that his first wife would be angry, but his love for Amina made him careless of any concern apart from that of his new happiness. In the staying season he chose a place some distance from the town of his elder wife, a place on a high bank beside the deep river, and there he built a hut for Amina and her coming child. An area of thorns between the hut and the banking was shaped and cut to make an enclosure for a few animals. At the back of the thorn enclosure, he cunningly hollowed out, in the centre of a dense clump of the stabbing growth, a concealed space large enough to hold one cow. He also carefully made a dugout canoe with paddles and a pole. In the prow of the canoe, he made a little hidden hollow place with a covering. In this compartment he placed a flask of oil, a leather bag of meal, and a pouch of cowrie shells. He covered the canoe with thorns and left it near the river. He showed Amina all that he had made. She did not understand the purpose of the secret cow place or the need for the stored meal and oil in the canoe, but she smiled at Abubakar for the cleverness of his designs.

A son was born to Amina and Abubakar. He was given the name Shehu in a joyful celebration. The reserved manner of the proud herdsman, the bravest of his generation, melted as he rejoiced loud and long in his great happiness. Word of this reached the elder wife, and her bitter resentment that had smouldered within her since the news of Abubakar's second marriage was fanned by jealousy into flames of rage.

In another year a girl child was born to the contented couple. At that time the old town chief died, and disturbing stories began to reach the hut beside the river at the edge of the small encampment of nomads. The new chief of the town Fulani was the son of the old chief, the brother by the same mother of the angry elder wife of Abubakar. Nearby villages were being raided and captives were being sold to northern slave traders for prices that were enriching the household of the new chief. It was nearing the time when the cattle would begin their movement to the grasslands and Abubakar was anxious, because of the worrying news, to be moving.

On a still day, a hot and heavy day, in the year of the death of the old chief, Abubakar was working on leather thongs at his hut's entrance, his new daughter sleeping soundly in the shaded interior of the dwelling. Amina was below the hut at the river's edge with Shehu. She was washing clothes on a rock while her child threw pebbles into the pools that formed in the channel at low water time. She did not hear the horses approaching because of the height of the bank behind her, but sounds of confusion, of horses neighing, of screams, of clashing and of clanging came to her. With terror in her heart, Amina scooped up her son, scrambled up the bank, slipped into the thorn enclosure, and crawled into the secret cow place. She realised with a flash of understanding born to her in danger that horses could not penetrate the enclosure and human eyes could not see into her hiding place. She crouched there, shaking, with her hand clamped over the mouth of her crying child.

The sounds of horses and of voices grew fainter until there was nothing but the crackling of fire moving through huts made dry and brittle by the season of no rain and of Harmattan winds. Tears and sweat mingled in a rolling stream that poured from her eyes and her face onto her hands and her arms that wearied of binding into stillness the writhing, whimpering child. Finally, she crept out through the thorns to the smoking and ruined place that had been her sweet world.

Abubakar, the bravest of the Fulani herdsmen, a man to be desired by a princess, her own husband, lay, arms splayed out before him as if he had fallen while pleading or grasping. She turned him over. His face was contorted. A spear had pierced his throat. She ran into the hut and began to tear like a crazed thing at everything in sight. Making an anguished, gurgling sound, she searched every corner, every edge, for the infant that was not there. There was no sign of the baby, not even the clothes that had wrapped her.

She ran from hut to hut. Amid the smoking, smashed ruins, she found a few bodies, but life was gone. There were no people; there were no cattle. There was only a little goat that peered at her from around the corner of one of the huts. Nothing else moved or breathed but curling smoke and crackling flames in the shell of the empty village.

Her voice rose in a terrified scream just as the storm, as if it had been waiting to join her in chorus, burst upon her with a blinding flash, a mighty roar, and the howling of a wind matching in intensity the passion of her grief and rage.

That long black night she crouched, shivering, in the corner of her broken hut, rocking, moaning, howling, twisting her hands together, frantically rubbing her arms and legs. Water poured from the sky. All the waters that had flowed past the hut seemed to be returning in a night. The little goat crept near her for comfort. It ignored her frenzy but bleated with fear whenever the lightning flashed, the thunder bellowed, or a tree crashed to the ground.

By morning's first light the world and the woman were calm. She gathered all she could find of any value from the huts. She took a rope and a leather strap and fashioned a halter and lead for the goat. The goat had milk and she took some for the waking child who had slept, as only an exhausted child can sleep, through all the storms of the night. Her own milk had vanished with her baby.

She carried her bundles of cloth and some stores of fruit and dried fish, down to the bed of the river. She uncovered the hidden canoe, ignoring the pain of the thorns tearing her hands and arms. She dragged the heavy dugout along the sand into the channel where the river, already risen from the rains of the night, was flowing. She lifted the child, the salvaged goods, and then the goat into the canoe and, still in the half light of the early morning, she began to pole the dugout downstream and away from her home, from her husband's abandoned body, and from the memory of the girl baby snatched to slavery.

Amina made a pattern of her days of flight, driven by the need to be far from this place with her child. In the day's light, between storms, she poled her way along the edge of the increasingly swollen river. When she saw or heard signs of village life, she paddled further into the stream and ignored all calls from people on the bank who saluted her passing. She needed to find a place and a people far from her own and her husband's to be safe from the raids and from the anger of the first wife.

At the approach of night, she looked for sheltered places where she could land, drag her canoe ashore, tether the goat for grazing, feed her son, and sleep a little. Her husband's provision of meal and oil in the hollow place at the front of the boat, with fish and fruit, gave her enough food to last many days. She thanked her dead husband for his care for her. She asked the one God to protect her now and to guide her and Shehu to a safe place.

One day she paddled furiously into the middle of the river to avoid a large group of slithering alligators, and the current swirled her canoe until she found herself on the opposite, southern bank of the now-broadened river.

A quiet, grassy bank with a bustling village clustered behind it at last drew her to land. She was afraid, but weariness from the journeying was so great in her that she could go on no longer. She took her child from the canoe, tethered the goat nearby and, carrying her most precious bundle with Shehu in her arms, moved through curious people towards the market space in the centre of the village. She was alone and unprotected, but her fear vanished when she saw at the market the familiar face of a travelling Ibo trader who had often visited the village far upriver. She did the only thing that she could do. She bowed herself down at the feet of the astonished Ibo, grasped his ankles, and wept.

★

The Ibo trader was a good man. He accepted the helpless woman and her child as his responsibility. He found for her a broken, empty hut at the edge of his own family compound near the river's side. She mended the hut, installed her few possessions, and set her little goat loose to graze in the abundant grasses nearby. The child and the goat grew fatter, and Amina found calmness returning to her

11

heart like the quiet that comes to the world after storms. The Ibo trader, in the river village of many tribes, supplied her with her needs for a time until she grew stronger. His wives became her friends and their children played with Shehu in the shady green market place. The Ibo encouraged Amina to use her cowries to buy a cow and to sell her cow's milk and her goat's milk at the market. The tall, graceful Fulani woman with light eyes and skin like the sand of a golden desert became a familiar sight at the market place as she sat beside her great bowls of steaming, frothy milk, seeking trade. Shehu remembered nothing of their life before this place. The hut beside the river and the grassy place under the great baobab tree where he and his friends scampered in play with kids of goats, were the places of his home.

The Ibo trader treated Amina with respect and kindness. He did not take her for his wife or look into her eyes at all. He cared for her as he would for his sister who was the daughter of his own mother.

★

To the south of the village by the river, more than a day's journey away, the softly rolling grassy land with its foliage of bushes and little trees folded away under a canopy of towering trees at the edges of the rainforest. Inside the darkness of that world hidden from the open sky, in the village of her husband's people, Iye the Ibo woman shook with terror when she realised that the birth time was near. She knew from her great size and from the tumbling and twisting of too many limbs inside her that she would bring two children to birth. Others in the village had watched her closely as she grew so large with child, and she had heard their dark mutterings. She pretended that she suspected nothing, but now she must act. She would not allow her children to die, pronounced the offspring of an evil one by the powerful chief elder of the village. No hands must seize her newborn to snap their tiny backs; their lifeless forms must not be left in jars in the jungle to be eaten by the creatures there; she must not be driven into the terror of that dark world to fend for herself until killed by a beast on the prowl.

She had prepared her unsuspecting husband for weeks now for what must happen. She had begun by whining and wheedling in the nights until he had wearied of her sulking and pleading and agreed that she be taken to the village of her mother's people, a good distance away, for the time of her childbirth. Now, with her husband gone on a hunt in the forest, and with her time almost at hand, her terror drove her into action. She gathered a bundle of clothes and food. She chose a charm to carry for protection. She left word with her neighbour that she had gone to her mother, and she slipped into the secret world of the forest. She headed north and west, not north and east towards her mother's village. She moved with fear nipping at her heels, fast, as fast as she

12

could, and even faster. She had no fear in her of enemies, of spirits, of animals, or of snakes; her all-engrossing dread was that of losing her babies.

As she came out from beneath the canopy of trees on the second day, into the heat of the sun and the blazing of its light, the pains of the birth began. She crouched in the long grasses off the path until the pains passed, then resumed her flight with grim desperation to be yet farther from her people.

In the night, in a deep hollow she had found beneath the roots of a clump of gnarled trees, she strained and gasped and delivered a perfect boy child who howled his arrival to the stars of the black sky. Iye rested quietly, then as day came, she gazed at her soft, nuzzling newborn son, hoping that she had been wrong. The gripping pain began again and, crying out with despair as much as from the powerful force that seized her body for a second time, she gave birth to a baby girl.

She wiped the babies and herself with soft grasses, and she wrapped the infants in strips of cloth she had brought with her. She sat with her back against a palm, and she put the babies to her breasts. The children were soft and beautiful, like little flowers at the first, perfect opening of the bud. The boy, eyes shut tight, sucked furiously at her, his fists clenched. The little girl's open eyes fastened on the face and on the heart of the new mother. Iye wept.

After strength had returned to her, the mother of twins walked slowly on with her warm bundles of child, until she saw the signs of village life in the distance. She found a well-branched tree away from any path and, with fallen palm fronds she had collected, she made a simple cradle which she wedged into the branch at her head's height. There she securely tied her newly fed and sleeping son. She placed the charm on him. The beautiful girl baby she wrapped up entirely, covering even her head in cloth, and she moved into the village holding the precious bundle close to her.

The market square of the village was full of life, of people and animals, of sounds and smells, of shouts and laughter. She moved through it all as in a dream until she saw, beneath a great baobab tree, a beautiful Fulani woman sitting beside large bowls of frothy milk and smiling as she watched a copper-skinned child playing in the misshapen roots with a goat's kid.

The Fulani woman looked up to see the Ibo woman standing in front of her, staring at her. She was used to people staring because of her unusually light-coloured eyes, so she nodded to the stranger, and she wondered what was in the bundle the Ibo would offer for sale. Iye the Ibo handed Amina the Fulani her bundle and then disappeared through the market crowd back the way she had come, back to the tree that held her baby son.

Amina slowly unwrapped the tiny, warm mound of cloth, and she found within the soft coverings a perfect baby girl looking up at her. The god who had brought her and Shehu in peace to this green place had now sent her a girl child to replace the baby lost to slave raiders from the hut made by Abubakar. She gave him thanks in her heart.

Her children had grown together. As Amina watched Shehu and Minna sleeping in her hut, she remembered the paths of her life that had brought her to this place. There had been sadness, but now there was a certain kind of contentment. She had children to love and care for; she was safe. Amina no longer feared the coming of the season of storms.

CHAPTER TWO

Every year during the dry season, Iye the Ibo woman came again, alone, to the village beside the dark river where she had left her baby. She brought gifts to Amina and Shehu, to her own child Minna, the Ibo girl child who bore the tattooed marks of the Fulani on her face, and to the Ibo trader who served as interpreter between the two mothers of Minna.

In her Ibo village in the rainforest, her husband had received his son and had not doubted her story that she had given birth to the single child in her journeying towards her mother's home, or that it had taken several days for her to gather enough strength to find her way back to her own hut. Iye ignored the muttered suspicions of her neighbours and the dark glances of the village elder. As she gave her milk to the boy baby, she thought of his twin, the baby safely far away. Her husband died in the next year, and she took her son to live in the village of her mother. No one there knew of the too-large pregnancy.

Now she came, each year, to feast her eyes upon the little girl who grew strong and fat on the milk from Amina's cow, the child who bounded about in play under the great baobab tree with the goat's kids and with her teasing brother Shehu. The two mothers were as sisters in their mutual love for the lively child Minna, and in their gratitude to each other for the gift of her life.

Minna grew older and abandoned her playing to enter the dreaming thoughtfulness of approaching womanhood. In the busy market place she often sat alone in the world of her own imaginings, her back resting on the trunk of the giant tree, children and animals playing about her feet.

Amina and Iye together discussed the future of the child. They decided that Minna should accompany her Ibo mother into the forest for a visit to the Ibo grandmother to hear the stories of her tribe and the ways of women, as was the custom. For the journey time, about four days, Minna was to abandon her Fulani clothing and wear Ibo cloth. Beads of fine work and food from the market for the grandmother were sent as a gift from Amina.

Iye and Minna moved northwards towards the dark world of the forest. They passed through land of small trees and tall grasses, over hills and into valleys, and waded across streams of shallow water. They saw the dark outline of the great forest ahead and, as they moved under its canopy and the bright sky disappeared, the child panicked. Then, as her eyes grew accustomed to the gloom, the playful monkeys and bright birds in the branches and among the heavy vines near the path made her laugh, and she forgot her fear.

They came to a broad and deep river and the Ibo woman signalled the child to wait while she disappeared off the path. She returned with two large gourds obviously hidden earlier, and she showed the amused child how to lie across the hollow while paddling herself to the opposite bank. There, the gourds were hidden again, this time in bushes behind an outcrop of rock back from the river's bank.

On the second day, they came in the evening darkening to a village which they skirted carefully until they reached a hut on the edge of the farther side. No one seemed to be about, and the sounds of drums, singing and dancing feet in the distance explained the general air of desertion around the huts. They crept inside where, in the gloom, Minna could see an old woman, a blind old woman, her head turning slightly sideways as if to see their approach through her hearing.

Iye spoke quietly to the old woman who gazed at her with sightless eyes, but with an astonishment in her expression. Minna was pulled forward and soon the old, wrinkled, bony fingers of her grandmother were stroking her face, gently probing at her eyes, her forehead, her cheeks, her nose, her lips, her chin, her ears, and even feeling her teeth. Her hair was patted and pulled;, the hairline followed right around her head. Minna could not stop herself from laughing, and the old woman laughed with her.

Then the sightless eyes began to leak tears, and words that Minna could not easily follow began to pour from her lips. In a stream they came, on and on like the rains. Minna felt in them the drama and the force of this passing on from the old to the young all that is known and that must forever be told and known again, but she understood only a little. She did understand that she was the young and that this old, scrawny, bony, leaky, rasping person was part of her being, of her past, and connected with her future, so she sat motionless and took in the sounds of words she did not comprehend with the conviction that it would be her task one day to pass on to another what she would then know.

After the old grandmother had fallen asleep with the contentment of her work done, Iye and Minna ate some food and prepared to sleep. In the night the dancing, singing, and drumming grew louder until it seemed that a procession was passing by the opening of the hut. Iye stood in the entrance to watch, allowing Minna to peer carefully out, hidden behind her mother. Men in leopard skins with wooden masks of terrible faces danced by, followed by young men of Minna's age, obviously celebrating their entrance into manhood. As they chanted and roared in their festive abandonment, one of the boys moving by the doorway looked at Iye and grinned. Minna saw that his face was her face. She grew hot and cold all together. The face that had been reflected to her from the face of a boy stranger dancing in the firelight in a village distant from her known world. She was not one person, but two.

Before light came in the morning, the Ibo woman and the girl fed the grandmother, left her with more food beside her for the coming days, and crept back into the jungle to begin the walk northwards. Minna moved quickly and lightly, longing to see the sky beyond the jungle canopy again, eager to share with her Fulani mother and Shehu the stories of what she had seen. She had been touched by her own grandmother and had discovered the twin face of a brother. She had travelled into the strange world of the hidden forest, and she had slept undiscovered in a village of the Ibo.

When Minna reached the stream of the hidden gourd place ahead of Iye, she ran on to drag the vessels to the bank, wanting to please her Ibo mother by her remembering the hiding place and with her helpfulness. She was smiling back up the path towards the approaching footsteps of Iye when a canoe shot suddenly and silently out from behind the curved upstream bank. A large black arm grabbed her from behind and she was lifted, howling with terror, into the dugout before the Ibo woman, who screamed with fear and rage, could reach her. As the canoe rolled away from the bank, Iye plunged into the water, grabbing frantically at the boat with her bare hands. Two men held the struggling girl as another raised his pole high, then brought it down with a crunching sound onto the head of the woman. Iye disappeared under the dark green water.

★

The child was pinned into the canoe's bottom by the stout legs of the huge man who had snatched her from the bank with the ease of an alligator clasping a fish. There was a screaming and a sobbing inside her head and from her heart, but her lips allowed no sound to escape them. With animal cunning, she tried to watch the passing banks to see detail, to remember, so that she could find her way back. She longed for beautiful Amina, for teasing Shehu, for warm milk, for the smell of her hut, for the noise of the market place under her baobab tree, and for the bright light of the sun. The Ibo mother was gone, but she must get back to her Fulani mother somehow.

The darkness of the stream's channel in the forest broadened out, and the sky opened above the canoe. They came to a great stretch of water, greater than she had ever seen. The men set their poles into holes at the bottom of the dugout and hung cloths on them with ropes. As the wind billowed into the white cotton, the canoe seemed to use its power, as a gliding bird uses its wings, to float across the broad black river. It would be too far for Minna to swim back across when she could get free.

A clearing on the other side showed signs of life, and men appeared, calling out to those in her canoe. The dugout was pulled up onto the banking by those on the shore, men with the faces of another tribe, the same kind of faces as those of her captors. She was peered at and there was much noise of the clattering of tongues she could not understand, neither the sound of Amina's words, nor those of the Ibo trader or the blind grandmother.

Men, women and children were tied and penned at the edge of the clearing, like animals waiting for slaughter. She was tethered tightly, arms together and ankles hobbled, at the edge of the pen. She curled up into a ball and slept, exhausted by her terrors and her watching and her despair.

In the morning they were moved off after a rough feeding of gruel and water, prodded into motion by spears and knocked into an orderly line by clubs, along a path that led again into the deep darkness of the rain forest. Staggering and stumbling, moaning and crying, the captives were kept moving as quickly as a chained line of people were able to move. Persistent stumblers who delayed the progress were speared and removed from the line, which then continued to move on past the discarded bodies. Smaller children who could not keep up the pace or howled their misery were also speared and left abandoned. A mother who screamed out her grief as her child was thus dispatched soon lay dead beside his body.

Minna was young but strong, and she kept the pace. Numbed by the horror of it all, she kept her eyes forward and gazed hungrily at the scenery beyond this path of blood and cruelty, trying desperately to imprint the sights on her mind so that her memory could lead her back when she could escape. She could leave no marker at forks in the trail, so she tried with all her might to memorise every join and turn until the hopelessness overwhelmed her with the awareness that they had gone too far for her to remember her way back anymore. She fixed her mind on a picture of her village under the sun's light. Her memory of the place would help her find her way back sometime, somehow.

For days and days there was the clattering, jolting movement of the line of running prisoners followed by dark forest nights of heaving, exhausted sleep. They finally came to a massive wall, covered with green creeper and rising high above the jungle floor. The captors danced and sang, pumping their spears up and down in triumph and rattling the chains that bound their prizes.

From an entrance through the wall came others, people like them, who sang and danced in answer, gathering drums beating a powerful rhythm to accompany the procession. Into the gateway they passed, and the captives found themselves to be at the beginning of a long, broad avenue that went straight on, as if forever, into the heart of the greatest city they had ever seen. Fear was swallowed up in awe. Men, women and children, dogs, goats and monkeys gathered to cheer before the huts along the road as the line of slaves jogged past to the tempo of the drums. Along the way there were tall sharp stakes on which were impaled bodies or heads of bodies. Even these seemed to be grinning and jeering. There was a smell of blood, of death, of grief, and of deep, dark terror in the place. The young girl thought she must be dreaming in an ugly sleep or that she must be dead and in a place of torment.

The road came together with other roads in a large central space around which was clustered a group of magnificent, pillared buildings declaring, by their size and ornateness, that here dwelt a leader of power and wealth. The main building glowed in the light of the sun reflected off elaborately decorated copper panels covering the pillars.

The procession halted and silence descended on the noisy crowd. From the main doorway of the building the gathered throng were facing came two men with coral strands around their necks, each bearing a pole surmounted by the handsomely carved shape of a vertical fish. Between the pair walked a king, a powerful-looking man with a tall coral crown and bands of coral ringing his neck from his chin to his chest. The attendants solemnly led the king to a carved ivory throne shaded by rich silk hangings. After he was seated there, a group of richly dressed men, women and children gathered around him. Separating the throne and royal household from the assembled people of the city with their captives was a pavement of large, round stones.

The king smiled and nodded towards the crowd that filled the open central space at the heart of his great city. At this sign of his pleasure, the silence was shattered by an ear deafening roar, the surge of sound made by a multitude of voices accompanied by the beating of many drums. A chant began, 'Oba! Oba! Oba!' Everyone began to dance to the rhythm of the drums and the chant, and the captured people from the other side of the great black river, caught up in the noise and excitement, were chanting and dancing with the rest, their clanking chains working to the pulse of the drums.

The newly captured slaves were pushed to the front of the crowd and signalled by their guards, who prodded and pulled at them, to run before the king. The crowd roared afresh at the sight of the prizes to be presented to their sovereign in a running line before his throne.

When Minna reached the stones, the toes of her foot stubbed into them with such force that she yowled and collapsed in a heap, bringing those tied before and behind her sprawling and crashing to the ground in a tangle of flailing limbs and chains. She could not know, as she swooned, that guards and royal attendants had panicked, screamed, and begun flogging the fallen slaves. Some of the floggers had waded into the chaos of falling bodies and had themselves, tripping over legs and arms and heads, become part of the tangle, a writhing heap of helplessness right in front of the solemn throne.

She did not know, either, that the Oba's most precious and favourite little son, seated on his own miniature ivory throne near his father's feet, had started to laugh with his squealing, infectious laugh and, as the crashing and tangling had increased, had laughed harder and harder until the tears had run down his fat little cheeks, or that the Oba, watching the little boy, had begun to laugh also and had infected the entire household with his merriment until the whole of the royal group had been as helpless in their mirth as the slaves were in their tangle.

★

Minna woke to consciousness in a large, cool hut. Her face was being gently bathed with sweet-smelling water. Brightly clad women and children were gathered around her, watching her curiously. They were smiling and chattering. Her foot throbbed. She fainted again.

The Oba's little son wanted the new girl slave as his companion, for she had amused him. Minna was tended carefully, fed, examined by gentle hands and then decked out in fine cloth before she was introduced to her young charge. She quickly realised that in the occupation of amusing this powerful child lay not only her responsibility, but also her safety.

She learned words so that she could speak with the small prince and follow his commands. She learned ways to make him laugh. She knew that if she tried to leave the central palace area of the city, the beautiful, sumptuous royal place of her confinement, her life would be worth nothing. She was cautious, obliging and attentive. And she was very funny. She tried not to think of Amina who would be grieving the loss of her, of Shehu, of her dead Ibo mother, or of the quiet she found beneath the reaching branches of the baobab tree in the otherwise lively market place of the village that had been her home.

There were other servants of different tribes who shared with Minna the sleeping hut in the Oba's palace complex. One was a timid, quiet girl who answered her questions about life in the city kingdom.

'Were the people hanging on the stakes because they had been bad?'

'They were put there to appease the gods.'

'What is the fish sign on the poles?'

'The sign of the nation of this king.'

'Who are the great bronze heads at the shrine?'

'They are the Obas from earlier times.'

The girl also told her strange tales from her own home place deeper in the jungle to the south of the city. She said there was an edge to the land, a great blue water beside it. She said that men came from another world to the edge place, men with white skin, and that some of her people had disappeared with these men in huge sailing canoes into the blue water, never returning. She said that many ages before, at the time of the making of the beautiful bronze heads of ancient Obas, her people had learned from other people of white skin of a god's son, greater than the little Oba prince and more deeply loved, who had died on a crossed stake near the wall of a wonderful city somewhere else. He had been put on the stake by enemies, and he had died, but he had killed the death and had

20

come alive again. She said that the secret sign of his followers was a fish, but not the fish of the Oba's kingdom, she thought. Minna did not know if there was truth in the stories of her new friend, but she kept the strange secrets as the bond of their friendship.

★

Minna's friend came into the sleeping hut late one night troubled by news. The Oba's son child was ill, and Minna must not go to amuse him in the morning. For days Minna was told to stay in the hut, and the city became a tense, silent place. Drums then began to throb all around, with an ominous, heavy beat like a slowing down heart. The friend came in one night weeping. 'There must be a sacrifice. Pray to the god's son.' Minna did not understand.

In the morning, attendants came to bathe her with sweet water and scented oil. They put rich clothes on her and wound beads around her neck and her arms. They brought one of the royal child's ornaments and hung it over the beads. Women and children were weeping around her, and Minna realised that it was for her they wept, not for the sick child.

She was taken out in a litter accompanied by drummers and chanters as guards, and she saw a man waiting for her, a large knife in his hand, in front of the entrance to the prince child's hut. Her friend wailed as the litter passed by her.

Suddenly, above the sound of drums, she heard a thundering, cracking sound, and booming like the thunder of the storms. Horsemen of the Yoruba, shooting blasts from metal poles in their hands, swarmed into the area of the Oba's palace from all sides. Her litter crashed to the ground, and she was scooped up by one of the riders. She saw her friend fall beneath the horses' hooves and fail to rise. There were screams and explosions and clashes of metal, but it was all like a dream to her.

The Yoruba horsemen escaped back through the wall of the city with loads of captured booty, and they rode through the forest until they came to its edge, the place where there was for Minna again sky over her head and grassland under her feet.

They turned the wrong way, though, away from the dark river and further westwards for many days. Other groups of horsemen gathered with more captives. Again, she was moved in a chained line, a growing line of captured people of many tribes moving somewhere away, always away, from her known world.

The land changed. It became dry and scrubby of growth. They turned southwards so that the sun was not followed but rose to one side of them and sank to the other. One day the air smelled different. Wind blew in her face and her licked lips tasted salty. They came to the edge of the land. The stumbling, shuffling, jogging line of captives was transfixed by the view of water reaching so far that they could not see the other bank, of huge, rolling waves making a noise like thunder as they crashed in rage against the white sandy shore. The light and the sound were blinding and deafening, as in the worst lightning flashes and thunder rolls and crashing of trees in a jungle storm. Only there was no storm. The light was from the sky and the thunder was from the water.

Some distance away in the water was a ship rolling about on the huge waves. Minna saw that it was larger than even the largest canoe on the greatest river she had seen. Poles holding the sails on the ship were as tall as the tallest palms near her village, nearly as tall as the trees that formed the canopy of the rainforest.

On the shore was a large pen for the men captives with a smaller one for the women and children. Men with the explosive rods in their hands were all around. Water and food were brought, and the tired captives settled to wait for whatever would come.

At the next day's light, a large canoe came to the shore from the great boat. It was paddled by many men, but one man who wore strange dark clothing did not paddle. He wore heavy garments that almost fully covered him, and a shaped cloth, not like a crown, was on his head, and Minna was shocked when, as he came near, she saw the white colour of his skin. She was afraid, but she was also filled with curiosity. The servant of the Oba who had been her friend had spoken of men like this in her tales, and Minna had not understood her.

The women were pulled out of their enclosure to stand before this man. The covered up white man moved down the line of women and children, examining them closely: their teeth, their eyes, their breasts, their stomachs and even below, between their legs. Minna shivered with fear and embarrassment. She would not look into his eyes when she felt his hands on her face, but when he examined her teeth, she glanced up and discovered that his eyes were light, like the eyes of Amina. He kept looking at the tattooed marks on her cheeks, and feeling them, as if puzzled. He spoke to the Yoruba man beside him, looked again, shrugged, and continued with his interrogation of her body's secrets. She knew that he could not understand how she looked like an Ibo but was marked with Fulani marks. She was glad that he did not understand her; she could keep her knowledge and memory safe from his prying, probing hands.

Certain women, always the younger and fitter ones, and older children were finally selected from the line. Minna was a chosen one. In small groups these selected ones were moved down the white sandy incline to the edge of the pounding surf where they were roughly shoved through foaming waves and hauled aboard the large canoe waiting there. As strong paddles began to move the canoe out towards the huge ship lying in deeper water, some of the women wailed, shrieked, even screamed.

Shehu had told Minna that only women showed fear or pain, happiness or sorrow, to others. She struggled now to maintain her composure, to retain her pride, to stop herself from screaming too with fear and grief. She longed as never before for her light-eyed mother Amina, for the tormenting teasing of Shehu, for the shade of the wonderful baobab tree, but with every stroke of the paddles and every plunge of the canoe into another wave, she knew with more certainty that she could never find her way back. She knew, with a great, cold block of terror filling her heart, that her sweet world was gone from her forever, that it had been gone from the moment that the head of Iye, her Ibo mother, crushed by the smashing of the pole, had slipped below the green waters of the gourd-crossing river.

PART TWO

BARBADOS

CHAPTER THREE

The ship's surgeon hauled himself aboard the Polly with the greatest of difficulty. The blasting heat of the African sun, even offshore where breezes lightened the oppressive furnace-like burning sensation in his lungs, was killing him. Duncan envied the blacks their light draping of bright cottons, even the bound slaves in their nakedness, but he would succumb to the heat in dour misery before he would expose his tender pink flesh to the searing gaze of the southern sun.

He dragged his completely and heavily clothed frame across the deck and disappeared into the oven of his cabin, leaving his self-important young surgeon's mate Morris to oversee the hauling onto the deck of the day's acquisition of slaves. The quota was filled, and they could sail now for the West Indies. While the new slaves were being branded, manacled and separated by sex and age into divided compartments below the deck, he would stay in his cabin. Better the stifling heat in his cramped accommodation than the stench of burning flesh in his nostrils, the screams and groans in his ears from the wretched captives while they were marked, chained and sorted like beasts in the marketplace, or the sight of the leering crew members searching among the female section of the loot for a young mother or a girl child to use during the voyage.

Once Thomas Duncan had been full of a sense of purpose about this triangular passage, satisfied to contemplate the reward of his work at the journey's end; now he was sickened to think that there could be profit to him or to any of the scum with whom he sailed in such a business as they conducted. The knowledge that two legs of the three of his hated contract remained to be completed filled him with utter, inconsolable melancholy. He wished nothing more now than to be able to fly back to the land he had spurned in pursuit of his notions of becoming a qualified and respected physician. As a penance for what he had done, he would abandon his half-finished studies, forever loathing himself for his own betrayal of his professed ideal to be of service to mankind, an ideal that had nerved him to defy his responsibility, as an elder son, to take his place on the family land. He yearned now to play the part of the prodigal and to beg his father's forgiveness, to seek a place at home.

Gregson was at it again. He could hear the noises coming from the next cabin. The massive third mate couldn't leave the child alone. Since the Ibo girl with the strange Fulani markings had been loaded aboard the week before, Gregson had kept her locked in his cabin. All the while the man was with her, at her, groaning, grunting and bellowing like a bull, there was no sound from the child. Always later, when the man had gone back up on deck, Duncan heard eerie wailing, keening sounds seeping through the wooden partition, the plaintive noises penetrating the wall like water pouring through cloth. Someday, Duncan knew, he would forget much of the horror of this journey. He would forget just what the heat felt like, the taste of the foul food, even the smell of slimy sickness that came from the deep, dark holds. He would never, though, be able to forget the sound of the African girl, the sound of the child's pain, terror, loneliness, grief, and of her young, impotent rage. That tragic music would forever ring in his ears and haunt his peace.

★

The two men prayed many prayers during the fifty-day passage across the great, dark, swelling ocean. Gregson prayed loudly and publicly each night after his day's work was done. Under the starry sky, cooled by the blessed westerly winds, he thanked God for his position on the ship, for the good financial prospects in a safe and swift voyage, for his sweet wife Dora and his three young children waiting at home in England, and for the peace he felt in his heart. Sometimes he sang aloud for joy and from his overflowing sense of well-being. He was not like other poor, wretched souls who had no satisfaction in their lives. He had worked his way up the ladder of authority at sea, from cabin boy to seaman, and now to third mate. There would be pay for him, at the end of the contract, equal to that of an educated surgeon. Life was good and getting better, for he was known as capable and reliable. Dora was proud of him and would love the fine new china he intended to purchase for her on his return to Liverpool. She was worthy of the very best. After he had prayed his long and happy prayers, he would go contentedly to his cabin and there again enjoy the soft, warm young black girl. Other slaves, on previous voyages, had responded more to his attentions. This one angered him sometimes for, though she did not struggle, he could feel her loathing of him, and he regarded her continuing physical tension as an insult to his manliness. No matter how he turned or moved her about, she managed to keep her eyes, if not her face, averted from him. She had some spirit, this one. She would not cower, even when he shouted at her. He had paid good money to the captain for the use of her, and he meant to have full satisfaction for his ten pounds during the crossing.

Duncan's praying had nothing in it of the joy or triumph of the third mate's. He prayed for forgiveness for his very existence; he prayed that the great brute in the next cabin might fall overboard; most of all, he prayed mightily for a merciful deliverance for the young African girl whose keening song of sorrow daily drilled a deeper hole in his heart.

★

Weeks went by, one folding into another with hypnotic monotony. The winds did not fail them. and the Polly made steady, plunging progress through the dark waves. The swaying vessel creaked, the sails flapped in the wind, and there was the ever-present smell of hot wood and hot tar. Eventually, despite careful daily sloshings down in the hold using endless buckets of salty water, the smell of wood and tar was overpowered by the creeping up stench of excrement and sickness from below the decks.

Each day the holds were emptied of slaves, a section at a time, for the cleansing process and the exercising of the slaves in the fresh air. Dead or nearly dead slaves were slipped overboard at this time, their numbers carefully noted so that insurance claims could be made for the lost cargo.

Each group brought up on deck was inspected by the surgeon for injuries or signs of developing sickness. Then the slaves were doused with water and given food and drink. Morris, the surgeon's mate, was also the ship's fiddler. He carefully tuned his fiddle every day, so carefully that often the Master roared, 'Get on with it!' As jigs and airs, lively and trilling, poured from the fiddle, the watching seamen cracked whips and thundered curses to force the slaves to move their stiffened limbs in time with the music's rhythm. To the crew, there was always a sense of danger at these times, for some of the African men were large creatures, surly animals, and ships had been known to come to grief when such westward-bound savages had mutinied. Thus, at exercise times, the entire crew stood guard, tense and alert until the last of the cargo was safely stowed below again, chained leg to leg, hand to hand, even neck to neck, for another night in the nailed-shut bowels of the Polly.

In the quiet of the evenings, some of the ship's officers brought out the women they had taken apart for their own use, and these female slaves were allowed more freedom to walk the deck than were the men or the women normally kept in the slave compartments. One such woman had a soft, sweet smile about her lips, but her eyes had the look of a hunted animal. She was a tall, elegant figure, and her placid young child clung, creature-like, to her even when they were on deck.

One evening, when the wind had gathered strength and those on deck were enjoying the coolness of the stiffening breeze, the ship suddenly rolled severely. The slaves below the deck began to groan and then howl in anguish as they were thrown sharply against each other in their stinking, stifling black holes. The sweetly smiling woman, with her child in her arms, emitted a piercing, ululating cry and, before anyone could get near her, she plunged over the side into the black swell. Seamen yelled and slaves on deck screamed, but the woman and her child were gone. The captain snarled something about diminished profits. Other crewmen quickly ushered their distressed female slaves to their cabins or back into the hold. An old, bronzed seaman muttered to Duncan that the savages believed their souls would be lost if they died away from African soil. 'Reckon she'll drift back from this distance, Doc?' he asked, and grinned.

Gregson never let his child slave see the light of day during the entire crossing. He kept her chained to his bunk, only releasing her daily to use a bucket, to sponge herself down, and to eat. He seemed to think that everyone aboard the ship would forget he had her there, himself forgetting the thin cabin walls. He often lectured the child, while she ate, on the subject of his kindness to her. But for him, she would be in the blackness of the hold, sliding about in the putrid slime that could not be washed away, eating only pig's swill instead of the tasty scraps he brought from the seamen's mess. She ate without looking at him, always ignoring the stream of meaningless sound that poured from the lips of the stranger she despised.

More than a month's distance from Africa, the Ibo girl became ill. Duncan heard retching sounds through the cabin wall. After several days he approached Gregson on deck.

'Your African girl is sick.'

'It's only the motion of the sea.'

'She's long past that. Let me check her.'

The bushy eyebrows contracted as the mate glowered at the surgeon, 'Nothing wrong with her. She eats.'

'If she has the sickness, man, and she dies, you explain to the captain why you wouldn't let me see her. You'll have to pay up for the lost cargo.'

The brute nodded sourly and handed his cabin key to the surgeon. Duncan found the girl retching distressingly, her head hanging over a foul-smelling bucket she could barely reach at the edge of the bunk. The surgeon touched her gently, and she flinched, but she did not look at him. He spoke to her, but she did not respond to his voice. He apologised as he began to examine her hunched form, and he felt foolish knowing that his speech would be unintelligible to her. He softly touched her hair, as if in blessing, sighed, shook his head, and left the cabin. He tossed the key back to the mate and growled, 'You were right – seasick.' The big man snorted and resumed his work.

A week later, Polly approached the teardrop island of Barbados, a tiny, lush world all alone where the dark ocean cradled snowy shorelines inside a lapping boundary of warm emerald waters. Majestic palms waved in the cooling breezes, as if welcoming the exhausted mariners, and the sturdy warmth of the east-side mountains of the island gave promise of solid land for the journey's end. The ship rounded the blunt southern end of the island. Everywhere there were whirring windmills and gorgeous blossoming bushes. Polly moved northwards past a guardian citadel and towards the watery entrance into Bridgetown, their destination. They anchored some distance offshore and waited while the captain went in a small boat to arrange for their docking, the sale of the cargo and the purchase of fresh food and drink for those on board.

For several days the slaves, kept closely under watch on the deck day and night, were cleansed and groomed. They were fed fresh fruits and vegetables brought from the town. The stinking holds were scrubbed and scoured and scrubbed again until the ingrained stench of the weeks of voyage had begun to lessen. The sickly Ibo girl and the other used females were quietly slipped back in among the others for the cleaning and feeding up process. The retching of the child continued, and, despite the grooming and the extra food, she remained thin, a picture of pitiable misery.

At last, the generally cleansed and fattened stock was pronounced ready for sale, and the ship was moved into the harbour area where the Polly touched land on the dockside along a tidal inlet. The Africans on the deck, chained tightly to each other and to rings in the deck, strained for a look, and stared in wonder at the new world they had entered.

The large bustling town had shops and fine houses of several storeys lining its main thoroughfares and streets running from and parallel to the harbour area. There were several large stone churches, lofty and imposing structures, rising above the other buildings. Elegantly dressed white men and women strolled through the streets and along the dockside where hawkers were calling out in singing tones their superior claims to hoped-for customers. Children played. Dogs barked. Many men were astride handsome tall horses equipped with beautifully tooled leather bridles and saddles. There was the delicious smell of roasting meat, and there was the sound of people laughing. It was, to the slaves from far away, a place of many rich kings. In fact, all the white men seemed to be kings. There were men and women who looked African or half-African everywhere too, but these seemed somehow not African. They wore a simple form of the luxurious and complicated dress of the white people. Some seemed to dress as grandly as the white people. They spoke the words of the white people, not African tongues. They did not look afraid, or even unhappy.

White men came on board the ship for several days. Some left with one or two Africans. Others left with many. No one took the miserable, retching Ibo girl child. The captain shook his head and mumbled something about 'overboard' and 'insurance'.

Duncan finally left the ship the third day after it docked, and he began to walk through the streets of the lively town. He loved the feeling of solid, unrocking land under his feet, and he longed to be back in Liverpool for good and all. He searched the faces of people as he walked, as if he were looking for someone. In a quiet side street, he saw a middle-aged man leaning against the open doorway of a saddler's shop. The sandy-haired man was small, but he was sturdily built. He was watching a little dull-coloured bird on the street. He had dropped a crumb of bread near to his foot and was standing very still, chuckling away at the shyness of the creature that wanted the bread but feared the foot. 'Don't worry, little birdie. It's for you. Come on,' the man urged, gently. A cheeky green lizard came from nowhere and snapped up the morsel, causing the bird to flutter away further. The man laid another piece of bread out nearer to the nervous bird and he spoke again, softly, to the feathered creature. Then the saddler noticed the stranger who was watching his game, and he looked embarrassed. 'Greedy lizards!' he exclaimed, grinning.

Duncan moved forward to stand beside the man, chatting away in minutes as if to an old friend. He ended up enjoying a late-night glass of rum in the kitchen of his new acquaintance, James Stenhouse, Saddler of Bridgetown. The surgeon returned late to the ship, a happier man with a lighter step. He even whistled a song.

Early the next morning, the saddler appeared at the side of the Polly and watched the ship being loaded with its Liverpool-bound cargo of rum and sugar. The surgeon met him beside the ship and led him aboard. Thomas Duncan explained to the captain that Stenhouse wasn't looking for much, just a girl for a bit, and was prepared to take a chance on the child who was poorly. He was quite good with sick animals, it seemed, and might just get some good from her. He would only pay ten pounds, though, considering the uncertain state of the creature's health. The captain mulled over the proposal and, considering that Gregson had given ten pounds for his use of the girl already, decided to accept the offer. It was more than insurance would bring.

Minna, the daughter of Iye the Ibo woman and of Amina the Fulani woman, was handed over to James Stenhouse with a proper bill of sale. She was described on the paper as 'Negro girl, sickly.' The ship's surgeon walked the pair back to the saddler's home. There the men toasted the bargain with a rum. They laughed together, for Duncan had given the saddler the assurance that the child was not sick, only pregnant. He had, further, slipped the man five pounds towards the cost of her purchase. For five pounds, James Stenhouse had acquired not one slave, but two.

'Why have you done this, Thomas, my friend?' asked the rum-warmed saddler. 'For your kindness to little creatures,' slurred back the surgeon, whose heart had shed a part of the burden it carried.

★

On the voyage of the Polly back to Liverpool, the towering third mate of the ship collapsed with the fever. He shook with the rigours, he sweated, he ranted and raved, and he finally turned a hideous yellow colour. The surgeon attended to him, but he died. While the captain intoned solemn and holy words over Gregson, the surgeon was one of those who helped to tip the massive, enshrouded form of the man over the rail somewhere in the middle of the swallowing ocean.

Dora Gregson was given the sum of money earned by her brave, capable husband on his last triangular voyage from Liverpool. The sum was ten pounds less than she had thought he would have received, but his share of the profits of the successful venture made up for that.

CHAPTER FOUR

The Port, Scotland 1790

A child with rosy cheeks and tousled golden hair sat on the edge of the harbour wall, watching, fascinated, as boats were unloaded below him. He was holding a bag of sugar and, while he watched, he jabbed a fat finger into the bag and then into his sugar-coated mouth. As gulls screamed and dived overhead, boats rocked and creaked, waves slapped gently against the stones beneath his swinging feet and men called out to each other in their work, he sucked contentedly on the sweet stuff.

Two streets of houses and shops ran from the harbour, one to the north and one to the south, both following the shoreline of Luce Bay. A third road came from the east, from Laird Maxwell's fine estate house. It wound down a massive, raised beach embankment to meet the other roads at a pretty little square which formed the heart of the laird's new town.

A finely dressed young man walked purposefully into the square from the street of the embankment, and entered the shoemaker's shop in the square. The little boy gripped his precious bag of sugar tightly and scrambled down from the wall, darted across the street, and slipped into the shop behind the gentleman. The shop was rich with the aroma of leather and melting tallow. The child entered as his uncle rose from a workbench to greet the customer.

New boots were ordered and discussed as the little boy, noting the softness of the gentleman's shirt, the quality of the wool of his jacket and trousers and the suppleness of his boots, continued to work away at the sugar.

The man glanced down to see bright eyes regarding him with admiration and, patting the curly top, he remarked, 'Sugar! Good stuff! Young man, mark my word, get enough sugar and you can be as rich as Sir William. Get enough sugar, and you can live in a castle! How would you like that, eh?'

The shoemaker looked towards the child and muttered, 'Leather'll no' get him a castle, but it'll suffice.'

After the well-dressed man left the shop, the child ran back to resume his watchful seat on the harbour wall. He gazed beyond the small boats there with dreamer's eyes. Little John McGuffie could picture them – castles built on mountains made of delicious sugar, far off, beyond the horizon of the bay.

CHAPTER FIVE

1804

She gracefully turned before the long mirror to check that she was perfect. With creamy light brown skin and a face framed by glossy black ringlets, with sparkling black eyes and perfect white teeth, with a crisp, neat gown, a carefully tied bonnet, and with a basket balanced artistically on her forearm, she was absolutely perfect. She curtsied to herself in acknowledgement of the fact.

As the door opened and she emerged from the shade of the house into the blinding sunlight of the Bridgetown morning, the cry went up, 'Pretty! Pretty!' Whistles and calls went in waves before her as Mary Ann Stenhouse moved through the crowds towards the marketplace. Her routine excursions had become the daily highlight for the Bridge Town young men from Broad Street to Cheapside. To be smitten by her beauty was the latest fashion and, though she blushed as they sighed or applauded at her passing, she revelled in it. Life was delicious.

★

Minna, her African mother, was glad to be relieved of the shopping trips. In the home of the saddler, she was the lady who moved with confidence and serenity about her tasks, proudly presiding over the efficiently run household. Whenever she emerged from the doorway into the bustle of Bridge Town's streets, however, her confidence melted away. On the outside she became an African slave in a foreign world. She was treated, at best, with condescension; at worst, she met rudeness. The paper of freedom given to her by James Stenhouse could not lighten her skin, alter her features, or remove her fears.

There were times when Minna longed for air and sky, and there was a place then to which she was drawn. Inland from the bustle of the business streets and harbourside, behind the church of St. Michael and near a swampy area, there was an imposing and important house. In the grounds of the house stood an ancient baobab tree. Sheltered under its strange, gnarled branches, with her back pressed against its massive trunk, Minna would gaze up at the sky and remember again her birth land. She would be for a time in her memory a child beloved of Amina, the light-eyed Fulani woman, scampering with Shehu and the goats among the roots of an ancient baobab tree in an African marketplace.

Many years had passed since the wretched, pregnant slave child had been received with kindness into the house of her new master, Stenhouse the saddler. Her misery had been forgotten quickly in the need he had for her to nurse his dying wife, a sad quiet woman of white skin. After the death of Mrs. Stenhouse, Minna had given birth to a beautiful baby girl with skin lighter than her own and hair, though black, of a softer curl. The saddler had loved the child and had given her the name of his dead wife, Mary Ann. With his surname, he had also given the baby and her mother papers of freedom.

They were his family, and Minna, after some time, had looked into the eyes of her kindly benefactor, becoming his wife according to the ways of her people. She would not leave this man, for he needed her. Even if he were gone, she could not have found her way back across the vast waters that separated her from Africa, and she had forgotten the memory of the paths that would lead her back to the village of Amina and Shehu. This Barbados would be her dying place.

James Stenhouse had patiently taught her the words of his language and the ways of his peoples' living. There were many more things to know here than in her first village. There were more kinds of people, and all of them had stories of places far away. There were more things, most of them made of materials and substances she had never seen in Africa. There were more kinds of food, and more kinds of clothing. There were many more rules of what must be done and how and why. She had learned much, but she would never be finished with the learning. Each time a ship landed at the harbour there were more tales of places and peoples she must learn to understand.

Minna had taken, with the love of the white man and the language and ways of his people, the God of this land as her own. She found that He was the one God, as Amina had told her. She had also learned that this God had a son who came to kill the power of badness and of dying, just as the friend in the Oba's palace had told her. To this new God, Minna often prayed for the care of those she loved in her old world, as well as those in her new world.

CHAPTER SIX

1804

The occasional visits of Cedric Collins to the Stenhouse home in Bridgetown were dreaded by the entire household. The brother of the deceased wife of the saddler had followed the couple into the colonial world of the West Indies as a seaman. Whenever he docked in Barbados, he had descended to claim free hospitality at his sister's house. The first few visits after her death had been marked by his noisy expressions of outrage that an African slave had filled the place of Mrs. Stenhouse in the home. His sense of outrage was not great enough, however, to keep him from claiming free lodgings there and, as the years passed, he continued to appear at sporadic intervals, uninvited, unannounced and in disagreeable form. James Stenhouse was disgusted by the man, but endured him for the sake of the memory of his late wife. Minna was miserable during his visits, but she always quietly and meekly served him for the sake of her kindly Stenhouse. Collins, for his part, recompensed them for their tolerance of him with rudeness and ingratitude. Mary Ann did not fear the terrible uncle, but she loathed him and treated him with haughty indifference which he sometimes found amusing and which sometimes made his blood boil.

Early in the season of storms in the year when Mary Ann's loveliness became the talk of Bridgetown and when she had newly discovered her power to charm, Collins appeared. He was more sullen, more silent than he had been during previous visits, and Minna served him with nervous meekness. Mary Ann was aware that his eyes scarcely left her, and she could not resist the temptation to inspire his admiration by practicing pretty, feminine ways in his presence.

On the last evening of his stay, a sultry, heavy evening, Minna slipped away just before dusk to breathe fresh air beneath the branches of her tree. James was in his workshop, taking advantage of the last hour of light to add finishing touches to a saddle due for collection the next day.

Mary Ann, alone with the uncle, complained about the excessive heat and pushed her sleeves up to her elbows. She stretched her beautifully shaped arms and fluttered her soft fingers. She excused herself and went out to the back to get some air, but Collins was behind her as she emerged from the house into the yard. He roughly grabbed her and shoved her into a stone store shed. One hand clamped firmly over her mouth and the other pinning her against him, he hissed, 'Make no sound or you'll feel my knife.'

She was brutally shoved to the floor and, as he raped her, the pain of the dying of her sweet dreams was greater than that of the physical force which overpowered, crushed and invaded her. When he had exhausted himself, he squashed her small face in one large, dirty hand, and growled with hot, rummy breath, 'You ever tell, and I'll finish you and your Ma, n***** child!'

Mary Ann was numb and helpless with shock. She felt nothing; she could do nothing. She eventually crept back into the house, took water to her room, and washed herself until her skin stung. She cowered in her bed until the sounds of movement in the house had ceased. She slipped out then into the street, and she walked north past the town, then west to the shore. She sat on soft sand, watching the moon's light reflected on still water, a beauty that seemed unreal in a world of such ugliness. There was no anger in her yet, or fear; there was only bewilderment. She wished that she were dreaming, but a coldness in the pit of her made her know that the dreaming was of the past and that now she was awakened fully. The pretty was gone. Thinking must begin.

Her ambitions would be dashed if anyone found that she had been used. Admiring glances and soft sighs would cease. She felt that she could still rise above the level of her beginnings, the level of her slave blood, but the softness and sweetness that would have been her chief aids in rising were gone. Loveliness of appearance was left with her and now to it was added, in the moonlight by the sea, a newborn cunning.

★

In 1805 Barbados was astir with fear and excitement as news came that Napoleon and the Spanish were coming with invasion forces. In that time, Mary Ann Stenhouse gave birth to a sickly girl child who quickly succumbed to fever. Few noticed the young beauty's absence from the streets and those of the household nursed their tragedy privately. She would tell no one how she had come to carry the child, and she seemed determined to behave as though nothing had happened.

In the summer there was delirious joy throughout the town as the British naval hero, the Admiral Lord Nelson, brought his fleet into Bridgetown harbour. For twenty-four hours their presence inspired cries of support and congratulation from throngs of people, black and white, who flooded into the town from all over the island to catch sight of their champion, his men and the magnificent ships.

Mary Ann was among the crowds as the fleet, having received word of Napoleon's return to the coasts of Europe, sailed out. Wildly patriotic cheers rang out with bells from the churches as the hope of the British nation sailed east again in pursuit of his peoples' enemy. The watchers dispersed and there was time again for the young men of Bridgetown to notice the beautiful saddler's daughter gliding proudly through the streets back towards her home.

★

Later that summer, Cedric Collins returned. Mary Ann avoided him as carefully as she could, and Minna noticed that there was terrible tension in her daughter's manner. Twice, unknown to anyone but Mary Ann, he came to her room in the dead of night to forcefully violate her as he had done the previous year. With the vicious assaults he repeated the vicious threats, and she knew that he meant them. Each time he crept from her room, she was left shaking with terror and with hatred, but she told no one. Again, she conceived a child.

★

Lord Nelson saved Britain from the French, but he gave his life to do so. Barbados, the most English of all the Caribbean islands, in patriotic fervour grieved the loudest and longest over the death of their protagonist. Invasion fears passed with Trafalgar's battle, and the peoples' grief became, in the strange mingling of sorrow and joy, a celebration of mourning. St. Michael's Parish Church was thronged at Nelson's memorial service and the island buzzed with plans to commemorate the Admiral with a statue on the bridge of the town he had visited just before his renowned victory and much-lamented death.

★

Mary Ann Stenhouse cradled in her arms a little, dark, wrinkled girl child whose very existence reminded her of the fear now dominating her life. She feared that she would never be free from the threat of the coming, the cruelty, and the physical power of her tormentor. She feared for the life of her helpless baby, for her own life, and for the life of her African mother. She feared the memory of the smell of the man, the monster. His first invasion of her world had crushed her dreams into plans; his second had obliterated her plans, even her hopes.

When Minna rocked little Caroline Stenhouse, a healthy, black-skinned child with tight black curls, she mused over the contradictions within her feelings. She grieved for her daughter's shame; she was alarmed by her daughter's dark mood and secrecy,; yet, she loved with all her heart this tiny person who was the visible evidence of all the hidden sorrow. She murmured to the infant in African sounds as she pledged herself, in the way an African grandmother must, to protect her children.

CHAPTER SEVEN

1800

The second son of McGuffie, the draper of Mochrum village, was a dreamer. He was bright, attractive, and an obedient child, but the whole village knew that the boy lived more in a fanciful world of his imagining than in the cold, grey practical world of Scottish reality. The dreaming and the scheming were always in his head and their overflow tumbled out in his words as he worked with his uncle in Port William making leather into shoes. He would grow out of his nonsense in time, said the uncle.

When he was fifteen years old, John McGuffie was allowed to go to the county town with his older brother William for the Lammas Fair. As they crossed the peninsula between the Solway's bays of Luce and Wigtown, William noted that his young brother was unusually quiet. 'Building one of your castles, John?' He nudged the dreamer and laughed. Merry eyes answered his teasing.

Wigtown could not be seen on approach from any side but its sea side. The brothers climbed up the hill that rose from the side of the winding tidal Bladnoch River and entered the town at the top of its broad central square near the West Port. A large tolbooth with handsome assembly rooms dominated the street where crowds, animals, stalls and goods filled every available space. The crush made progress difficult; the din made conversation impossible. William plunged into the thick of things to begin to attend to his business while John moved slowly through the throng to his merchant uncle's house beyond the tolbooth.

He found his favourite cousin there and together the boys slipped out of the East Port, at the bottom of the main street, to the quiet of the Jedderland. Beneath great, sheltering trees marking the site of Lady Devorgilla's ancient monastery, the excited boys chattered and plotted together. The bay and the port of Wigtown lay just below them.

They were not missed until the next day, when William, ready to return home, discovered that neither John nor the cousin could be found. The adventurers had managed to stow away the previous evening on a boat leaving for English ports as the high tide had receded from the Bladnoch's channel.

Some months later, after a frightening voyage from Liverpool, the excited boy who had dreamed and schemed so blithely in the safety of his homeland watched in horror as his cousin died of fever in Jamaica, their first port of call. It was a sobered and more thoughtful John McGuffie who disembarked in Bridgetown, Barbados, a much older version of the boy who had crept from his family with no goodbyes and no thought to make them. Two letters were sent back to Liverpool with the ship. One, to his aunt in Wigtown, told of the death of her son in Jamaica; the other, to his mother, begged forgiveness and promised a return some day with wealth enough for the whole family.

He had never forgotten the words of the young Maxwell gentleman, the words about sugar and the riches it could bring, and John McGuffie had learned that Maxwell's sugar came from the island of Barbados. When he asked the way to Maxwell's land, he was directed to cross the bridge above the harbour and to follow the coast until he reached the part of the island called 'Maxwell's.'

The heat was overpowering for the fair-skinned, golden-haired boy, and everything seemed unreal to him as he trudged along dusty roads towards his long-cherished goal. The sky was brilliant, the ocean was like the colour of a fabulous jewel, and the foliage was luxuriant.

There were no Maxwells on Maxwell's lands. The family's mills turned to produce the sugar from their property for their profit, but no Maxwells were resident on the island, waiting, as he had imagined, to welcome the Scottish lad to a home far from his homeland. Sugar was not going to fall at his feet and turn to gold.

Lying along the curve of a bay was a bustling fishing port with a community of businesses providing services for the surrounding plantations and mills. For all its alien feel, it was a village like Port William. Attracted by a familiar, pungent smell of leather, John McGuffie entered the open door of a saddler's shop along the street, and he begged the Barbadian saddler to give him a chance to prove himself in work as an apprentice.

★

For six hot years, John McGuffie worked in Oistins village learning well the skills of harness and saddle making. He grew tall and strong and bronzed from the sun.

He sometimes delivered commissions to nearby plantations, and he learned on those trips how the plantations and mills operated, how the slaves lived and toiled, how the colonists lived and played, what strange, luscious fruits grew on strange trees, how bright colours could be, and how the same ocean that roared on one side of the island only gently lapped the soft beaches on the other side.

When his contract years were completed, John McGuffie was given a week of freedom and the loan of a horse. He explored the island to its far rocky tip and discovered it, in its length, width and shape, to be almost identical to the shape and size of his home peninsula in Scotland. The journey took him much longer than a similar exploration would have taken him at home. The days were not lengthened as summer days stretched in Scotland, so night's fall came quickly; and the great heat of the West Indian midday sun made travel impossible for a few hours. As he moved slowly around the island, he filled his eyes and his memory with exotic sights and sounds, and he searched all the while for inspiration that would provide the key to making his dreams a reality.

His search finally brought him, at the end of his circling of the island, back to Bridgetown. Among a jumble of neglected buildings at Egginton's Green near the bridge itself, he found a cheap inn, and he booked a night there. To the north and east of the green, inland from the swampland at the bend of the river above the bridge, rose the great church of the parish. Beyond it lay a large house with a baobab tree in its park. To the west of the green lay the busy port, the bustling Cheapside marketplace, and the thriving businesses of Broad Street. More businesses lay to the south of the bridge in Bay Street, the street that led to the fort.

Around Egginton's Green were many buildings even more neglected looking than the cheap but lively inns there. Peering in windows, John McGuffie could see that the narrow street frontages did not give an indication of the spaciousness of the long, almost tunnel-like premises that stretched back into the darkness. Upon enquiry, he found that plantations once used the buildings, some of which had lain empty for a long time, to store their produce while awaiting the arrival of ships expected from Liverpool. As smaller plantations, over the years, had been amalgamated into larger holdings, some of the storage houses had been abandoned, if not entirely forgotten.

The young Scotsman wandered further west into the bustling heart of Bridgetown's commercial district. He noted that only a few lanes separated the neglected area around the green from the port, business and market streets. As he stood watching the bustling crowds of townspeople, he saw a beautiful mixed-race woman walking out from the marketplace with a heavily laden basket on her arm. All eyes were on her as she passed. People smiled, and many nodded when they caught her glance. She walked proudly, with a little swing in her movements, as if she were in defiance of the world. The young saddler followed at a distance as she left the main business area and turned up a quiet side street. She entered a shop with a sign over the door reading 'J. Stenhouse, Saddler.' He chuckled to himself.

John McGuffie worked two months' notice in Oistins and parted from his employer there on good terms. He then entered the employment of old James Stenhouse of Bridgetown, who had been persuaded to take him on as an assistant. He worked hard and long hours with great diligence and skill, and he soon saved enough to place a deposit on one of the empty properties in Egginton's Green. After his daylight labours with leather at the saddler's shop, he returned in the darkness to begin a second working session, toiling by candlelight in the cleaning, clearing, and improving of the long, narrow neglected building of his choice. He was never too exhausted, as he worked, to dream his dreams and weave his schemes.

CHAPTER EIGHT

There was nothing about the way he moved through his days that betrayed the restless energy and intense purpose at the core of John McGuffie. His golden curls, even features and quick grin made him seem delightfully boyish and carefree. His strong arms and skilful artistic hands made his steady, expert work with leather seem second nature. The bright, interested expression in his eyes and the ubiquitous sound of music that accompanied his work as he hummed, whistled, or even burst into full-throated song while alone in the workshop, made him seem to be a man contented with his present lot, a great rejoicer in life exactly as it was.

James Stenhouse regarded him as the son and heir to the work of his life. The African Minna received him as needed light in their shadowed existence, a gift from a benevolent God. Caroline adored him, pestered him, quizzed him, and snuggled in against him while he hummed his way through his work. Mary Ann tried very hard every day to disregard him completely. She was grateful to him for her stepfather's sake, amused by his effect on her mother, moved by his tender humour and even temper with her child, relieved from fear by his presence in the household, and yet determined with iron in her will not to fall prey to his charms for a single second. She had greater ambitions than to be the woman of a saddler, of any saddler, even one who looked like John McGuffie, who betrayed the artistry of his nature in his work, and whose singing made the world seem strangely sweet again.

She did not know the John McGuffie who went back, after his days of work, to his own secret world at Egginton's Green. In that place he did not sing, and he did not smile, for there his furious single-minded purpose absorbed him into a frenzy of activity. After several years of work, the room at the front of his building had been opened out into the cavernous storage area behind, and above the cleaned and freshly laid out space he had created comfortable living quarters of several rooms.

John McGuffie had begun then to socialise with the young men of business in Bridgetown. His easy charm, good looks, and air of confidence had quickly taken him into the centre of the social life of the island's commercial people, and there he had established potential business connections with many, and real friendships with two. John McAra was another young Scotsman who was making a name for himself as a coach painter almost as successfully as he was becoming renowned for the hilarious tales of misadventures accompanying him through his chaotic life. Wonderfully full of fun and naturally gregarious, there was no room left in his nature for caution or concern, and he was forever falling into holes of his own digging and taking other people with him.

George Whitfield, by contrast, was considerate and temperate in his manners, serious-minded to a fault, and seemingly wise beyond his years. Whitfield was an Irishman who owned a successful dry goods merchant business which he had recently moved to a site in Broad Street, in the very centre of the town. His connections throughout the island were unrivalled, for he inspired trust, confidence and absolute loyalty in any with whom he had contact. His integrity was such that men found themselves conscious of guarded speech in his presence, almost as if there were suddenly revealed to be a lady in their company. Unlike most men of such obvious virtue, George Whitfield was genuinely liked as well as respected, for his purity was honest entirely, not assumed for occasional show or conscious display. No one could hate him or despise his unusual, childlike innocence; some pitied him, though, and few desired to emulate him.

CHAPTER NINE

Returning home from an afternoon session under her baobab tree, Minna chose one day to take a route that cut across Egginton's Green. There was a bustle of activity around a cart in front of John McGuffie's door, and she watched as men unloaded crates, barrels and rolls of cloth.

She rushed home and burst into the workshop where she found the young man finishing with care the work on a beautiful saddle. 'John! Men put tings in you door at Green! Quick, quick! You go dere! '

He just smiled at her and stood up from the bench to take a towel and wipe the sweat from his face and arms. 'That's good, Minna. They were supposed to come today. I know about it.'

'What de cloths and boxes for? Saddler's not needing de cloths off a whole ship.'

'For George Whitfield. I'm storing some for him, but some are for me, too.' He fixed her with the bright blue gleams and lowered his voice to a conspiratorial tone, 'I'm starting up a new business. I'll carry samples around the plantations on my days off.' He chuckled when he saw the fears betrayed by her expression. 'Don't worry, Minna, dear; I'm not leaving you all!' He took her hand, turned it over, and gently traced the lines of her individuality in the pink palm. 'You're my family here. This is for all of us together. Old James and I will take on an apprentice and we'll share the teaching of him. As my business grows, he can take on more of my work here. I'm not leaving you, really!' He patted her cheek and she, in turn, patted his.

Caroline bounded into the room, gazed at her grandmother with her liquid black eyes, grinned up at John, and leapt to be caught in his arms. She merrily rubbed her tight black curls in his face, and he tickled her until she squawked. Minna shook her head, as if confused, and left the workroom.

★

They went together in a grand procession to inspect the new business six months later. James Stenhouse and African Minna, dressed in their best, walked in front, followed by a dull-spirited Mary Ann holding the ever-scampering Caroline firmly by the hand. The new apprentice boy brought up the rear.

John opened the door to his callers and led them into the spacious long storehouse he had created. It seemed to go on forever, and was stacked from ceiling to the floor along the walls, and in racks as tall as a man running down middle aisles, with every imaginable kind of thing to sell. There were bolts of cloth and trimmings for dressmaking, rolled up carpeting, tools and gadgets, household utensils, the makings of soft furnishings, bags of nails, coils of ropes and wires, lanterns and candles, all stacked neatly from the window frontage to the faraway back wall of the amazing treasure-filled cave.

Caroline squeaked with delight as the apprentice boy began to chase her up and down the long aisles. James Stenhouse became engrossed in examining a selection of the latest ironmongery items from England. Minna was absorbed in the material section of the shop, fingering and stroking the bolts of fine cottons, linens, shimmering satins and silks in rolls reaching up to the ceiling. John manoeuvred Mary Ann into a corner beside the front window, just out of sight of the street.

Light from the window fell on her face as he addressed her with a directness and seriousness she had never known he possessed. 'All of this is for you, as well as for me. You filled my head as I built every inch of this place. Do you remember the first day I came to see James?'

She just stared at him, nodding mutely.

'I saw you in the street, and I followed you home.' She started to look amused, and he pressed on, 'That's why I came to work for him -- – because of you. No more just a saddler, Mary Ann. From now on it's big business. I'll be a big man here, and I mean to have a castle for my home. I want you here, beside me in it all. I love you.'

Caroline, making the noise of an escaping pig, cannoned into Mary Ann's skirts, and she plunged over into John McGuffie. All three crashed onto a roll of carpeting and a box of candles, hit by a flying elbow, cascaded over the tangled heap of limbs and skirts on the floor. Everyone but the horrified apprentice, who had skidded to a halt, burst into peals of laughter. As they untangled themselves and began to gather up the debris around them, Mary Ann glanced up at John McGuffie and gave him a smile that flashed such joy as to ignite an explosion of happiness inside him.

★

No formal marriage took place, but the beautiful mixed-race girl and her handsome Scotsman were feted at a dinner where friends and family publicly pronounced their union as acknowledged, and at the table the kindly, grave George Whitfield asked God's blessing upon their joy.

★

In the summer of the year of 1813, a statue of Nelson was built at the newly declared Trafalgar Square situated at the edge of Egginton's Green. In that August, Mary Ann Stenhouse gave birth to her third girl child, a baby with pale cream skin and soft, silky black hair. The child was christened Margaret McGuffie. Her proud father held his treasured first child in his arms, whispered to her that she would be a princess for his castle, and planned in his heart that the son yet to come, the one that would complete his happiness, would be heir to an empire worth owning.

CHAPTER TEN

Only in her childhood had Mary Ann witnessed the activities of slave trading from Africa. She had but dim memories of slaver ships docked at the harbourside in Bridgetown and of the tense atmosphere of business being conducted, of deals being struck, near the ships, on the streets, or in the doorways of inns as she had passed with her mother. She had seen Africans then, nearly naked, led away in chains down the roads leading to the plantations where sugar and cotton were grown.

Those sights, those pale recollections, had nothing to do with her She was not African. She was light-skinned. She was considered a 'free mulatto' from her birth, never a slave. Her mother Minna was at ease in her home, always dressed in good cotton dresses, neat and sleek with health; Minna looked nothing like the defeated, bony, glistening black creatures she had seen, with the unknowing eyes of youth, in distant days past.

In the year when Caroline had been a baby, the British government had abolished slave trading to its colonies. None of Mary Ann's children would witness the selling of Africans in Barbados. All slaves were now Barbadian, were British. Many were as dark-skinned as the Africans of her memories, but they were fed and dressed and spoke in English. They knew where they were; where they had come from had ceased to matter. Others were light, as light as she was, and there were many, both black and mixed-race, who were now free, able to rise to new heights of attainment in business success and in education with increasing prosperity and dignity of status in their sights.

Freedom for all, it was constantly whispered around the island, was only a step away. The abolition movement in England was powerful, and word of its impact on the British government was as eagerly seized by the slaves as it was dreaded by the plantation owners. There was endless discussion about the jeopardy to the economy of the island inherent in the freeing of its slaves. Those who walked as superiors by virtue of birth or acquired freedom were less than wholehearted in welcoming the mass of the remaining slaves into their free company. The slaves, and their friends the abolitionists, pressed on daily with more intensity and excitement as they believed increasingly in the imminent realisation of their dreams.

★

Mary Ann conceived again before baby Margaret was a year old. On the anniversary of Margaret's birth, she felt the quickening of the child. John touched the swelling part of her body and he, too, felt the movements of the infant. With pride and deep happiness, he looked forward to the birth of his son.

Only days later, as he was preparing to leave the island for a journey to other islands to sell his goods and then on to England to replenish his stores, Mary Ann fainted at his feet. When she recovered consciousness, she complained of pain. A doctor was sent for, and the young father was pushed from the room when he arrived with a nurse in attendance. The brusque-mannered nurse appeared sometime later with a bowl, and she presented it to him without comment. In it lay a tiny child, far too tiny to breathe. He looked at it with wonder. It was a pink creature with closed lids, and he could see that, had it survived, it would have been his first son.

The young couple wept together over their loss. Very soon after, he took his leave from her sorrowfully, for the departing ship would not wait for his grieving to be done. He promised Mary Ann that, upon his return, all would be well and that they would have another son. Before he left the house in the care of Minna, he cradled and kissed his beautiful sleeping baby daughter, and he held close to him his much-loved stepdaughter, charging her with the care of her mother and little sister. He warmly embraced Minna, who bore her share of the day's sadness with her customary stoicism. As the ship glided out and away from Barbados, there was no lifting in him of the sense of mourning; rather, there was a feeling of foreboding added to it, a feeling he could not shake.

★

Two months later, Mary Ann was startled to feel again within her body the sense of quickened life. She was puzzled at first by the movements and by the accompanying swelling, as if a child grew again within her. Minna understood the presence of a second child. There had been tales in her African days of twins born of separate conceptions. She remembered the twin brother she had never known but in one glance, and she rejoiced that one of two children given to her daughter might yet be safely brought to birth.

Eight months after John McGuffied had left on his voyage, Mary Ann was delivered of a smaller, weaker child, a boy like his lost twin had been. He was dusky of colour and soon deepened in hue to a blackness more like the colour of Minna and Caroline than that of Margaret or Mary Ann. His hair, straight and soft at birth, began to curl and, within two weeks, was as tightly coiled to his little head and as jet black as Caroline's.

The tiny baby did not feed well, and he screamed continuously. Mary Ann, remembering the loss of her first child and the baby's twin, struggled with tears to keep life in her new son, to feed him, to nurture him, so that she could present him with pride to his father.

When his father returned home, the child was four weeks old but not thriving. John McGuffie's evident joy at seeing Mary Ann again was just as evidently quenched when he saw the child in her arms, the wizened, screaming dark-skinned infant. 'That is not my son,' he muttered under his breath.

Mary Ann, uneasy from the moment he had appeared, countered with alarm, 'It is! Of course he is your son!'

'You lost my son before I sailed, and that was ten months ago. I have not slept with you since. This cannot be my son. Look at him, besides!'

'John, I was already carrying this child when I lost the other. They were twins,
but of different times!'

'This child is not big enough to have been a twin of the other. Mary Ann, do you think me a fool? He's too small, and he's too black. He is like Caroline, not like you, not like me, and not like our Margaret!' He shot a look of rage at her as he referred to the girls. A subject never raised between them had been that of Caroline's natural father. He had taken the child as his own and loved her so readily that Mary Ann had almost erased the memory of the horror of the child's conception from her mind.

Mary Ann, Margaret, Caroline and the baby son moved back with Minna to the
Stenhouse home. Little James Stenhouse was christened with his mother, his grandmother, his sisters and old James Stenhouse present as witnesses. John McGuffie would not acknowledge the child as his and did not seek the return of Mary Ann to his home.

★

War was raging between Britain and America over slave trading. America sacked and burned British cities in Canada and Britain retaliated by burning America's capitol. Two peoples who sprang from a common root and spoke a common tongue, who together could form a great alliance, hated and burned each other as if they were natural enemies.

CHAPTER ELEVEN

1815–1816

With one last surge of political energy, Napoleon tried to return to power. He was dispatched fully, firmly, and finally from the world's scene by Wellington's dramatic victory at Waterloo. In the year of the final settling of peace, of freeing of lands and of reconciliation with enemies, nations made a pact with nations to cease the traffic in slaves from Africa to the New World, and to regard as unlawful such traffic by other nations.

The same winged words that brought news of victory and peace in England to Barbados also brought stories that the slaves of the island were to be registered. As if they were individuals worthy of being named and numbered, the facts of their existence would be marked down in legal documentation and listed somewhere. They would no longer be as anonymous as stones on a hillside, as trees or bushes to be grown or cut down without explanation or apology, or as animals to be named, fed and watered but never to be acknowledged as of the same significance as real people. Behind and within the news of the coming compulsory registration, the island's slaves understood the impact of Wilberforce's long-fought campaign for total abolition of slavery in every land called British. From mouth to ear and mouth to ear, from the town of the port to the plantation house and on to the slave huts, into the fields buzzed the whisper, 'Freedom is coming!'

In fact, the conditions of their slavery had improved dramatically already in their own generation. Since the trading of slaves from Africa had ceased, each slave had become more precious to its owner. They were not expendable any longer, not easily replaced by a fresh crop being sold at Bridgetown's harbourside. Deaths must be balanced by births among the now-local slave population if the workforce of the island were to maintain, never mind increase, its numerical strength.

It had become fashionable to treat one's slaves with consideration, even with kindness. There were published writings on the subject of keeping slaves healthy, happy, and in contented working form. Labouring hours were broken with appointed rest times and food provision. Ample quantities of food were provided, even prepared for the slaves. Pregnant slave women were treated with favour and gentleness, even to the extent of being given a companion of their own choosing for their confinement period. Children were not allowed to work until their young bodies were mature enough to suffer no ill effects from hard labour in the fields. Indeed, young children were given the lightest and easiest work available to gradually accustom them to the world of adult labour. Slave houses were strong and commodious by design, and good clothing was provided regularly. Slaves were given extra ground on which they were encouraged to grow produce, either for their own consumption or for private profit. Punishments, where deemed warranted, were carefully regulated. Old slaves told young slaves that they were soft.

The planters of Barbados were puzzled, even hurt, by the obvious interest stirring among their slaves in the whispered news of coming freedom. 'What could they want further in life than what we give them? We are already generous to a fault with them!' They discussed their wounded feelings with each other in muted tones, always careful to be out of earshot of ungrateful slaves.

★

Mary Ann had eventually crept back, alone, to John McGuffie, and he had embraced her, silently, receiving her back into his home, with forgiveness in his heart. Minna, grieved by her daughter's utter misery, had pressed her to go, offering to keep Caroline, Margaret and baby James if the attempt at reconciliation were not spurned.

Alone together in the months that followed, the young couple grew closer than they had ever been. She travelled with him as he toured the island in pursuit of business orders. She would ride behind him, arms wrapped around his waist, her chin resting on his shoulder, and they would talk, as they rode, of their memories and their dreams, of the distant lands of their parentage and of the plans they made for their own 'someday' grand house. Behind them trudged John's apprentice boy, a 'free mulatto', who led two horses carrying samples of cloths and tools. They rode from plantation to plantation, through cane fields and cotton plantings, past whirling windmills, up rises and down into green valleys, under great old trees and between rows of newly established mahogany stands, beside grazing cattle with egret birds for companions, along with scurrying flocks of brown, goat-like sheep, through banks of bushes ablaze with blossom, along the steep clay-red ridges of the potters' mountain, and then wearily back to teeming, steaming, clattering Bridgetown.

★

The slaves of Barbados believed, they really believed, that on New Year's Day of 1816 the announcement would finally come that their freedom was accomplished. The announcement was not made, and they awoke, on the 2nd of January, still slaves. Later that month the most influential men of the island met to discuss and to reject officially the demand from Britain that their slaves be registered. A story began to spread, coming first from some free men of colour in the town to mixed-race free tradesmen in the country and finally to the ears of the slaves that a paper had come from England, from Wilberforce and the King, granting freedom to all, but that the white owners were not going to tell the slaves that they were free.

In huddles, wherever and whenever they could gather, the slave people discussed their problem. Someone told them that an island called Domingo had given its slaves their freedom only when they had rebelled and seized the prize in their own determined hands. The idea of rebellion took root and gradually worked into the shape of a plan. With a man called Bussa at their head, and with two others called Sarjeant and Cain Davis as Bussa's chief supporters, with heaps of cane trash already in place waiting to be fired as a signal of general revolt, the slaves could almost smell liberty in the wind.

John McGuffie and many others like him were puzzled by the slaves' behaviour in the weeks leading to Easter. As they travelled throughout the island, slaves kept asking, in a persistent and even aggressive way, 'Any good news for we?' The customary deference in their manner was gone and even the black women confronted visitors to the plantations with demands for news. Friendly slaves confided their hopes of coming freedom; antagonistic ones openly challenged the right of the whites to keep them enslaved against the King's wishes. Plantation owners and mill operators expressed disquiet, even some fear. John refused to take Mary Ann with him into the countryside because of the mood of the time and because, again, she was pregnant.

In the same week, in Bridgetown, John McGuffie heard from a free man of colour, and James Stenhouse heard from the trusted slave of a plantation owner, that rebellion was imminent. Those who believed most firmly that their freedom had already been granted and was being unlawfully withheld would wait no longer than Easter Monday. It was said that one of the leaders of the planned revolt was to be installed in the governor's residence of Pilgrim House, that white men would be slain, and that white women would be kept for the use of the victors.

★

Minna and her trio of different-skinned grandchildren were brought to the house on Egginton's Green for safety, away from the tighter lanes of the town centre and nearer to escape routes to the north, east, or south, within easy reach of the ships. John McGuffie, James Stenhouse and the apprentices would not leave the house but kept guard, in turn, over its family and its stores.

In the late, dark hours between Easter Sunday night and Easter Monday morning, light sleepers heard noises of voices and clamour in the garrison part of the town. Early in the morning the whole town heard the sounds of soldiers gathering and marching, of guns rolling and horses' hooves pounding as the government troops went out in strength into the countryside. There was alarm in the town when the wind brought the smell of burning and the air cracked with the distant report of gunshots or rumbled with the boom of large guns. The people of Bridgetown were subdued and the only movement on the streets was when necessity caused someone to scuttle silently from one place to another. Conversations were conducted in undertones, within securely fastened doors, among friends and family. Servants and slaves of the town kept out of sight, afraid to be caught listening or even speaking among themselves for fear of being thought to be party to the rising.

The rebellion was easily crushed by the superior force of power and artillery used by the government's troops, but one white man had died, hundreds of black people had been killed or were later publicly executed and a fifth of the island's sugar crop had been destroyed. The easy peace of former times was not restored as talk about the incident raged for months on the island and in Britain. In Britain, writings blamed the cruelties of slavery for the rising on Barbados. On the island, the whites blamed the over-emotional and misguided claims of the abolitionist camp across the seas for inspiring unreasoned hopes for freedom in the hearts of their well-looked-after slaves. Slaves blamed each other.

Freedom had not come at Christmas or New Year. It had not come in the Easter rebellion. Yet, though the crushing of the rising seemed to spell an end to the hope for abolition, the underground current of the longing for freedom had been exposed. The owners had been shown in the burning of island wealth by the rebels that slaves did not want a more prosperous slavery; they wanted to be freed from slavery. They wanted, and they had screamed out their wanting to the sky, to be owned no more. There was a new realisation of the inevitability of the success of the seemingly never-ending march towards freedom.

As the island discussed, argued, investigated and reported its troubles, Mary Ann produced another girl baby who was baptised Mary Stenhouse and died, four days later, bearing the name Mary McGuffie.

CHAPTER TWELVE

1820

As soon as Margaret was old enough to straddle a small pony, she was riding horses. John McGuffie made an ornately tooled miniature saddle for the child he astutely designated his new travelling companion on his business trips around the island. The combination of the handsome, competent Scotsman and his pretty little daughter worked to charm the customers and beguile them into buying. Margaret's tiny, perfectly cut riding habits, always made in the latest design coming from London and in the best of cloth, complemented by the pertest of hats and the most beautifully fitted riding boots in the supplest leather, her outfits accentuated by her carrying of the daintiest little silver mounted riding crop ever seen by the ladies of Barbados, were admired and discussed by the fashion-hungry plantation wives and daughters. The child's sweet, dimpled face, her pale skin framed by a mass of silky dark ringlets, her solemn expression and her wonderful huge jet-black eyes, softened the hearts and loosened the purse strings of many planters and their managers.

She loved the rides. She was always happiest on those long days when, except for the accompanying boy with his pack horses, she had her father all to herself. Often, he chatted to her about all the things that tumbled about inside his lively mind. There was music all around her. Sometimes he sang to her in his rich, full and joyful tones. Other music filled her ears: the songs of the calling of birds, of the chattering of shy monkeys, or the thundering sound made by turquoise waters crashing into the sand of the shores.

When they rode in silence, even then there were the lovely sounds of the creaking of their saddles, the soft clumping of their horses' hooves, or the whispering of the wind in the trees, bushes and tall canes ripening before the harvest.

One day they set out in the early morning's half light, heading eastwards. 'We're going today to the place where they make men into priests,' her father announced as they trotted out towards the sunrise.

'How do they make priests?' she called forward to him.

He laughed. 'With a lot of study and, I suppose, a good bit of praying!'

Keeping to the low-lying land, they skirted the central ridge of the island and curved along below it on the eastern side before turning to ride northwards. A long, straight avenue bordered by rows of young palms dipped down to a building with an open central archway through which could be seen the sea. To the left of Codrington College, the island's seminary, was the Principal's Lodge. Margaret had never seen a house like it. Though its shape was much like that of the familiar large planters' houses, this one was built of stone – greyish, solid blocks of stone. Its heavy stone-pillared entrance seemed to embrace the doorway, promising shelter and strong refuge to those who entered.

She was left in the shade of trees with the tethered horse and pony while her father and his boy took the pack horses around to the back of the house to conduct their business with a housekeeper. Some minutes later, a pale, slender young boy came out from the shadowed porchway and stood, blinking, in the sun's powerful glare. He looked towards her, shading his eyes against the brightness with his hand, and then approached her. In the politest of tones, he said to the pretty little girl, 'Do come in for something to drink. My mother says that you will be thirsty. It's very hot today.' He extended his thin, pale hand and she, looking up shyly at him, mutely obeyed by slipping her creamy little hand into his.

John Nicholson, eldest son of the college's principal, gave her water with lime juice and sugar to drink, and then led her around the grounds, solemnly guiding his little visitor over rough places and explaining unusual things to her. In front of the college building, the children gazed together up the thorny trunk of a huge silk cotton tree. She reached out to touch a large, dark spike, and he gently pulled her hand back. He didn't speak; he just frowned a little and shook his head. Soft puffs of downy white stuff from the top of the tree lay about their feet. They picked some up, scrunched it in their hands, and tossed it about in the breeze.

'Like snow,' he informed her, wisely.

'Snow?' she asked.

' It is white like this, but very much colder,' he explained. 'It comes from the sky instead of rain in the winters in England. I expect to see some before very long. I think we might go to live in England soon.'

He said it without excitement in his voice. Margaret thought how immensely important it sounded to be talking so calmly about going to England to live. She didn't know what that meant, really, though her father sometimes spoke of places called Scotland and Liverpool. She knew that there were such other places somewhere, and that the ships went there from Bridgetown and returned from there to the island. She imagined that all the places were like Barbados, and she wondered why snow came to England when snow did not come to her island. She also wondered how snow could look like the cotton down that came from the tree but be cold. If she put snow in her pocket, like she could put the cotton down from the tree in her pocket, would it make her pocket cold? It all seemed very strange and mysterious.

CHAPTER THIRTEEN

1821

Mary Ann was on her knees in one of the shop's aisles, tidying shelves while her younger children scampered about her, up and down, chasing, rolling wooden spools, skipping down the long rows, and whining in turns for something to eat. The bell at the front door clanged, and she rose to her feet, smoothing her skirts. A tall stranger stood facing her as she turned. She looked towards him and into the light of the shop's front windows, unable to clearly see his shadowed face. A silky voice, in measured accents, enquired, 'Mistress McGuffie?'

'Mr. Lord? Mr. McGuffie is expecting you. I'll take you to his office.' She called out,

'Caroline, take Margaret and James upstairs, please.' A lanky black girl appeared, scooped up the thin little boy who was protesting noisily while clinging to his mother's skirt, then pushed before her the curious, light-skinned eight-year-old girl as she moved towards the stairs at the back of the building.

Mary Ann led the visitor down the central aisle of the store to the office room that John had created at the rear of the warehouse, a room stacked with ledgers and littered with papers. She presented the stranger to him there and turned to leave, catching as she did an impression of elegance of attire and the merest glimpse of brilliant, watchful eyes contradicting in their expression the shape of a smile on too-generous lips. As she climbed the stairs leading to their living quarters, she heard the friendly sounds of her husband's voice and the smooth sounds of the stranger's, already involved in animated conversation.

'I don't like that man,' she said, with a shudder, when John appeared for his meal much later.

'Oh, Mary Ann, don't be daft!' He chided her. 'That's Samuel Hall Lord, and he's going to make us wealthy, my girl. You'll like him well enough then!' He rubbed his hands together and grinned at her. 'He wants only the best, and it's only the best he'll be getting. Then it's only the best we'll all be getting!' He swept up all three children and swung them around in a whirl of heads and limbs while, as they shrieked with glee, he sang, at the pitch of his glorious voice, about castles and kings.

Highgate had always been the island house most admired for its perfectly classical proportions, its long windows, its sweeping circular drive, and its situation above the busy town. Sam Lord was building a castle. Its shape and size were the talk of the island. It crowned Highgate's gracious classical design with an ornamental castellation never before seen on such a home. On the eastern side of the island, facing out over the dramatic Atlantic shore, above the dangerous Cobbler's Reef, the new architectural wonder inspired talk throughout Barbados.

People guessed, but no one could prove, how the mysterious rascal had amassed his fortune. His wealthy English wife had left him once for his cruel behaviour, had returned to Barbados, and had finally left the island for good. Lord was suspected of deeds akin to piracy in daring and ruthlessness, but he was clever, he was determined, he had style, and he had built a fabulous castle in Barbados. The house, with its stunning exterior and fine detailed artistry in interior finishings, ceilings, staircase and pillars, required glorious furnishings to complete it.

The Scottish dry goods merchant John McGuffie had impressed Sam Lord. Both men were dreamers and schemers, but with differences enough to make them complementary figures instead of rivals by nature. John dreamed more strongly than he schemed. He had wedded himself to a great beauty for love, and love fuelled his continuing sense of purpose. Sam's scheming outpaced his earlier, younger, kinder dreams and took them over entirely. In his newly accomplished position near the top of the ladder, he was willing to fulfil his designs by any or all means that came to hand. His wedding to a wealthy, plain woman had suited his purposes and his loss of her, now that his original intentions were achieved, caused him no regret or embarrassment.

They agreed to do business between them. John McGuffie pledged to bring the finest of furnishings from England for the grand house. Sam Lord promised, in return, vast resources of funding for his purchases. It mattered not if he ran short of money; there were ways, he had learned, to get what he wanted. He wanted a house like no other on the island, a house that none but he would have dared to build, and he would have it.

★

John McGuffie left Barbados for England to begin work on the furnishing of Sam Lord's castle; he searched in Liverpool's vast emporia for what he needed. He examined, he enquired, he looked, and he studied; then he placed his orders and, in the weeks it would take to ready his acquisitions for the return voyage, he went for the first time in twenty years back to his home in Scotland.

A small schooner with general cargo and eight other passengers brought him across the Solway from Liverpool. A recently constructed, deeper channel into the Bladnoch River and a large new harbour replaced the old creek port at the base of Wigtown's hill. After disembarking, McGuffie hired a local lad to carry his bags to the coaching inn, and he walked alone up the lane that led to the county town. The road branched just above the mound where Wigtown's castle had stood in antiquity, the eastern route leading directly to the tolbooth by the

Mid Row Lane. The other route to the town rose along the southern flank of the burgh's hill to its junction with the road he had travelled so long ago to Wigtown from Mochrum village. In a wood of beech planting at the crossroad there, just at the edge of the town, Mr. James Simson, Collector of Customs, had recently erected a fine house high above the bay with a southerly aspect over the course of the Bladnoch River.

The royal burgh itself was grander, more impressive, than he remembered. Its large central square was dominated by the tolbooth and town assembly rooms. Yet, for all its loveliness, it seemed tiny compared with the hugeness of Liverpool or even with crammed, bustling faraway Bridgetown. He hired a horse and, in the long, stretched hours of light belonging to a Scottish summer evening, he rode westwards across the peninsula to his old home in Mochrum village.

The widowed mother of John McGuffie wept and shouted with joy as she embraced the beautiful man who came unannounced to claim the place he had abandoned so long ago, so casually, when he had been a golden-haired dreamer of a child. Beside a glowing peat fire lit in the chill of even a summer evening, he told his tales to his mother, to his brothers William and James, and to his sisters. He told them of his voyage, of his years as a saddler, and of his thriving, exciting business. He told them of rich plantations and of black slaves. He told them of characters and of riots. He did not tell them of his beautiful love or of his children. He told them that he was looked after by a capable coloured servant woman named Mary Ann, and how he acted as benefactor towards her three lively children. They asked no more, but one of his sisters studied his face closely as he spoke, and she saw the blush of colour that came when truth was tinted to the taste of its hearers. The aged mother, with dimmer sight and only optimism in her hearing, was amazed at him and all his great accomplishments. She pled with him, as she rubbed and patted his strong, brown arm and felt his fingers, to come home now, to marry a bonny local girl, and to give her more grandchildren to love before she died. She wanted no more dreadful fears for his safety to haunt her old age.

He gave them gifts of fine cloth and shawls for the women, and watches for his brothers. He said that his fortune was nearly made, that he could return soon, but that he had a task to complete first, an important commission to deliver for one of the grandest people on the island.

With his older brother William, he talked at length about local developments, land enrichment schemes, thriving shipping interests, mansions being built, enterprising lairds, and, with the most excitement, about the coming burgh and electoral reforms. There were great prospects for wealthy retired colonial merchants now returning to live in places like Wigtown. They commanded new respect and wielded power to a degree once attainable only by the sons of ancient, titled families. This was a new aristocracy, one that allowed entry to men like John McGuffie.

As he slept in his old house with Scottish food inside him and warm woollen blankets wrapped about him, with the sound of the accents of his childhood in his head and the smell of peat smoke in his nostrils, it was as if he had not been away at all. The sensation of familiarity with his long-forgotten past was powerfully seductive. Under its spell, it would be easy to forget as a dream the blaze of sunlight and colour on the other side of the ocean and the people he loved who were there.

★

He took return passage on a ship bound for America via Barbados. He sailed out of Liverpool past the new Princes Dock, a finer dock than the great port had yet seen, with high walls surrounding it.

A lively company of passengers on the ship made the time of the voyage pass quickly, and he hardly noticed when the cold grey skies and icy waters gave way to balmy blue skies and a different swell. There was a lovely, gentle, pale and timid Irish lady aboard. She was sailing towards a new life as the affianced bride of George Whitfield. John McGuffie won her over with his tales of the virtues of his old friend, and he kept her amused with stories of the antics of himself and John McAra, with George Whitfield always, in his narrative, coming to the rescue of his friends in his wise and careful way.

Another passenger was the strangely dramatic figure of one Julius Brutus Booth. Julius Brutus Booth seemed more explicably dramatic when he revealed that he was an actor of Liverpool fame seeking his fortune in the New World. No matter who he encountered, at table with fellow passengers, or colliding with servants below deck, or passing crew members while he strolled about, his loud and resonant voice would be heard when, as he bowed, sweeping off his flamboyant hat, he solemnly intoned, 'Julius Brutus Booth, at your service.'

They were all chattering, with an excited tumbling of words, when he returned to Mary Ann, to Caroline, Margaret and shy James. 'The East Bridge is rebuilt!' ... 'What did you see?' .... 'What did you bring us?' Longer tales were recounted later, when the children had fallen asleep. A liberal-minded planter, Reynold Alleyne Elcock, brother of Mrs. Nicholson of Codrington College, had made a will the year before leaving money to his slaves for the improvement of their lives after his death. Unable to wait for nature to take her course, his faithful valet had cut Elcock's throat, hoping to take immediate advantage of his master's generous provision. Execution had been the reward for his impatience. Napoleon was dead. The world was always changing.

Samuel Hall Lord was pleased with the rich and beautiful fabrics and furnishings John McGuffie had brought from Liverpool for his new mansion.

Mary Ann, dressed in a fine gown in the latest of English fashions, outshone all but the fair and gentle bride when she attended George Whitfield's wedding with her John. John McGuffie settled in as if he had never left and never would leave the exotic island and the people he loved there.

CHAPTER FOURTEEN

1824–1827

James Stenhouse died peacefully in his sleep. Minna, normally calm and inscrutable in her ways, exhibited a grief that terrified her daughter. She cried, she shouted, she rocked, she moaned, and, for a whole night, she uttered a continuous keening wail. Early in the morning of the next day, before the world was fully light, Minna slipped past the sleeping form of her exhausted daughter, through deserted streets near the cathedral, and to the great, silent tree from Africa. She lay down among its roots, her back against its trunk, and she fell asleep. When she returned home to her frightened family, she was calm again, and she began to live the life of the rest of her days, the life of widowhood, engrossed only in supporting the young of her family.

Caroline and young James were sent to live with her as a comfort and focus for her existence. Mary Ann kept Margaret with her at the home of John McGuffie. Together the beautiful mixed-race woman and her light-skinned daughter cared for and filled the world of the energetic, popular Scotsman who was increasingly involved in a lively social clique formed of the most popular businessmen of the island. The furnishings he had provided for Sam Lord's castle were wonderful, it was said, and all who aspired to be fashionable flocked to him for the materials required to adorn their persons and their homes.

George Whitfield and Jessie produced a daughter, and Margaret McGuffie loved to visit the Whitfield home to amuse the pale, quiet little baby for hours at a time. The infant was her mother in miniature. Margaret's lively sense of fun was welcomed by the lonely Mrs Whitfield, one of an unfortunate number of women who had discovered after their marriage that the climate and exotic ways of the island were more than they could bear. She had developed, with her physical intolerance of the place, a dread of leaving the familiar oasis of her home.

As Margaret grew older, her skin seemed to grow lighter. The only physical clue to her African ancestry was the deep, dark black of her eyes. Her speech became a curious blend of the proud English of the priest in the cathedral and the Scottish rolled 'r's' of her father's tongue. Occasionally, when she was excited or agitated, the African tones of her grandmother's talking burst forth from her lips. Then she would be angry, for she struggled hard and consciously to talk like a lady and, much as she loved her grandmother, Minna was not a proper lady.

Her pony exchanged for a neat little mare, her child's saddle for a small lady's side-saddle, she continued to accompany her father on his journeyings around the island. Sam Lord's castle was her favourite destination. She loved the handsome house with its fairytale top. She loved its hugeness and its arrogance. She loved the artistic details of its cornices and the grand sweep of its staircase. Most of all, she loved its proud position high above the ocean. The waves, however angry, could not roll as high as the castle, and she laughed into the wind as she looked out upon the desperation of their crashing against the Cobbler's Reef far below her. Her father had always whispered to her about princesses and castles, and when she stood beneath the walls of the home of Samuel Hall Lord, she always expected to see a princess looking down at her from a window.

She was budding into womanhood. One day in Bridgetown, her African grandmother bade her, with an uncharacteristic firmness, to accompany her on a walk. Margaret usually tried to give the impression, when on the street with her grandmother, that she was a young white girl with an old black slave as her companion and guard. On that day it would have been apparent to any but the most casual observer that the old lady was not moving to the bidding of a young mistress, but that the young girl was being commanded by her elder.

Past the big church, they entered the grounds of the great house. Margaret was uneasy, but Minna, a familiar and unthreatening visitor, was greeted by the gardeners as she walked across the parkland to her tree. She sat among the roots of the baobab, indicating to Margaret that she should sit also, facing her. In strange, sing-song tones, Minna then began to narrate the story of her beginnings to this girl grandchild who was about to become a woman. She traced her way in memory from childhood days under the baobab tree in an African marketplace, through the journey to the Ibo village where she had seen her twin and heard the speaking of her old blind grandmother, to the recounting of her capture on the dark riverbank and the drowning of her Ibo mother. She told of the forced march through the jungle, of the great city, of the magnificent palace of the Oba, of the raid by the Yoruba horsemen, and of her arrival at the white shore with the pounding sea. She told of the great ship, of the cruelties and kindnesses of her journey, and of her purchase by James Stenhouse. As she spoke, she laughed, she cried, she moaned, and she even sang, staring sightlessly through the branches of the tree and into the sky over the head of her granddaughter.

She finished the telling and, exhausted, bowed her head, sitting in silence. Margaret had been spellbound by the tale, sometimes enchanted, but mostly horrified. She looked at the black, tight curls with their crisp powdering of the white of advancing years, and at the slumped form; she saw the familiar black skin now warmed to a rich mahogany shade and, as Minna finally raised her head to meet her gaze, at the features of the African face that had always seemed so familiar.

No words were in her mouth or in her heart. There were only tangled emotions, jumbled together feelings of pity and pride, and a severe sense of shock.

The girl crept to her grandmother's lap and, enveloped by the comforting black arms, the pretty young white lady wept silently, distressingly. Minna rocked her and crooned sounds of comfort to her. All was well. A woman's heart was awakening in the child. The grandmother had accomplished her task.

★

With the preoccupations of a long war settling into the past, the world was moving onwards and forward. In Britain there were developments in industry, great mechanisations changing the patterns that life that had taken from ages too early to be remembered. Factories were opening, canals were being dug and railways were being planned.

In Barbados, restoration work at St. Ann's Garrison, the rebuilding of the fort needed since the devastation wrought by a hurricane forty years previously, was finally completed. In 1826, Bridgetown, always rebuilding the sites damaged by hurricanes, fires or floods, had another disaster to cope with, and it was of John McAra's making. Sergeant Major McAra, attached to the Artillery Company of the militia, had obligingly offered to store a box of cartridges in his premises after a parade, rather than return them immediately to the artillery store. He put them too close to a fire, and they exploded. The blaze which sped from McAra's place swept through the town with terrifying ferocity. Even the ships in the water were threatened by the extent of the inferno. Though no human lives were lost, many livestock perished and whole streets of houses were burnt. The newspaper later reported that the horror and tragedy of the great fire, 'was enough to make the most obdurate and unbelieving heart cast off all its pride, vanity, and self-confidence, and humble itself before an all-powerful God.' John McAra, his friends said dryly, had never dreamed that his careless ways would bring about a general increase in piety on a West Indian island!

Bridgetown received the prestigious designation of 'city' when, as the seat of a newly created Anglican diocese, its parish church became a cathedral. Being able to attend weekly worship at 'the cathedral' for a time had a further salutary effect on the piety of Bridgetown's inhabitants. The seats were as hard, the air was as warm and the prayers and sermons were of the same style as before, but the worshippers walked more proudly to their services and spoke more eagerly of having attended them for a time after the pronounced transformation.

★

There were subtle changes at the heart of the island of Barbados. From the days of the rebellion ten years before, white supremacy in colonial life had ceased to be taken for granted. Some of the clergy of the established church, seemingly echoing the tone of the early Moravians and Quakers and the more recent stance of the despised Methodists, were beginning to preach that, in the eyes of the God worshipped in the cathedral, there was no difference between black people and white people. The earlier liberals of the other churches had contented themselves with urging the whites to accept that the blacks possessed souls and should be taught of God's love and redemption. Now, even-more liberal voices from within the very established church were pressing further into realms of thought than ever heard before – that blacks not only had souls and eternal existence, but that they were equals, the same entirely in the sight of the Creator as the whites.

There was a revulsion and wild raging in the minds and hearts of those who had always accepted their superiority as a gift from God to their race, by His design for time and through eternity. Being kind to blacks, even turning a blind eye to skin tones of a paler sort was one thing, was behaviour now accepted as quite positively Christian; to make no difference at all between the races was another thing altogether. If that were to be judged right and true, then the whole of the history of slavery from Africa was not one of the development of an efficient and necessary economic system, but was one of a deep, hideous, sick evil, and accepting it in any way, profiting by it to any degree, had made the white colonials guilty, horribly, monstrously guilty of a wrong, a crime, a sin beyond their comprehension. It was easier to argue against the idea of equality than to face its implications.

★

John McGuffie felt the way the wind was blowing, both in Barbados and in Britain. New life was beginning to surge forth from the old, tired ground of his homeland. On the island, however, certain imminent change would mean an end of the natural advantage of white supremacy, economic instability that an egalitarian society would produce in the ordered world of colonialism, and the knowledge that, back home, there would soon be less prestige attached to the title 'colonial.'. He became thoughtful and he less frequently shared his thoughts with Mary Ann.

Part of the land at Egginton's Green was required as a site for the construction of grander public buildings and an extension to Trafalgar Square. Mary Ann did not know, until the papers had been signed, that John McGuffie had sold his entire shop and store premises for a handsome sum of money because of their prime location.

She was too proud to show her distress as he quietly organised for her and Margaret to be removed, with their personal possessions, and back to Minna's home. He stayed there with them for several weeks while he arranged his passage back to Liverpool. He placed his business concerns, officially and publicly, in the hands of George Whitfield and John McAra. Mary Ann pretended that she believed that he was only going on another business trip.

'I'll be back, my dear beauty,' he promised, his eyes full of love, 'and we'll build a fine place somewhere.' She turned her eyes from his. She knew that he was gone.

★

Letters came to them, frequently at first, telling with excitement about the great possibilities now developing in Britain, about electoral reforms, abut ships being built in tiny Scottish ports and about the founding of a steam navigation company in the old royal burgh near his home in Scotland. After the news of the death of his mother, there was a tailing off of letters until there was virtual silence.

At first, Margaret pestered her mother continually about when her father would return. She was sixteen, then seventeen, then eighteen years of age and, as she left the house to go to the Cheapside market one day, a call went down the street before her, 'Pretty, pretty!'

CHAPTER FIFTEEN

1831

One hot afternoon a stranger arrived at the Stenhouse home. Caroline answered
the sound of sharp rapping on the door and was startled when a shabby old man
she had never seen pushed past her into the dark hallway.

'Who is you?' she demanded to know, bristling at his rudeness.

'Who is you?' he shot back, mockingly, a tobacco-stained grin revealing
only occasional tobacco-stained teeth. He was horrible.

Minna appeared from her kitchen, surprised to see Cedric Collins again
in her home, then not surprised to hear him demanding a room. The four women
would need to share a bedroom to make space for the unexpected visitor. James,
now a gangly youth, had his own sleeping area in a small room under the wooden
staircase, an unwindowed place with only a tiny jalousie for air. Collins did not
enquire about his brother-in-law.

Mary Ann returned from a shopping expedition with Margaret and was
transfixed with horror to see the monster of her long-forgotten dreams, however
decrepit he had become, clumping down the stairs towards her on his way out to
the rum of the inns. When he had gone, she slumped into a chair, weak and
nauseous. Her head swam with a confusion of memories and fears. She vowed to
herself that he would not touch her again.

Caroline entered the room. 'Who that man, Momma? He is rude, rude
man!' She cackled with mirth. Mary Ann was silent, for the answer was
unspeakable. The man was Caroline's father.

Minna was puzzled and not a little alarmed by the nervous tension she
sensed again in her daughter, the same grim intensity she remembered from Mary
Ann's behaviour before the time of John McGuffie and never since. Even during
the experiences when she had lost babies, and since John had left the island, the
mood now evident had not been upon Mary Ann. Minna said nothing to her
distressed daughter, but she watched her.

★

One close August afternoon, Minna escaped from the noisy city streets to the
space and the air under the branches of her familiar tree. She breathed peace
there, but soon became aware that the peace was strange. There was no wind, and
it felt to her that the earth was holding its breath. The parkland was full of yellow
butterflies moving in swarms as she had never seen them before. Large seabirds,
normally glimpsed only at a distance in flight over the ocean waters, flew over

her, singly or in groups, swooping and diving as if searching for a place to land. Then she noticed, up through the gnarled baobab branches, a reddish glow. She remembered the story James Stenhouse had told her of a great hurricane in years past, a tale of fear and death and destruction beyond belief. She remembered that he had spoken of a strange, red sky over the island and of a hushed world before the storm had come.

She ran, aware of her shortness of breath in the oppressive heat, as quickly as she could back to her home. The streets through which she ran had become empty of people and were silent too. She rushed through her front door and out the back, where she opened and examined carefully the two stone storage sheds in the yard behind the wooden house. The smaller had a stronger roof and door, and she cleared as much space in it as she could, removing implements stored there and placing them in the larger shed. With the floor cleared, she began to prepare the chosen place. She drew water and placed it carefully in storage jars, wedging the jars securely in corners. She brought food and blankets from the house. She checked the door again, carefully examining its hinges and bolt.

'Dere be storm comin', Mary Ann,' she cried through the house. Mary Ann and Margaret appeared, fanning themselves, and Caroline came galloping down the stairs. 'Where James be?'

'George Whitfield's offices, pestering for work,' replied Mary Ann.

'Get he here,' commanded Minna, full of purpose.

'Where Uncle Cedric?' asked Caroline.

'Forget he,' replied Minna, curtly, and Mary Ann grinned.

Before her daughter could leave the house to search for James, Minna changed her mind. 'No way. You here wid de girls. I get de boy.' She shot out the door.

It was so very hot, so utterly airless, as Mary Ann went into the kitchen to prepare some food for them. Just before darkness, the unbearable sultriness was relieved by a shower of rain which drenched the returning grandmother and her charge. The family ate together quietly, glancing at their fiercely absorbed matriarch who said nothing.

Mary Ann slipped outside. There was only stillness as night came, and with awe she watched the inky blackness all around the sky's edges, the rolling, dense menacing cloud filling the dome of the sky. A strange, small, weak circle of light at the zenith of the heavens, directly overhead, a last, helpless beam of day, was being swallowed up by the heavy mass thundering upwards towards it.

When darkness had enveloped the world, they went to their beds, but they only tossed restlessly, the four women in one room and James in his cupboard space. Dogs were howling piteously through the town. Sleep had not come to the women when, several hours later, the wind rose. Soon they heard flapping sounds from torn roofs and the sound of debris being blown through the streets.

Suddenly the skies erupted with sheets of brilliant lightning blazing into the night. Streaks of fire stabbed incessantly, murderously, towards the island. The four women grabbed their blankets about them as the howling of the wind increased and the roof above them began to shift. Rain poured through onto them as they fled down the stairs, and Minna shouted to them to go to the small shed while she got James from his hole under the stairs.

Mary Ann misheard her mother's directions in the din, and she led the girls, clinging to each other for strength against the blasting, screaming wind and the lashing power of driving rain, into the larger stone shed. She heaved the door shut against the wind, but could not fasten it. Inside the shed, revealed by the light of a flickering candle, Cedric Collins, rum bottle in his hand, was leaning against the wall.

'Ah, my beauties,' he chortled, unaware in his stupor of the storm raging outside. He shuffled towards the soaking, frightened girls as Mary Ann struggled to hold the door closed against the power of the wind. 'Give us a bit,' he wheedled, and made a stumbling dive at Margaret.

'Leave she be!' shouted Caroline, pushing at him, as enraged at the huge filthy man as she was terrified of the blasting elements.

Mary Ann turned to see him shove Caroline aside while he groped at the skirt of Margaret's nightgown. She let go of the door and, as it swung open, a shower of slates from the roof of the house rained down on her. One flew straight into the back of her exposed neck, and she fell, a bloodied heap, in the doorway just as Minna appeared in her search for the missing three.

Collins did not see Mary Ann fall. He did not hear the noise of the roaring of the storm or the crashing of the buildings which obliterated the sounds of the screams of Caroline and Margaret, and he ripped at Margaret's skirt, pushing her down on the stone floor.

The candle blew out, but the skies blazed with light and in that light Minna saw it all, knowing in that instant all she had never understood. She grabbed the axe lying among tools beside the door, and she was upon him. She added her scream of anguish and rage to the swallowed-up chorus of terror rising from the throats of Caroline and Margaret as, with all the power of her fury in her strong black arms, she split open the head of her daughter's tormentor, her granddaughter's attacker.

The roaring of the hurricane was increasing. With shaking limbs, Minna moved to pull Margaret, now senseless, from beneath the bleeding head and fallen body of the man. She carried Margaret and led Caroline back into the storm where they forced their way against the wind, a step at a time, to the smaller, provisioned shed where a sleepy James, unaware of all that had passed, was slumped in the corner.

The door was pulled shut and secured. Caroline crept to her brother, wrapped her arms about him, and sobbed uncontrollably. Minna tenderly wiped the blood from Margaret, bathing it away with the edge of a blanket dipped in the water she had stored. She cradled the unconscious girl against her, crooning to her, as outside the whole world screamed and pounded, its elements gone insane. This horror was beyond her imagining, surely beyond their surviving.

★

Early in the morning, just before light, the wind died. Minna had not slept, but her three grandchildren, wrapped in her blankets, were deeply into the sleep that comes to those exhausted by grief or terror. She was a strange, greyish colour as she quietly rose, her blanket about her, and slipped out into an unreal world. Her beautiful Mary Ann lay dead among a pile of slates and through the open door of the larger shed she could see the body of Collins.

She moved like a ghost through deserted streets framed by piles of rubble where houses had once stood. She passed the proud cathedral, triumphant in its survival. She moved on through the blasted landscape of the parkland of the great house, seeing nothing but broken trees and uprooted bushes everywhere. Her baobab tree, gnarled and strange branches sprouting from the massive trunk, was there, alive, still upright, deeply rooted in its place. She sat down beneath it, her back against its strong body, and she began to rub her sore arm, shot through with pain all during the long night since she had wielded the axe in defence of her children. She saw again the face of Collins, but it became the face of Gregson. She shuddered and closed her eyes, so very weary she was, and she slept.

Gardeners, moving later that day through the devastated landscape of the great house's parkland, found the cold body of the old African woman, wrapped in a blanket, at the place where she had so often sat in contemplation, on the roots and beneath the branches of the ancient baobab tree. They lifted her body and carried her to the common grave that was dug for the unknown people found dead in Bridgetown, those whose identities had perished with them in the terrible storm of the night.

★

The morning was well advanced when the three young people in the stone shed eventually stirred from their sleep and emerged from their shelter into the waterlogged atmosphere of an eerie day. They crept across the yard behind their only-partially roofed home and stood gazing in horror at the flapping door of the other shed. Just inside the gloomy place, among the slates, lay the crumpled heap of their mother's body. Deeper into the darkness was the mound of the body that had been Cedric Collins.

Margaret's legs sagged, and Caroline supported her. Sleepy, dreamy James was rooted to the spot, just staring at the grisly scene. Around them they could hear sounds of grief and confusion. They stumbled over debris into the wreckage of Minna's home, searching for their grandmother, but they found only chaos and terrible destruction in their once-familiar rooms. Furniture not smashed stood in strange places, as if the pieces had been dancing across the floors and were frozen in the positions they occupied when the music had stopped playing.

They found some clothing and dressed themselves as best they could, then started to wander the streets and lanes of what had been Bridgetown, looking for their grandmother. There was tragedy at every turn. Bodies lay scattered about and houses had collapsed. People were calling out names as they dug crazily at mounds of rubble with bare, bleeding hands. Moans and screams could be heard coming from different places. A horse appeared from nowhere, in the middle of Bridgetown, galloping like a frightened, drunken thing, stumbling over wreckage lying in the street, its eyes, ears and nostrils clogged with sand. Dogs ran about madly, frightened, emitting strange howls and sharp, agitated barks. There were huge blocks of wood blown inland from the pierhead, lying as if dumped by a giant hand.

They walked on to the harbour and saw ships sitting askew on dry ground, as if they had been placed there by the same giant hand that had played with the massive blocks of wood in the night wind. The waters of the ocean were still boiling with the hurricane's raging, and bits of houses were floating in the choppy waters of the harbour area.

They returned to their own ruins and to the awful scene behind the house. 'They must be buried,' whimpered Margaret. It was already hot, and flies had appeared, quick to take advantage of the grievous wounds of the world in which they alone seemed to have survived unscathed.

Caroline returned to the street and asked passers-by where the bodies should be taken. An old gentleman, blank of expression, told her, 'To old St. Mary's churchyard.'

They tenderly placed their beautiful mother on a blanket, and they covered her with another. James walked at the head, his hands behind him gripping two corners of the improvised litter. The girls each took a rear corner, and the three moved slowly, picking their way through scattered rubble, to the church near the market where a great trench was being dug. Without a word, they carefully laid their mother's form, still covered by the blanket, into the opened trench and they watched, with tears streaming down their faces, as earth closed over Mary Ann Stenhouse.

As they walked away, they saw a group of people accompanying one such litter as they themselves had brought to the burying ground. At the head of the procession walked a priest and they heard him calling out the words written in his book as he came towards them, passed them, and moved away from them. 'Man that is born of a woman hath but a short time to live, and is full of misery. He cometh up, and is cut down like a flower. He fleeth as it were a shadow, and never continueth in one stay. In the midst of life, we are in death. Of whom may we seek for succour, but of thee ...'

They retraced their steps to the house where they next faced the task of the retrieval of the remains of Collins. Caroline made Margaret wait in the ruined house while she took James into the shed. He shuddered as Caroline told him, in a brief, staccato way, of the attack and of Minna's astonishing defence. The axe, still embedded in the skull, had to be pulled out. He gagged when it came free from the bone, and sweat ran with tears down his face. He handed her the weapon, and she carefully put it back in its place behind the door.

They prepared the litter for the second, heavier corpse and again, struggling with their burden, moved in the triangular formation through the streets to the busy churchyard. They made sure that the body of Collins was placed at the opposite end of the great trench, not being able to bear the thought that, even in death, he could be anywhere near their mother. No one questioned them, and no one comforted them, for hundreds of people were engaged in the same gruesome task that day and most of the bodies bore marks of crushing or cutting injuries, some even of the severing of limbs.

As evening approached, Margaret, desperate for news of Minna, remembered the tree in the parkland, and she sped there alone, hoping to find her grandmother seeking solace in her sheltering place. She asked a gardener who was moving sadly among the tangled, fallen trees, 'Did a woman come to the baobab tree today?'

'An old African woman was lying dead there this afternoon. We knew her. She often came here. She wasn't injured or anything. It was like she was sleeping, wrapped in a blanket. We buried her with the rest, because we never knew her name. Was she your slave, Miss?'

Margaret fled from him and back to her home. Her breath came in great, rasping sobs; her tears blinded her. In the house, she crept into a corner, locking her knees in her arms as she crouched, rocking and crying, and then a strange, keening wail rose from her throat. When Caroline and James heard her, before they saw her, they knew that African Minna was dead.

★

On 27th August, 1831, The Barbadian newspaper proclaimed:

'Whereas it having pleased Almighty God to afflict this colony with a most awful and destructive hurricane which has destroyed all dwellings and plantations of the inhabitants of the island; and whereas it is apprehended that some evil disposed persons may attempt to plunder the distressed inhabitants of the few articles and provisions which they have preserved:

'I do therefore hereby order and command all Magistrates and Constables to exert themselves to the utmost of their power in preserving on this melancholy occasion the peace and tranquility of the island and to prevent, as far as in them lies, the depredation and plunder by such evil disposed persons ....

'And whereas it has been represented to me that the principal merchants of Bridgetown have not enhanced the prices of the necessary articles of life: Now I do hereby strongly recommend that so laudable and benevolent an example may be generally observed: and I trust and expect that no advantage will be taken by Mechanics and other Tradesmen in the present lamentable state of the colony. And I do call on and command all the inhabitants of the island white, free, coloured and slaves, to demean themselves with propriety, order and decorum, and whatsoever person or persons shall be detected in committing any robberies, receiving any stolen goods, shall be prosecuted to the utmost rigour of the law.

'Town Hall, 15 August, 1831, second year of His Majesty's reign.'

With the Depute Governor's declaration in the newspaper came his instructions to the people of the island. All officials were empowered to preserve the subordination of the slaves. Men were appointed with authority to demand that slave-owning householders provide labour for the clearing of the streets. Treasure money was allocated for the pulling down of buildings left in a dangerous condition. The churches were appointed to collect money for the poor, the maimed and the starving. Slaves found wandering without passes were to be whipped with up to thirty-nine lashes and put on the treadmill; they were to be then employed clearing the streets. Mechanics employed to repair hurricane damage, if found charging higher than usual charges, were to be fined.

In September, 1831, the newspaper reported:

'Whereas it pleased Almighty God on the morning of the 11th August last past to visit this island with a most awful Storm of wind, whereby in a very short space of time the churches and chapels and other private buildings and dwelling houses throughout the Island were with scarcely an exception levelled to the ground or materially injured and many persons perished in the ruins or through the violence of the tempest and much damage was done to the property of the inhabitants: And whereas He was yet pleased in the midst of judgement to remember Mercy and to stop the fury of the Hurricane and to shorten its duration, saving the lives of thousands and sparing the fruits of the earth, and in the season of our most pressing need giving us favour in the eyes of our fellow colonists who readily to their power, yea even beyond their power, administered to our necessities: I do therefore by and with advice of His Majesty's Privy Council, appoint Friday, 7 October Next to be set apart as a day of Solemn Humiliation and Thanksgiving unto Almighty God: And I do most earnestly call upon all classes and conditions whatsoever within this Island to assemble themselves together on that day in such churches and other temporary places of worship as shall have been repaired or provided for the occasion to humble themselves before Him, and to offer up their prayer and supplications unto Him with Thanksgiving.

'God Save the King.
The Depute Governor.'

CHAPTER SIXTEEN

1831

At first each family visited by death, each home blasted to ruin, nursed its own grief alone, but, within a few days necessity drove people from the centres of their own broken worlds into making contact with others and, as stories were shared, the single sad cries of loss began to mingle and blend themselves into a tragic chorus, a sorrowful hymn, ascending into the very heavens from which had come the wind. Almost two thousand had perished in one night on the tiny jewel-like drop of land in the ocean.

While some people remained occupied with keeping alive the thousands injured, others commenced the huge task of rebuilding their world. Heaps of timber, piles of slates and beached ships with their wood and canvas were sorted through. The materials gleaned were used to erect tented shelters in open spaces for the homeless, or were carted to smashed homes to make rough repairs to them. Broken roofs were mended with the least damaged of slates from collapsed ones. Doors and shutters were repaired or replaced. Food was salvaged and carefully stored. Clothing was searched for and shared out.

George Whitfield found the three young orphans working on the broken roof of the half of the house that still stood. He was the first of their acquaintances to learn of their loss, of the deaths of Minna and Mary Ann. He gathered them to him, and he wept with them, but he asked them for no details, and they offered him none. He had come to seek out Margaret's help to comfort his nervously distracted wife and to assume care of his little girl. He needed desperately to be freed from the domestic crisis to get on with the business of helping to supply the needs of the island's people from his, albeit damaged, stock. At the Stenhouse home, though, he realised immediately that more help than temporary employment for Margaret was needed, and he offered clerking work to the shy, gawky James, who was so unlike his confident father. James, who had long pled for such a post, glowed with pleasure and eagerly accepted. Caroline would keep house for them, it was agreed.

Whitfield took time to survey the half-ruin before he left them. 'With some help from builders I employ on my property, we could construct a simple room or two here,' he said. 'Some of my apprentices are living in a canvas tent on the beach since the storm, and they could live here. If you would be agreeable to providing them with breakfast and supper, Caroline, I would pay the costs for food.'

Caroline narrowed her eyes and pursed her lips, then asked, 'Who own de house dey sleep in, Mr. Whitfield?'

He chuckled at her quickness. 'You three, of course, but in return for its building you let my lads stay for two years, no rent. Remember, you'll be getting food costs. Don't be too hard on me, Caroline; the island won't have a lot of money for a good number of years again.'

The three agreed, Caroline smiling sheepishly, and they thanked their friend, their benefactor, their father's good friend, for his help. He promised to send word of their circumstances to John McGuffie by the first ship leaving the island.

'Father will come back,' whimpered Margaret, after George Whitfield had left. 'He'll not leave us like this.'

'Yuh can't expec' he to come back here, Ma'gret! Nevah, nevah! Dis a done place and dat man not gon' be Big McGuffie in no done place!'

'Caroline! He's Father! He loves us!'

'You father never gon' say I is he child.' James was scowling. 'Might come to see Ma'gret livin'! Might even come to give dat Caroline a hug; but no place in he mind for James Sten'ouse!' The newly appointed clerk for Mr. George Whitfield spat out the words. 'I t'ink Caroline right. Big McGuffie not struttin' here no more!'

Margaret stormed out of the house, weeping as she ran down debris-cluttered streets. She headed away from her old happy home at the green, away from Minna's sheltering place under the tree, towards the docks. She sat there, on a tossed-up block of wood. She saw ships, like beached whales, with desperate people, dressed in rags, picking at their bones for what they could salvage. She saw fires of rubbish burning. She smelt death in the heavy air. She hated the world as it had become. This was not the home of her beginnings. She longed for Minna who was dead; she wanted her mother who was dead; she needed her father, the sparkle of his eyes, the rich sound of his singing, the warmth of his love, but he was gone, and he might not come back. She stared out past the harbour to the ocean, rolling and dirty with the dirt from a churned-up world. Her eyes could not see as far as the place where her father lived his life not even knowing of their ruin.

★

John McGuffie was entirely unaware of the destruction on the island he had left behind. He was busy. He had already sent a ship from Liverpool, laden with supplies, to George Whitfield. Work as his friend's buying agent was adding steadily to the sum of wealth he had acquired from his business for Sam Lord and from his sale of the land at Egginton's Green. He had decided to invest a considerable portion of his money in the newly formed and already-thriving Wigtownshire Steam Packet Company, which was cornering the market for modern, fast shipping trade between ports in the southwest of Scotland with Liverpool and Whitehaven. A shareholder and director of the company, he was establishing a base in its headquarters, the county town of the shire of Wigtown. He was building a fine new villa on the southern edge of the town, just below the customs officer's house in a wood of beech trees. McGuffie's villa, planned to be in the style of Bridgetown's Highgate House and Sam Lord's castle, would be the first seen by people arriving in the town at the harbour, and it would be the finest house ever built there. With his wealth, his home, and the promise of political influence about to be fulfilled through the voting and municipal reforms coming before Parliament, his was an enviable position. He felt that his greatest days were yet before him.

He was a handsome, unattached bachelor. Eligible ladies from fine families in Liverpool and the shire of Wigtown were responding to his charm and vying for his attention in fluttering, balloon-sleeved flocks. Invitations to dine were frequent, with his dinner companions invariably fair, free, and elegant. His wardrobe was updated, his hairstyle altered, his conversational skills exercised, and his melodious voice tuned for many social occasions.

Dinner parties in Britain during the summer of 1831 rang with excited chatter. There were so many topics for stirring conversation that voices sped on from one to another and returned again. The riots of agricultural workers over increased land mechanisation, Earl Grey's reform bills, the exploration of the North and South Poles, Belgium, the coming emancipation of the slaves in the West Indies, the growth of the railways, and the impending coronation with its planned pomp, ceremony and speculated guest list caused tongues to wag until the very air went shrill with excitement.

In the late summer, a terrible storm blew up and there was a great maritime tragedy. The ship Rothesay Castle, travelling from Liverpool to Bangor, sank with the loss of one hundred lives, many women and children among them. It was claimed in the newspaper reports that the crew had been drunk. The same papers discussed the problems of the impending emancipation of slaves in the colonies. The amount needed to recompense the slave owners to their satisfaction was being seen as a great drain on the British economy and possibly too high a price to be paid.

In September, the papers were filled with details of the Coronation of King William IV. There were terrible stories of a volcanic eruption in the Mediterranean and of cholera in Austria.

On the 4th October, while visiting his old home in Scotland, John McGuffie was stricken to read of a hurricane that had devastated the island of Barbados in August, nearly three months previously, leaving 'one entire desert of Oistins, Holetown, Speightstown and Bridgetown alike.' As he read of the many hundreds killed and thousands maimed, of whole areas flattened, of the horrors of the terrible wind, and the roaring storm on the seas, he felt ill with fear for those he loved. While he had been busy organising his shipping interests, discussing reform bills, planning his new home, dining out, flirting, and dreaming of future power and influence, they had been enduring nightmares and struggling to survive if, indeed, they had lived through the disaster. He took the first passage available from Wigtown to Liverpool where he found, awaiting him, a letter from George Whitfield.

John McGuffie wept bitterly as he read of the deaths of Mary Ann and Minna. He must go to his poor children! First, there were supplies to be gathered for rebuilding on the island and the reclothing of its people, and he flew through Liverpool's streets, a demon of energy, buying, ordering, demanding and bargaining. Among the goods on the next ship to sail for Barbados were special parcels for Margaret, Caroline, James and his friends the Whitfields and John McAra.

He stood on Princes Dock and watched as the fully laden vessel sailed out and away towards the stricken island. There was so much for him to do in Liverpool and Wigtown. Business could not run itself, and his house plans urgently required his attention. He could go later.

CHAPTER SEVENTEEN

1834

Slowly the fallen buildings of Bridgetown began to rise from their crumpled chaos until, capped by new roofs, the town stood straight again. Building work went on all over the island, for churches, as well as homes and windmills, had collapsed from one end of Barbados to the other. Even the roof of Sam Lord's castle had taken wing in the mighty storm.

Caroline ruled what remained of the Stenhouse world. Her sister, her brother, and the apprentices of George Whitfield alike danced to her whistle and quietened to her hushing. James worked hard at his clerking, determined, with an intense, dour commitment, to prove himself worthy of the father who had rejected him. Margaret spent her days shoring up the sagging spirit of Jessie Whitfield and delighting in the growing young Whitfield child who alone supplied her delicate mother with a reason for living.

Every time a ship sailed in to dock at Bridgetown's harbour, Margaret hoped afresh that she would hear the sound of her father's returning step, but no ship brought him. Sometimes she wept silently, for she loved him and longed for him to comfort her. She would weep forlornly, stuffing her fist in her mouth to stifle the sound. At other times, though, she raged at him, for she was angry, terribly angry, because he had left them, and he had not come back; even the news sent of the smashing of their world and of the deaths of the mothers of the family had not brought him back. His presents had come, but he, himself, was needed. Her anger spent, Margaret would sink again into the corner and weep with the flooding desolation that told her that he could not love them at all. Caroline watched the swinging moods in her sister with great, tender sorrow, but she always prodded Margaret on roughly, telling her to forget the man. 'Some Big McGuffie, he,' she would challenge. 'Scared to come for the wind gon' blow again!'

Jessie Whitfield sank so low in spirits that her gentle husband feared the depression would steal her soul out of her body. He decided, in desperation, to send her back to England for a change, hoping that familiar sights and cooler air might revive his poor wife. Margaret would look after the child at home in Bridgetown while she was gone. Passage was booked.

It was Caroline who had the idea: Margaret would go to her father, and Mrs. Whitfield would provide the passage. In earlier times, Margaret McGuffie would have been the most likely member of the household to have enjoyed favourable prospects of advantage in life on the island. She was the fairest, with the lightest of skin, and she spoke the most correct English of them all. Things were rapidly changing, and Caroline had sensed for some time that, with the coming of the long-awaited and now-promised emancipation, their world was about to be transformed. When all were free, equally, there would be more black than white on the island and, for a white girl with no fortune and no protector, there would be no advantage anymore. She was uneasy about her younger sister's plight, her lack of a future. Caroline could work. She had strength, a tongue in her head, and a natural cunning. She also had her own home. James had employment and was secure enough. Men could always make their own way. Margaret could not make her own way; she must go to her beloved father. Seeing her there, in his own country, he would remember his forgotten duty, and he would provide for her.

Caroline went to George Whitfield and pressed on him the concern, she said, that Margaret had often expressed about Mrs. Whitfield making the difficult journey alone in her present state of health. 'Yes, sir, Mar'gret say the lady not fit to dress sheself, never mind feed sheself. She too weak!'

'What about my daughter?' he asked.

'Yuh have no fear 'bout she,' Caroline nodded in a kindly and encouraging way. 'Ah'll care fo' she same as Mar'gret.'

George Whitfield readily agreed, for Jessie did always follow Margaret's directions so meekly and limply that he knew the girl would keep her from neglecting herself during the sailing home. He wondered why he hadn't thought of the plan.

Margaret was astonished to discover that she was booked to sail for Liverpool, but Caroline watched with relief as the colour flooded into her sister's pale face, as her eyes lit up, and as her step regained its bounce during the few days before the ship was to leave.

In those waiting days it was Caroline who felt the desolation, who crept into corners with her fist crammed into her mouth, who in secret sobbed as if her heart would break. Margaret never knew the grief that her departing caused her sister. She only saw the Caroline who bossed, shoved, pushed and ordered her about, to the very edge of the gangplank. She, herself, could only think that she would be seeing her father again. She never thought, ever, even for the tiniest instant, that she would never again see Caroline of the blasting, chiding, commanding manner, or James, or Barbados.

CHAPTER EIGHTEEN

1834

James Stenhouse laboured on, learning as hard as he could make his head learn, acquiring the skills of clerking. Sometimes he dreamed when he should have been working, though. He dreamt of one day owning his own business, being an important person in Bridgetown. He wanted to walk down the street with the casual swing of his father's easy elegance, to see peoples' faces light up as they met him, hats doffed and curtsies swishing. He wanted a house, too, a big, fine house sitting high on a knoll looking down over the port. He wanted money and admiration, style and position, and he wanted a fair-skinned, beautiful wife who could give him fairer-skinned, bright children who would respect and adore him.

He sat on his stool, lost in his dreams, forgetting to count the rows of figures in the ledger before him. Someone bumped his elbow and shattered his reverie. An old black African, William Taylor, Mr. Whitfield's general worker and obviously favourite employee, grinned down at James in his kindly way. 'Come on, young James. Get on wid you countin'. Dreamin' don' make money for we black people. Doin' do!' He laughed, his open-hearted, happy laugh, and moved away.

James was filled with dismay as he looked down at the hands holding his pencil. They were black. In his dreams, he looked like, felt like, was like, his father; in reality, he was nothing like the man, and he was not even acknowledged as his son. It was not right, but he would make it right. He would not forever be James Stenhouse. He was by right James McGuffie, and Bridgetown would know it. He would be someone.

★

Mrs. George Whitfield died before the ship could bring her to land in England. Despite Margaret's frantic efforts, the sad, weak woman just slipped out of life and was gone. The long days and nights spent nursing her, and the long, sorrowful, exhausted sleep that followed the tragic committal of her friend to the waves entirely filled Margaret's voyage.

She awoke, as if from a terrible dark dream, on the morning that the ship entered the waters of the Mersey and approached the famed Liverpool, a place greater than anything she had ever imagined, in the cold, grey light of a spring morning. The water beneath the ship was not blue, but was like frothing waves of dark, cold metal. The sight of huge buildings looming up behind a forest of masts of giant ships docked in rows beyond counting rendered her speechless.

She felt dizzy with sickness, and she shivered in the icy, cold wind. She had never been cold before. She had scarcely ever felt coolness, and she was frozen to her very bones. She shook so violently with cold and with fear that her teeth made a strange, clattering noise. A sense of terror engulfed her as gulls screamed noisily over her head, and she began to cry. She was all alone. She didn't even know where to begin to look for her father. Jessie was dead and George Whitfield didn't yet know it. She had no contacts at all. She longed, as she sobbed with great, racking sobs, to be home with Caroline and with James, and to be warm.

PART THREE:
BARBADOS VILLA

CHAPTER NINETEEN

1834

The house of John McGuffie's dreams was rising, week by week, towards the crowning of its roof, and all of Wigtown buzzed with the news of the progress of its building. At the beginning stage of its construction, a strange storm of hurricane force had blasted the town and had shifted the rising western gable of the new house, but the damage had been repaired. There were no more hitches during the winter and into the spring of the new year, and the impressive villa took its beautiful shape before the eyes of many admirers. A young lad from Port William, they said, had made his money from tea or sugar, or slaves, and he had come back to settle in the county town among his own folk. Quite right, they said.

The house was positioned on the southern edge of Wigtown, sideways onto the bay. It faced into the sun's light, towards the dipping and stretching of ever green fields bounding the winding River Bladnoch's wooded banks. To the side of the house, eastwards, the ground fell away quite steeply into flat acres of mossy seashore inks and blue—grey Solway waters. The busy harbour of Wigtown lay at the foot of the road that passed by the front of John McGuffie's new house.

Approvers of the edifice murmured their quiet applause as they noted the elegance of the circular drive, the graceful flare of the stone steps, the long windows, and the dignified entrance portico. Disapprobation from detractors, generally spoken in louder tones than those heard coming from any supporters, included lamentations about the ostentation of a too-grand triple-gated entrance, the strangeness of the heavy wooden shutters being erected outside the long windows, and the very peculiarly shaped coach house with an entirely nonfunctional ornamental castellation effect. Each feature of the building was pondered, debated, and voted upon in the houses of Wigtown, in the inns and upon its streets. The discussions were reconvened daily, the subject of the house nudging 'the weather' out of its accustomed place as prime topic of conversation.

Wigtown could not know the resemblances the strange new house bore to other houses, other places, in the far-off world of the West Indies. Wigtown did not know of the dignified house called Highgate, a building of classical proportions sitting high above the port of Bridgetown, a house hidden behind a wall and approached through a triple-entrance gateway and a circular drive. Wigtown had never heard of Samuel Hall Lord, or of his 'castle'. It had not seen those long front windows with heavy hurricane shutters framing them, the beautifully moulded plasterwork of the ceilings, the grand staircase. Wigtown thought all the intriguing designs for Barbados Villa had come from the imagination of the enterprising John McGuffie.

Not only for his house was he discussed. No such wealthy, interesting, and completely unattached gentleman had come to live in the town for many years. Each unpromised maiden, be she six or sixty years of age, considered her chances, nursed her hopes, of presiding as mistress within the world of the wonderful new house beside the custom collector's house on the road leading to the harbour.

The men of the town were divided into two distinct camps of opinion about McGuffie, as about his house. Those that smiled on him delighted in the evidence of the fellow's success, admired his house, wished him well with the lassies, and wondered what use they could make of him in the town's affairs. The negative party, comprised mostly of short men with plain countenances, men who had not been the object of a good flirtation for a long time, considered loudly among themselves that the house was ridiculously showy, and they privately nursed hopes that the man would keep his nose out of burgh business.

John McGuffie had returned to the district of his early years, and he was reunited there with relations who were now strangers to him. In his memory they had remained young, just as they had been when he shared with them a common family home. The parents of that home were dead, and the children of those years were grown people with children of their own. Tentatively, he made his approaches to brothers and sister-in-law, to sisters and brother-in-law, and to nieces and nephews who knew nothing of him or of their dusky cousins across the ocean.

McGuffie's sister Margaret had married and borne five children before her death. Grace, his older sister, had married a respectable businessman in Port William and had a respectable family of respectful children. His sister Mary, though still Miss McGuffie, was the unrespectable mother of a lively and enterprising young man named Peter Clokie. The charming nephew Peter won the heart of his newly discovered uncle in a way that the man's own son, the shy and stumbling dark-skinned James Stenhouse, never had.

Of his brothers, William, the eldest, remained in the family business and had never married. He had prospered, acquiring other properties in Port William and near Wigtown along the riverside. The younger brother, James, had recently married the daughter of a prominent Wigtown family. With her, Jane Dalziel, he had established a draper's establishment in a corner position on the main street of the county town of Wigtown, the town that was rumbling with gossip over the recent return of John McGuffie

The stranger uncle brought his sister Grace's three children and his favourite nephew, Peter Clokie, all young people near in age to his own forgotten son and daughter, to share with him the first ascent to the new McGuffie roof in

Wigtown. They began their approach sedately, but enthusiasm overcame reserve as their footsteps echoed through the empty hallway, the sounds magnified as they filled the spaces of the empty shells of rooms. Up the strong stone staircase they clumped, then further clattered up the carpetless wooden stairs leading to the servants' attic floor and, finally, there was a noisy and high-spirited scramble up the ladder leading to the flat roof itself. They all squealed with delight as the wind caught at them, and they shouted out excitedly as they pointed out to each other the sights they could see from their exalted position above the town and surrounding countryside.

'See, Uncle John,' young Mary Johnstone cried, tugging at his elbow, 'there's a ship coming in.' A small sailing vessel moved steadily into Wigtown Bay as they watched. It turned and glided carefully and slowly into the river's channel and soon came to dock in the t-shaped harbour. They watched, fascinated, as passengers, like little ants in the distance, disembarked and moved up the harbour lane towards the town. Some turned to cross the fields below them and enter the town near the tolbooth. Others stayed on the new road, and they passed the front of the new house. Each of these paused, as he did so, just for a moment, looking in through the impressive gateway towards the new house. Each one was acknowledged with a nod and a smile from the owner on the roof.

The excited cousins returned to the main street where a meal awaited them in the kitchen of the draper, their Uncle James. Verdicts on the house came in loud chattering and delighted whoops. Jane Dalziel approached her brother-in-law with a letter. 'This just came off the boat, John.' He broke the seal and scanned the writing. Jane saw that his face changed colour. He rose from his chair without a word and went to his room.

She rushed after him. 'What's wrong, John?'

'Nothing,' he mumbled, turning his back on her. He sank down into a chair, leaned forward, and gripped his curly hair in both his hands.

'Of course there's something wrong! Tell me. Have you lost all your money or something?'

He looked up at her oddly, and then grinned. 'My daughter has landed in Liverpool.'

It was her turn to blanch, and she sank down on the edge of his bed. 'What do you mean? You don't have a daughter!'

'This very eligible bachelor, sister Jane, does indeed have a daughter, and very possibly a son as well.'

Jane Dalziel McGuffie, raised in a town where everyone knew everything there was to know about everyone else, was not easily shocked by the reality of people's supposedly private lives. As she reflected, she realised that little had been asked of John about his years abroad, as little as had been offered by him.

'Jane, I'll need to go to the Port with the young ones and I'll have a talk with Grace. She's the wise one among us mad McGuffies. We'll sort something out.'

★

Alone in conference with his middle-aged sister, John felt like a naughty puppy creeping to its mother, fearing a scolding but hoping for some comfort at the same time. Grace was a gentle and calm person, like their mother had been, and she was greying, ageing, wearying before her time, like their mother had done.

'My daughter has arrived in Liverpool,' he blurted out. ' I wasn't expecting her, to say the least, and I'm in a quandary, Grace, my girl.'

She lifted her eyes from the sock she was darning. She is too calm, he thought. She just gazed at him for a moment, and he could hear his breathing getting louder. 'Mary Ann's?' she asked.

He was stunned. 'How did you know?'

'Oh, John! I've always suspected. All that talk, too- bright chatter, to Mother and us about your housekeeper and her children, and how you took them under your wing. You never had wings, and you aren't a good liar. I could read lies on your face since we were bairns.'

He grinned at her. 'You old sly fox of a creature!' he exclaimed.

'You old sly fox yourself,' she countered abruptly, unamused. 'So, tell me, and this time tell me true, John.'

He told her then. He told her of lovely Mary Ann and her mother, the proud black African Minna. He told her of kindly Stenhouse and lively Caroline. He told her of the joy of his Margaret's birth and of his rejection of James. 'He probably is mine. She wouldn't have lied. It seemed impossible because of the time, and he was so dark. He still is utterly unlike me in my ways, as well as his looks. You would never believe that he was my son, Grace! ... But he must be mine.'

He went on to tell her of the news he had received after the hurricane, of the deaths of Minna and Mary Ann, just as he had heard it all from George Whitfield's letter.

By this time, Grace was grief-stricken, not with the sorrow of the tale, but from the glimpse she was getting into the depths of the heart of an always-adored brother. 'You didn't go back to see the children, even then?'

His narrative interrupted, he looked up to see that she was staring at him, tears running down her face. 'Oh, Gracie,' he knelt at her feet and took her hands in his. 'Don't be like that. They're all right. Really! James has employment with George, and Caroline keeps boarders. Margaret gets some money from me and will be acting the part of a lady. I couldn't help it. I couldn't go back! I was too busy. The house ... the business ...'

There was a wrenching sob from her, and he became angry. He dropped her hands and jumped to his feet. 'Well, what do you expect? I cannot do well if I have them hanging around my neck here, because they just would not be accepted in this country. They wouldn't like it here, anyway. Well, Margaret might do. She's so fair-skinned that no one would know she has colour in her. It would be misery for James and Caroline in this country, and I cannot go back there now. Things are changed. The whole economy will collapse when full emancipation is declared. I have to be here, or I can't provide for them, never mind for myself.'

He whirled around, 'I've got it! Margaret can come to Wigtown and house-keep for me. I'll say that she's my ward from Barbados. No one will be any the wiser. She might even be an asset.'

Grace was not impressed. There was an unusual note of harsh sarcasm in her voice as she asked, 'What will her name be?'

'Margaret – Stenhouse!' he exclaimed, triumphantly.

'How very clever of you, John; and everyone will declare her to be your mistress. Your daughter! Your mistress? Your slave? Your coloured woman?'

He was severely jolted, and sat down again. 'You're right. That's that, then.' They sat in silence for some time, John looking miserable and Grace blowing into her sodden handkerchief. Eventually he twinkled across at her, 'Well, that's the end of my eligible bachelor image. All those lovely, lonely ladies!' He wailed in mock despair, and she laughed, inspite of herself.

The next morning, John McGuffie rode back to Wigtown and booked passage on the next boat sailing for Liverpool. He was accompanied, at Grace's suggestion, by his niece Mary. The uncle charmed his niece, as they travelled, with carefree chatter, diverting tales, and joyful outbursts of singing. The niece, indeed, the whole world, might have been given the impression that John McGuffie was not only sublimely happy at the prospect of reunion with his West Indian daughter, but that all his plans had been drawn from the start with this very purpose in mind, and that the new house under construction in Wigtown had always been intended to be her home as much as his.

CHAPTER TWENTY

Margaret, distressed and alone when the ship had arrived in Liverpool, had been taken home by the captain, like a piece of unclaimed baggage. It was he who had written to her father, and it was in his home, cared for by his bemused wife, that she waited to discover what would become of her.

The girl could not be warmed. On a fine, mild day, with sunlight glowing through the curtains, she sat alone in the front parlour, her chair pulled as near to a coal fire as it could be pulled. She shivered violently. She pulled a borrowed woollen shawl tightly about her shoulders. She touched the tip of her nose with her finger and felt it cold. She held her hands out beseechingly to the flames.

The neat stone house with its dark colours, its polished surfaces, its tiny coal fireplaces in every room, and its ordered existence was a kindly place, but it was not warm. It was all she had seen of Liverpool, for she would not be enticed from its safety into the clamour of the streets of England's famed port city. From behind the curtains at the windows, she had shyly watched people passing along the street, and she had several times been lured out to stand in the open doorway for a few moments, but she would not leave the house.

The days were strange, semi-dark hours to her, the skies never lightening into full, bright daylight. The world seemed to be caught in a permanent state of twilight, or a never-ending stormy-coloured season. The gloomy greyness was made unbearably miserable for her by the accompanying coldness of the very air she breathed. Even the furniture in the house was cold to her touch, and her clothes seemed permeated by the chill, as did the bedding into which she burrowed in the dark nights.

A carriage halted outside the front gate, and there was the sound of people in conversation. The timbre of a man's voice sent a flood of joyous warmth through the frozen girl. Colour rushed to her face and tears to her eyes. It was her father. She knew his sound.

She jumped to her feet, clutching the shawl, stumbling over her skirt. She smoothed her dress and then her hair, started for the door, and turned back towards the window. 'Father! Father!' The words tumbled about in her head and were tasted on her lips. There was a roaring in her ears, and it sounded like singing. Suddenly shy, she peered out from behind the curtain, and she saw him approaching the door with a lady on his arm. Her heart and stomach lurched with the sudden, sickening thought that he had married.

The captain's maid answered the door's bell. Quiet words were spoken in the hall. The parlour door opened slowly. Margaret was still standing, silent, beside the window when they entered the room.

His eyes gleamed with pure delight. 'Margaret! You're such a lady! You're so like your mother, so lovely!' He reached out for her and, just as she had always done in the years of her childhood, she rushed to be enfolded in his arms. Tears, long restrained, threatened to soak his jacket. 'Now, now, now,' he soothed her. He patted her hair and then, with his large handkerchief, he began to mop at her face and at his jacket. He laughed softly, teasingly, 'What's this? Such misery at the sight of me?'

She eventually controlled her sobs enough to be able to look up at him, and then she glanced past him toward the stranger watching them from just inside the door.

'Margaret, this is your Aunt Grace's daughter, Miss Mary Johnstone.' Margaret McGuffie flashed a brilliant smile across the room.

Mary grasped an offered hand in both of hers and said softly, 'Cousin.'

★

As if extra candles had been lit and extra fires were set blazing, the world seemed brighter and warmer in an instant to the Barbadian girl. In the hours that followed her father's arrival, she felt that she was beginning to awaken from a dark dream, one during which days and weeks had disappeared from her life. The captain and his wife were thanked heartily for their kindness to the young woman. The waiting carriage took Margaret McGuffie, with her father across from her and her new cousin beside her, clattering away into the streets of the city that no longer frightened her.

John McGuffie had regular lodgings for business trips in the street called Mount Pleasant, and he had organised an extra room for his niece and his daughter in the comfortable town house there. Within several weeks, the Scottish girl and her exotic kinswoman became as close as sisters. They helped each other to dress, brushed each other's hair, and tried to avoid each other's knees and elbows while sharing a great, soft feather bed.

Margaret needed new clothing of every kind;, clothing suitable for a proper young lady living in northern climes. She was measured and fitted for dresses, undergarments, boots, hats and gloves. In free hours when measurings were done and John McGuffie was engaged in his business dealings, the cousin friends often walked together in the great city, exploring broad streets or tiny hidden lanes, even venturing to the dockland to watch ships arriving or departing, loading or unloading. There were fashionable avenues lined with grand houses displaying the rewards of the wealth involved in the merchant trade based in Liverpool. The elegant men and women who lived in these homes travelled about the city's streets in luxuriously appointed carriages, and there were so many of them that the sight of them and the rumbling sound of their wheels on the cobbles was everywhere, all the time.

The country girl from Scotland was as astonished and charmed by the wonders of Liverpool as her Barbadian cousin. Like children, the two young ladies wandered and stared and talked, always talked. Alone in their room, they mimicked the fine airs of the ladies they had seen, they minced as they walked, like the daintily shod, swished their skirts, tossed their heads disdainfully, and then became helpless with laughter at their own antics. It was not long before Mary Johnstone forgot the sad image that had touched her heart in the captain's dark parlour, that of a dull, frozen and frightened stranger half-hidden behind a curtain. The girl of that day was no more.

Margaret, almost constantly bubbling with happiness since the moment of the reunion with her father, found nothing in the magnificent city, in the friendliness of the people she met, in the accents of the voices she had heard, in the abundance of luxury all around her, in the wonderful cultural delights that were daily experience in Liverpool, or in the comforting sense of safety in the old, secure civilisation around her to allow any room for any thought that a single second of the new life stretching before her forever could be anything less than perfect. She forgot homesickness; she forgot cold; she forgot the overwhelming sense of strangeness upon her arrival; she forgot James and Caroline; she forgot Barbados.

CHAPTER TWENTY-ONE

A coach was needed for the castellated coach house being built in Wigtown. Like the house itself, it must be the finest of its kind in the county town. Messrs. Varty and Wilson of Lime Street were recommended to John McGuffie and one day he took his daughter and his niece with him to visit that establishment. The three strolled together down Mount Pleasant, turned right to pass the city's grandest hotel, and walked along the bustling, infamous Lime Street. The ladies would not have walked there alone. They soon came to a wide and open doorway leading into the coachworks.

Before them was a scene of great activity. A blacksmith worked in the far back corner of the large working space, but the heat from his forge and the sounds ringing from his anvil filled the place. The central part of the room was filled with coach frames and bits of frames, and the floor was littered with fragrant wood shavings. In a corner a saddler was working on the pieces of leather upholstery and with stout leather straps. The smell of the leather evoked in Margaret memories of the saddlery in Barbados and made her feel strangely at home.

A tall young man of about eighteen years was bending over long shafts of wood at the front of a new carriage. He had a fine paint brush in his hand, and he carefully drew a delicate line of black paint all the length of the shiny green shaft.

'Bravo!' shouted a burly older man as he passed the younger lad.

'Hush, Barton,' the painter protested. He grinned up at his tormentor. 'You nearly spoiled the perfection of my line! You haven't the soul of an artist, or you'd take more care when you shout.' The young painter saw the three strangers looking in from the doorway. He swept them a bow and invited, 'Come in. Watch the genius at work!'

'Genius? He wishes!' exclaimed the laughing man called Barton.

John McGuffie shook hands with Barton Wilson and then with young Thomas Varty, the painter, who was the son of the other partner in the business. The subject of the new carriage was raised, and the girls wandered off, looking at the various parts and pieces of coaches, and at some almost-completed ones in different parts of the large room. They admired lovely carriages as beautifully finished as any they had seen on the city streets, some with sumptuous, buttoned upholstery, cleverly hidden windows, dainty door handles, and lamp fittings of the most modern designs. They had thought that people occupying such carriages as these were from a different world altogether than their own.

As they returned to the place where the men stood in conversation, Margaret heard her father say, '... Barbados, until recently.'

'I had a cousin in Barbados,' said Barton Wilson. 'Perhaps you knew him? Reverend Mark Nicholson of Codrington Seminary?'

'Oh, yes,' replied McGuffie. 'I did have some business dealings with Codrington, and I heard often enough about your cousin. I believe that I may have met his wife. It was very distressing when her brother was murdered. The Nicholsons left the island just about that time, didn't they?'

Codrington. Margaret remembered. She remembered a tall, pale boy who held her hand and guided her along a rough walk. She remembered the silent forbidding shake of his head when she reached her hand up to touch a thorny spike on the trunk of a large silk cotton tree. She remembered hearing about snow and about living in England. He had seemed so wise, and had been very kind, she remembered. She looked at Barton Wilson in amazement, for the world of that remembering had been so very far away from her thoughts and yet, here she was, looking at a cousin of the boy from that dream-like past, and she was standing in the England of that long-ago discussion. A strange feeling swept over her, like a feeling of half-sleeping and half-waking, and she shuddered a little.

'Well, Margaret, my dear, what colour shall the coach be?' Her father's question to her brought her from her reverie.

She blushed and answered shyly, 'I have never really thought of a colour for a coach, Father. What colours are there?'

Thomas Varty chimed in, 'All the colours of the rainbow,' and then, lowering his voice to dirge-like tones, 'plus black, and brown, and white.'

They all laughed and then decided, after a session of lively discussion, that John McGuffie should drive a coach of yellow, bright canary yellow, with black trim. The buttoned upholstery would be black leather with finishing touches of ivory for handles and knobs. The spokes of the wheels would be striped with black and yellow.

Mary clapped her hands in excitement and exclaimed, 'Wigtown will have never seen such a coach!'

'I certainly hope not,' laughed her uncle.

★

That night, at home with his wife, Barton spoke of the charming Scottish merchant and the two girls. 'His daughter is coloured, you know,' he mused to his Cecelia. 'I certainly hope that she doesn't find life too disagreeable when she goes to live in Scotland.'

'And why should she, Barton?' asked Scottish-born Cecelia, somewhat defensively.

'In Liverpool, with her being so fair-skinned, you wouldn't really notice or care about her colour, but small Scottish towns might not be so unseeing or so uncaring as we are in a big city like this. Here, she will just be seen as rich and pretty. There, -- well, it could be a very different matter.'

'Penrith is a small place, Barton, and your people there aren't like you seem to imagine small town people to be. Penrith would be kind and welcoming to the girl, especially if she is as light in colour as you describe her.'

'Penrith would if she were as black as coal,' said Barton, 'but not every town has had a Thomas Wilkinson to mould its conscience.'

★

Barton Wilson's father had come from a tiny hamlet lying within sight of the northern market town of Penrith. During his childhood in the place called Barton, he had experienced something that had marked his memory, remained a moving force in his life all his days, the effect of which had been passed on to his children.

Young William Wilson had been taken by his father, Barton's grandfather, with him to the market at Penrith one day. There the child had noticed a tall, thin man with long hair, a man in the plainest of clothes but with buckles shining like jewels on his shoes, addressing a large crowd gathered in the square. The small boy had slipped free from his father's hand and darted between people, even through legs, to get himself to the front of the crowd so that he could see what was happening there. He had listened to the man who had gathered the crowd. In a plaintive voice, in a quaint form of speech, he told a tale of poor African people being taken captive, being forced by the hundreds into the dark holds of ships, being kept in chains as they crossed the ocean in great physical distress for weeks, being sold like horses or cows in a marketplace on the other side of the world, being made to work in the hot sun to grow sugar, and finally dying of disease and maltreatment far from their homes and families.

The compelling storyteller had then unrolled a chart on which was drawn the shape of a ship with the outlines in it of hundreds of human shapes lying head to toe, side by side, rows and rows of them. The picture had burned its image on William Wilson's tender memory. The speaker had concluded his address with an appeal for people to sign their names to his long piece of parchment so that the King and Parliament could be pressed to make this cruelty to the African slaves come to an end. As the people of Penrith crowded forward to sign the paper, the little boy, his heart pounding, had forced his way back through the mass of people to his father's side. Tugging at his father's jacket, he had pled, 'Please, Father, sign the man's paper.'

'I have already put my name to Thomas Wilkinson's petition, William,' he had been assured.

'May I sign, Father? I would like to. I can write my name very well.' The child had been full of entreaty, his eyes large with solemnity and full of tears.

'You are too young, my little man, but, when you are grown, you must do your part. Remember what you have seen. Remember the words and the pictures of the Quaker poet, William, and you can help to make sure someday that slaves become free men.'

Barton Wilson's father had never forgotten, and he had faithfully passed on his passionate concern to his own children. The Wilsons celebrated as a family on the day that slave trading was officially abolished in the British empire. They now awaited, as a family, the long-anticipated day, this very year, when slavery itself was to be abolished in all the lands ruled by Britain. Still, the Wilsons of Penrith and Liverpool knew that the legal abolition of a thing would not eradicate its curse, at a stroke, from the human heart. Many who freed their slaves would never call them brothers, and some who had been slaves would never, in their hearts, be free.

CHAPTER TWENTY-TWO

1834–1835

Barbados Villa was nearing completion and John McGuffie left the girls in Liverpool while he made a brief visit to Wigtown to organise final details of the building. While he was away, Margaret and Mary often accompanied their new friend and confidante, Cecelia Wilson, in visits to art galleries and concerts. Margaret had quickly realised what her African grandmother had also learned, that beginning life in a new culture involved a great deal of learning, and that the learning was very hard work. Margaret's head would often be spinning with the amount of information she was trying to absorb. She had to learn the names of people and places, discover unfamiliar ideas, beliefs and attitudes, learn a great deal about history and politics, understand new customs and styles, and adapt to new kinds of personalities, sights, sounds and tastes. There was more to know about in a large country full of so many different kinds of people than there had ever been in the everyday life of her tiny island home where everything had been simple and familiar.

In Barbados, just a drop of isolated land in the middle of an ocean, news from the outside world had been ranked in its significance according to how it would affect the lives of the people living there, in that place. In Britain, news from anywhere and everywhere was immediately relevant to peoples' lives, for Britain's fingers touched every place on the entire globe. From Liverpool, England's great port and so near to its industrial heart, a pulse could be felt beating, it seemed, from anywhere on earth, and far-distant events were discussed with as much interest and eagerness in homes, among friends, on the streets by strangers, in businesses and in the inns as was news about Liverpool itself.

Margaret was fascinated by this sense of being part of the knowing and the caring about everything that went on in the world. She avidly read the papers that came, following the developments in politics as prime minister after prime minister resigned in a period of national turmoil. She read with concern of the rising and defying of authority among union leaders and, equally, of the dispatch of leaders of common working men to colonies in banishment. She worried over the pressures on the workhouses, problems caused by the new poor laws. She was shocked, along with the nation, when the great Westminster Hall in London burned down.

One day as she read her papers, the print of one particular article seemed to deepen and sharpen before her eyes. The day of emancipation had dawned, had passed, in the British colonies. She read that throughout the slave colonies, on the night of 31st July, 1834, the churches had thrown their doors

96

open and the slaves had crowded into the places of worship to await their moment of release. 'As midnight approached, they fell on their knees, awaiting the solemn moment, all hushed in prayer.' On the first stroke of twelve from the chapel bells, they had sprung upon their feet, and through every island had rung 'the glad sound of thanksgiving to the Father of all, for the chains were broken and the slaves were free.'

There was a soft surge of emotion within her as she read the words, a catching of her breath, a momentary misting of vision; the feeling passed quickly. She hoped that things would go well for them, that there would be no risings and no terror. She wondered if Caroline and James had been part of the celebrations. It all seemed so very far away from Liverpool.

Her eyes glanced past the article to another. She turned a page and, when her cousin came into the room a little while later, Margaret was absorbed in reading a description of the correct fashions for the month as they were detailed, including hat shapes and ribbon colours.

★

As spring approached, the weather softened and brightened. Cecelia proposed that the girls accompany her on a visit to Barton's family in the north of England. June was the month appointed for occupancy of Barbados Villa in Wigtown, and John McGuffie readily agreed that the trip to Wigtownshire could be made, by Margaret and Mary, in two stages.

They carefully packed fashions and furnishings acquired over the months into stout trunks and boxes and set sail for Whitehaven. There, with only enough personal baggage for the trip, the young ladies disembarked. The rest of the goods went on to Wigtown with the ship.

During the twenty years of Margaret McGuffie's life, she had never been any distance from the open sea or a tidal estuary. Nowhere in the tiny garden island of Barbados was far from sight of the blue Caribbean, and nowhere in the loud, busy clamour of Liverpool was any distance from the wide, rolling, salty Mersey. Now, travelling eastwards from Whitehaven towards Penrith, the travellers entered a terrain entirely unfamiliar to her. They were soon encircled by mountains, and the sight of the sea was gone. Even the air was different. At first, surrounded and enclosed by the mountains, Margaret felt a strange claustrophobia, but the shapes and colours of the majestic mountains, the deep stillness of the dark lake waters, and the sense of wildness in huge tracts of unsettled land began to work a spell on her. She could hardly believe that the landscapes she saw were real; they were like nothing she had ever seen or imagined; they were breathtakingly beautiful. Something in her heart ached strangely.

They left the mountains, but were still within sight of them when they arrived at the tiny hamlet of Barton, their destination. Here they were received by Wilson relations, and several days were spent resting. As they explored the lanes near the old church of the village, they could see, not far away, the shapes of the buildings of the market town of Penrith nestling into the side of Beacon Fell. They were close enough to see smoke curling from the chimneys of the houses there.

One morning they set out quite early to walk along a footpath that led from Barton Church to the market town. They passed the farm settlement of Thorpe and near the Quaker village of Tyrill, and then they dipped down into the hamlet of Yanwoth which lay just across the river from Penrith. Here Cecelia insisted that they pause to rest and take time to pay their respects to the Quaker poet, Thomas Wilkinson. Just off the path, a drive curved towards the front of a two storey house. In front of the house, wrapped warmly against any threatening chill from a spring breeze, sat an old man alone. When their feet crunched on his pathway, he turned his sightless face towards the sound of their approaching.

'Friend Thomas,' Cecelia called out loudly, 'are you well? I have brought ladies to meet you.'

Margaret saw a face with an expression of wonderful sweetness, a very old, wrinkled face framed by long white hair reaching down past his bony old shoulders. The man's spotless, well-brushed clothing was plain, even threadbare. Bright silver buckles on his shoes caught the sunlight and made it dance.

Cecelia gripped the man's hands in her own, and he smiled at her tenderly, with pleased recognition. She took Mary's hand and guided it into his, calling loudly into his ear, 'Mary Johnstone, from Scotland,' as she did. His face lit with delight, and he echoed, 'Scotland,' in a dreamy sort of way, as if remembering.

Margaret was signalled to come closer to the old Quaker's chair, and she knelt beside his knee to touch, in her turn, the ancient hands. 'Margaret McGuffie, from Barbados,'

Cecelia shouted into his deafness, 'Barbados, in the West Indies, Friend Thomas.'

Curiously, the old man lifted his slender fingers to her face and then, having explored her features, to her hair. He stroked its silky ringlets and finally rested his hands on her slightly bowed head. 'Barbados,' he said softly, sadly. 'God bless thee, my child, and keep thee.'

Margaret could not move. There was something in his face, in the loving touch, in his words that caught at her. It seemed, for a brief holy moment, that the world went still around her in acknowledgement of the simple blessing.

When she finally drew back a little and looked up at the face of Thomas Wilkinson, she saw that tears had escaped from his unseeing eyes, were coursing down his face, and were dripping off his chin. Her own eyes flooded in sympathy with his unnamed distress, and she looked up at Cecelia in embarrassment.

Cecelia knelt beside him and took the aged, now trembling fingers in her own warm and supple hands. She put her mouth against his ear and said firmly, clearly, loudly, 'Friend Thomas, all the slaves have been set free!'

★

The footpath from Yanwoth to Penrith wound alongside the Eamont River to a group of houses by a bridge that crossed the water into the market town. They passed ancient stones and ruins of castles, as they walked, all testifying to the civilisations that had existed and vanished in this place from beyond the times of remembering. This was a crossroads place and always had been. Celtic peoples had centres here. Roman roads had joined here. Scotland and England, now enjoined in a century-old union, had always touched somewhere near here. People travelling to the enchanted world of lakes and mountains, a part of the country that inspired artists and poets of world fame, often passed this way. Penrith, though, had no energy to ruminate on its past or take much notice of the famous visitors who passed by. It was a busy trading town full of practical people. Their chief concern was the need to adapt to the quickly changing way of life sweeping away, with the dawn of the age of mechanisation, all that had always been familiar in the workings of the world.

The three visiting ladies explored the marketplace in the heart of the town. When they were satisfied with their chosen purchases, they headed north, along the road that led from the Sandgate up the side of Beacon Fell. They passed a simple but beautiful Wesleyan chapel, a building that somehow reminded Margaret of the Jewish synagogue in Bridgetown's Swan Street. She had the strange sensation, as she had experienced in the coach works of Lime Street, of familiarity in an entirely unfamiliar setting.

As if she had read Margaret's thoughts, Cecelia remarked on the building, 'The chapel was built by Thomas's father and uncle in memory of his grandfather. He was the man who first invited John Wesley to preach in Penrith, they say.'

Mary asked, with surprise, 'Is Thomas a Wesleyan, then? I thought he was Church.'

Cecelia smiled, 'He is Church and only Church. His grandfather was Church as well, but, not content to be only one kind of Christian, he was Chapel too. There is a stone in his memory at the door of the parish church, in fact. The Vartys were all very devout people. An old story,' and she panted and puffed as she went on narrating while climbing the hill, 'is that Thomas's great-great grandfather was working in a stone quarry when he heard a voice telling him to leave. He did, and the quarry walls came crashing in around where he had been standing. It must have been a widely believed story, mind you, because that is recorded on a plaque at the very church door as well!'

They reached a lane running along the side of the Fell and turned to look back over Penrith, over the winding Eamont River, and past rolling countryside with nestling pockets of hamlets to the layers and layers of mountains, misty blue, misty grey, and deep, dark blue which framed the horizon. They went on a short distance, turned into a smaller lane to the north, and reached a gateway in a woodland on the east side of the fell. They soon came to a strong, plain stone house, the home of the Varty family, – Stagstones.

This house in the woods was the place that Thomas Varty of Liverpool inhabited in his dreams. The family home that had been established by a pious line of folk welcomed the friends of the young dreamer to its warm fireside and tea was taken with the Varty aunt and uncle while greetings and news were exchanged between city and country. Thomas's father had retired from his Liverpool business already, but he had no desire to return to this quiet, albeit beautiful, world . He had established his presence in a gentleman's town house in a square between the business and dock districts in the teeming heart of his adopted city, and there he would stay. His brother at Stagstones, father of daughters only, looked to the young nephew Thomas as his heir. Thomas longed to return to Stagstones. The place was his joy, all he ever really wanted from life. While he painted his coaches in Liverpool, he painted imaginary pictures of his life as a gentleman in the family home high above the Eden valley near Penrith. He told everyone about his dreams as he worked.

Margaret McGuffie understood Thomas. From her earliest days she had heard her father express such dreams, and she had always shared the longing for just such a life as the one that filled his fantasies. She now felt a certain sense of smug superiority, for she was only days away from the fulfilment of her own such dreams. She would very soon take up her position as mistress of the elegant home that her father, a wealthy and personable gentleman, had built in Wigtown. Stagstones was an almost puritanically plain edifice. Thomas was young, a boy, really, and still only a coach painter. His future as a country gentleman seemed a distant prospect, and his fine house just a dream.

Mary Johnstone had seen what Margaret had not. Thomas was quite besotted with Margaret and, whenever he had spoken of his life at Stagstones, he had implied the presence of another person there with him to share in it. Before their departure from Liverpool, he had presented Margaret with one of his own paintings, a hauntingly beautiful landscape in oils. With unaccustomed solemnity, he had asked her to remember him whenever she looked at the picture.

Margaret had responded lightly, thanking him prettily for his gift and assuring him that she would do as he bade her, but that she would also think of him whenever the yellow and black coach hit a bump in the roads of Wigtown.

His wild adolescent blush and crestfallen air had betrayed his heart to the watching Mary who had realised, by his reaction, that Thomas had hoped for some tender look or comment of regard from Margaret. Margaret had seen nothing of this. After teasing him, she had turned away to speak with Cecelia.

CHAPTER TWENTY-THREE

1835

Margaret and Mary stood at the port railing of the sturdy ship that steamed across the Solway towards Wigtown. The afternoon crossing meant that they headed straight towards the sun and against its brilliance, and as the boat approached the coast, the passengers could not catch an early glimpse of the town. When the ship slowed and turned to make its entrance into the Bladnoch River channel, the watchers on deck moved to the other side where, their hands shading their eyes against the sun, they could begin to make out the shape of a lush hillside, of dark green mounds of summer foliage crowning large trees, of handsome houses and thatch-roofed cottages, of groups of grazing woolly sheep and contentedly chewing sleek cattle in lush pasturelands.

They sailed on up the river, first between tide-washed grassy flat land, then alongside strong embankments, and finally into the open space of the t-shaped harbour. There were people waiting beside the dock and, among them, Margaret could see her father standing beside the yellow coach. The ship stopped, churned and puffed itself into a turning place, and wheezed into silence. The cousins quickly gathered their travelling cases and scampered down the plank.

As Margaret stepped ashore, her father took her hand in assistance, and she smiled up at him gratefully with eyes full of love and happiness. His eyes did not quite meet hers; he looked distracted, flushed, ill-at-ease in a way she had never seen before.

People scrambled busily about them at the side of the boat. Men were there to unload cargo. Boys were waiting to be hired to run errands or help passengers with their luggage. Some, like John McGuffie, were there to meet family or friends off the steamer or to collect parcels. Others, standing near the bustle in the pleasant evening sunshine, were just there out of curiosity. They were the regular boat-meeters, people who always came to see what and who came off the ships and why, so that the waiting curious in the town could be informed of these things. These last ones saw John McGuffie give his hand to a beautiful young woman who had dark, silky hair and strangely black eyes. They saw her expression of love and his of discomfort. They watched as she, with the niece from Port William, was carefully settled into his amazing new yellow and black coach, and they watched as the vehicle moved away, slowly and cautiously, up the road that led from the harbour to the fine new house. They looked at each other in a knowing way, clucked their tongues, nodded little nods, and disappeared back up the road and across the fields to the town as fast as they could, their clucking tongues burning to tell the tale.

★

The coach ascended the hill, turned into the opened gateway and swept around the gravelled circle. It crunched to a halt beside the stone steps leading to the front door. Margaret looked up at the sandstone-fronted villa with its elegant, pillared porch and, for the third time, felt the strange sense of a familiar thing in an unfamiliar place. She was at Highgate in Bridgetown, at Sam Lord's castle, and at the Principal's Lodge at Codrington, all at once. She felt like a dreamer in someone else's dream.

Mary was laughing and talking with her father. A boy was collecting bags and parcels, her bags and parcels. A smartly dressed maid stood in the doorway looking down at her. She was dragged from her daydream by Mary, who pulled and tugged at her, 'Come, come! I cannot wait to show you!'

They entered a large hallway with walls of pale sandstone blocks. The floor was flagstones, and from it rose an open curved stone staircase. Wrought iron stair railings were topped by a richly polished mahogany handrail. It was like a castle. Mary pushed open a door and beckoned her to follow. Margaret peeked around the corner into a drawing room full of light. A welcoming fire glowed from a handsome white fireplace. There were three windows in the room, each reaching from the floor to the ceiling. The ones on either side of the fireplace looked out past gardens of shrubbery and flowers to the harbour down the hill. People were still there, moving about the docked ship and up the road. They looked like little ants. Beyond them could be seen the shining waters of Wigtown Bay with soft green hills defining its eastern shore. Mary pointed upwards and she saw lovely cornice work, not as elaborate as that she had admired in Sam Lord's house, but with deep rich mouldings, nonetheless.

Across the hallway was a dining room with panelled walls and gracious furnishings. The richly polished table gleamed reflected light from the long, south-facing window in the room. On the other side of the hallway, behind the drawing room, there was a small morning room facing out into a walled garden. Through its window Margaret could see a kitchen garden, more flowers and shrubbery, fruit bushes and the beginnings of an orchard in the sunny, secret space behind the house.

They continued their tour by ascending the stairs, following the sound of John McGuffie's voice. The staircase was lit by a huge window looking out over the walled garden and, beyond it, the houses and trees of the town. When they reached the first floor, they found McGuffie in conversation with a severe-looking woman, and the young boy scurrying about placing bags into rooms as he was directed.

On this floor there were five principal rooms and a small, very modern water closet chamber. John McGuffie's bedroom, spacious and with views out across the harbour and bay, was to the immediate left at the top of the stairs. The three rooms at the front of the house were interconnecting as well as each opening into the hall. The central and smallest of these was furnished as a dressing room. A little bedroom on the farthest right, the room that faced to the west of the house, looked out over a courtyard, the castellated coach house, and into the woodland in front of the neighbouring house. In that garden, Margaret could see two young girls playing with a tiny kitten. One of the children, laughter on her face, glanced up and saw her. The elder of the two smiled a pretty little smile and then could be seen saying something to her companion. The second child ceased her playing, stood up, put her hands on her hips, faced the window squarely, and scowled. Margaret burst out laughing. The late sun streamed in the window, making the room a golden, lovely place. Just then her father entered the room.

'This will be your room, Margaret. We will leave the front rooms for guests?' She readily agreed.

The stern-faced housekeeper spoke politely to her, but seemed unbending in her sternness. The maid, flustered and shy, appeared with word that she had been instructed to help Miss McGuffie and Miss Johnstone unpack their things.

It had been a very long day and they were weary. After a simple meal served at the shining table in the dining room, Margaret and Mary went to Margaret's new room which, so used to each other's company, they had agreed to share until Mary returned to her family. Mary slept quickly and deeply, but Margaret could not sleep. The sun had set, eventually, but light lingered in the sky, it seemed, almost forever. When the world finally went dark, the exhausted young woman still tossed and turned, too excited to sleep. Soft daylight had crept back into the room and the birds had begun to sing their hearts out before she finally slid into slumber.

CHAPTER TWENTY-FOUR

Much of a year had passed since Mary Johnstone had left Port William and travelled to Liverpool with her uncle. She was now summoned home by her impatient mother and Margaret McGuffie was plunged alone into the task of learning about yet another new world and its ways. By title she was the mistress of Barbados Villa. It was her place to preside, as such, over any social occasions her father saw fit to arrange in his new home. These were multiplying with his increasing involvement in the social and business life of the town.

The real brain behind the management of the household's affairs was the one that was housed in the head with the stony face, that of Mrs Grey, the housekeeper. Mrs Grey, Margaret soon discovered, was most anxious to firmly establish the fact of her authority in the minds of all she encountered. No one must be allowed to think for a moment that the newly arrived strange, foreign female figurehead John McGuffie had introduced into the arrangements at Barbados Villa had any real responsibility. Margaret, perhaps contrary to Mrs Grey's expectations, had no desire to challenge anyone's authority or rule over any part of their shared domain. She had other struggles to occupy her.

Margaret McGuffie could not understand a word these people said. Her ears hurt, and her head spun with her efforts to concentrate on their speech and force some meaning from their words. The young boy who came daily from his family's farm just a field away from the house, the gruff gardener who clumped down from the town to do his work each day, as well as the maid Annie, and Mrs Grey who had rooms in the attic of the house, all spoke easily with each other. Her father, also, spoke with these people and seemed to have no difficulty in communicating with them. Indeed, he spoke their language not only with his staff but also with the well-dressed and polite visitors who called to see him at the house. She had no idea what they were saying, any of them. A foreign language seemed to fill the air and she only occasionally caught the sound of a comprehensible word from all the speech around her. It seemed strange to her that her father, familiar in his speech to her from her babyhood, spoke this way in this place and no other. She could not fathom how her cousin Mary had spoken so plainly, always, in her hearing, for she realised now that this was the true speech of Mary's people, of her father's people. For some weeks she felt adrift from reality and shut out from this world that was to be her home. Gradually, she came to understand them. Individual words made sense at first, and then some phrases became familiar. Finally, whole sentences fitted together for her and, when she could understand what people were saying around her, she began to feel more settled and less frightened.

★

Mr John McGuffie and his daughter were invited to dine with Mr and Mrs John Black at the British Linen Bank house. The invitation obviously impressed the housekeeper and the maid. They were animated in discussion about it for days before the event. When the evening arrived, Mrs Grey and the servant Annie muttered together over the dressing of Margaret for the occasion; they fussed and fretted over her ruby red dress, her dainty shoes and over the placement of ribbons in her hair. They continued with their fussing until she was safely installed in the carriage that waited, newly scrubbed and polished, at the door. Margaret carried a black lace shawl at the insistence of Mrs Grey who, for the very first time, had actually smiled at her.

Their destination was only on the opposite side of the town, and could have easily been reached on foot, but the opinion of the household was that Miss McGuffie's black satin slippers would become dirtied by walking the length of the town's square, no matter which route they took. The carriage had been decided upon to save her shoes.

Margaret had not yet seen the main street of the town, for she had spent her days thus far completely in the security of the new house and its grounds. She was excited as the carriage rumbled out the gate, passed the front of their neighbour's house, and turned up the main road into Wigtown. There was a large warehouse just behind the custom collector's house, the house that adjoined their property, and beyond that there were a few cottages scattered along the curving street that led to the corner of the High Street.

As they turned into the broad main thoroughfare, John McGuffie pointed out the shop and home of his brother, Margaret's Uncle James, on the corner. Clusters of people standing about in the evening light of the mild midsummer season turned to look at them. Margaret looked back, just as curiously, at first, but soon was overcome by a sense of shyness and turned to look towards her father's face for comfort. He stared straight ahead, gently slapping the reins up and down on the horse's back, keeping it moving steadily along.

'The courthouse', he said, quietly, nodding forward in indication. She looked at the large building with its prominent tower, a building that dominated the sloping grassy open space that was the central square of the old market town. 'Provost McHaffie and I have some plans to get this square cleaned up and planted,' he confided as they rode past more curious townspeople. 'There is a lot to be done here; it will take time…' he rambled on, as if to make the point to himself more than to her.

They passed the courthouse with its assembly rooms and continued down a street to the left of them, turning right in front of a house pointed out as the manse of Rev. Peter Young, before entering a drive that swung left behind the manse and entered a handsome gateway. They approached a large red sandstone house, even larger than their own, but somehow much plainer.

The banker, John Black, and his wife, Susan Couper Black, were standing at the door themselves. In a Barbados house of note, only black servants opened the door to visitors; Margaret had noticed in Liverpool that white servants always admitted any callers to a house,; but guests of the most deeply respected gentleman of this town were received with no ceremony but that of genuine, unselfconscious hospitality. Margaret began to understand the honour that was granted in the evening's invitation.

During the evening, the Blacks entertained Margaret, with infectious enthusiasm, by telling her many stories about the life and the people of the town that was to be her new home. They told her of ancient battles which, according to traditions passed down from generation to generation, had been fought in the field adjoining their own house and not far from Barbados Villa. They told her of the castle, now vanished, that had stood sentinel over the bay from near the harbour. They told her about a monastery and its monks, established by a mysterious lady and famous for its apples, not far from the churchyard. They told tales of kings visiting the monastery as they rested in pilgrimage journeys to the shrine of Saint Ninian in Whithorn. They told of the saddest days of all in the town, the period known as 'the killing times' in the Covenanter struggles. They told the story of how two women who shared her own name, a Margaret of eighteen years and a Margaret of sixty-three years, had been executed by drowning in the old river channel that had run its course beneath the church, not far from their house.

'I left the town from that very place,' mused her father from across the room. 'The new river channel had to be made because the old port was too shallow for modern boats. It was very difficult, even when I was a child, to load and unload cargoes down there.'

'The women,' asked Margaret, with persistent interest, 'they really drowned two women here, in this quiet place?'

'Oh, yes,' replied her hostess. 'Old Susan Heron has died just this year. Her grandfather was actually at the execution, and he described the scene to her most vividly. She always spoke of it. She must be one of the last who remembers hearing the tale from a witness. They are all passing, and some would like us to forget forever what happened. That is why the Balmaclellan man made the gravestones. He was determined that we must never forget what was done.'

'Are there gravestones here?' asked Margaret.

'Would you like to see them?'

'Susan, dear,' interjected the gentle banker, 'the girl does not want to go tripping about in a graveyard when she comes to dine with friends.'

'I would like to,' Margaret assured him, ignoring the way her father was rolling his eyes towards her in a signal of protest. 'It is light so very late here. I would love to see the stones.' Her shawl was fetched by a maid who looked entirely used to the idea of guests slipping out for a walk in the graveyard, and the four of them trooped out into the soft twilight, concern for satin slippers entirely forgotten.

The ubiquitous neighbourly eyes were upon them as they crossed the street at the back of the house and entered the churchyard by its top gate. Susan Black chuckled and remarked quietly to her husband, 'That's the topic of conversation settled for tomorrow: the pretty girl in the lovely red dress,' and she smiled warmly at Margaret, 'being taken for a walk in the cemetery by that strange wife from the bank,' and she laughed merrily.

Margaret was shown the grand tomb of the aristocratic Vans family, the cracked tombstone staid to cover the remains of the wicked and feared Provost Coltrane, and the stone telling the story of the beloved Covenanting minister Rev. Archibald Hamilton; finally, she was led in reverent silence to the north side of the church where she was shown the poetically inscribed stones placed in tribute to the two drowned Margarets and three Covenanter men who had been hanged at the same time.

The party returned to the house and chatted on together long past the hour when etiquette decreed the polite departure of guests was required. Little children kept appearing, and a tiny baby wanted settling in the nursery. Margaret accompanied her hostess into the upper floor of the house to tuck in sleeping cherubs, to admonish mischievous imps, to mollify a tousle-haired and sleepy-eyed boy who was grumpy because he had been wakened by his little brother, and to take turns rocking a fretful baby until he went limp, and his breathing came in soft, regular puffs. Margaret's favourite among the children was a funny little fellow with bright eyes and curly hair. His name was Ebenezer, and he was far too wide-awake for a three-year-old, insisting that he be read to sleep by his favourite nurse who should have been in her own bed.

Eventually, very late and in almost complete darkness, the yellow coach rumbled back through the town. The street was deserted and the houses in darkness. Margaret heaved a contented sigh and informed her father, with great satisfaction, that such a town and such people must be without equal. 'The town is handsome; the people are good and charming, not a usual combination, I think; the history is fascinating; it will be lovely living here, and it is quite warm!' At that point in her complimentary recital, he burst out laughing. She hushed him crossly, 'You will waken the place, Father!'

CHAPTER TWENTY-FIVE

1835–1836

The village of Port William had been designed and built by the enterprising laird of Monreith estate only ten years before John McGuffie's birth. The same laird, Sir William Maxwell, had organised the construction of a coach road between the county town of Wigtown and his lands on the shore of Luce Bay. Before he had built the new road, no wheeled vehicle had ever been seen in the area called the Machars of Wigtown's shire.

On a fine, dry summer's day, the shoemaker's son from Mochrum, his Barbados-born daughter with him, returned to his home parish. They drove there in the yellow coach built in Liverpool, using the road made for the late Sir William. The journey reminded Margaret of the almost-forgotten days of her childhood, of the journeys she had made with her father around the island in the Caribbean. She sat at his side, entertained by his chatter and bursts of happy song as the coach rolled along the road south of Wigtown, across the Bladnoch's bridge, ascended a wooded hill, and came into open countryside. The peninsula they crossed was the same size and shape as the island of Barbados and almost entirely bounded, like the island, by a sea. She was a little girl again, dressed in fine and showy clothes, travelling out with her cheerful, handsome father, required by him to make an impression on those he wished to impress. This time he intended to impress his own family.

On Wigtown streets, her father was acknowledged, always as 'Mr. McGuffie, Sir,' with courteous nods, caps removed by the men and respectful curtsies bobbed by the women. Entering his home parish, in both villages of Mochrum and Port William, Margaret was disconcerted to hear her father hailed by roughly dressed country folk and passing tradesmen, even by cheeky-faced children, as 'Johnny'.

At their first stop, the Mochrum home of her Uncle William, Margaret was presented to her Aunt Mary and met her cousin Peter Clokie. Peter reminded her immediately of her father as he was in her memories of the in the days of her early childhood. He had the same even features and firm jawline, curly hair, sparkling eyes, and happy confident air. He looked ready to burst into song. Peter was full of his new ideas about the acquisition of land. He wanted to own farms, to be a powerful and influential man in his community. His uncle heard his plans with obvious pleasure, his own face lighting up as he urged the eager boy on and offered him advice.

They finally took their leave of the McGuffie house in Mochrum and moved on towards the coast, to the village of Port William. There the carriage drew up in front of a small cottage. Margaret's cousin Mary rushed out to meet them. There were hugs and squeals of pleasure as the cousins were reunited, but Mary quickly sobered and turned to her uncle. She spoke quietly., 'My mother's not well, I think. She has been asking for you, Uncle John. She's in her bed.'

The girls chatted together amiably in a little parlour until Margaret's father emerged from the small bedroom at the back of the house. He motioned for Margaret to come with him. In the darkness of the quiet room, Margaret saw a pale, grey-haired woman beckoning her to approach and then, patting the bed beside her, indicating that she should sit nearby. Grace McGuffie Johnstone strained forward to see her face, touched her hand, and whispered hoarsely. Margaret leant nearer towards her aunt, her glossy hair sweeping around her face. The dying woman touched the curls, tucked them back for her, and looked into the black eyes of the niece she had never seen. For this girl she had prayed each day since she had known of her existence. She whispered, 'Thank you for being so kind to Mary in Liverpool, my dear.'

'Oh no, Aunt Grace,' protested Margaret, 'rather, thank you for sparing her. I did not know that you were ill, or we would have come home more quickly. I'm sorry.'

'It was good for her,' said the aunt, swallowing often as she spoke. 'She has now seen something of the world and will settle better.' She studied the young woman's face with interest and kindness in her expression. She was pleased to hear Margaret refer so easily to Wigtown as 'home'. Perhaps it would work out for the girl, just as she had steadfastly prayed, but hardly dared to hope, that it would. The girl had not chosen her parents, or been party to their decisions. She should not be made to suffer for what others thought of her heritage. Yet, it was certain, in some measure she would not escape untouched. Foreigners always found life difficult in the country; Grace had seen that over the years. There was so much adjusting to do and there was always prejudice to overcome. There would be prejudice against this child's very foreignness, more against her illegitimate status and, if it became known, most and deepest of all, against the colour that ran in her blood, the colour of a slave. 'Oh dear,' Grace whispered.

'Have you pain, Aunt? Shall I call Mary?'

Grace shook her head gently and again touched her niece's hand. Then she drifted off to sleep and Margaret and her father slipped quietly from the room.

★

Within the first year of Margaret's life with her father in their new home, her draper Uncle James and his wife Jane produced a son whom they named, in honour of the uncle who had returned as a wealthy man from the West Indies,

John McGuffie. For all her natural pleasure over the event and in the young child himself, a new baby cousin, Margaret was not entirely pleased with her father's reaction to the event. He was ecstatic. He took as much pride in the appearance, the naming, and the growth of his infant namesake as a man would normally be seen to take in those of his own firstborn son. James Stenhouse of Barbados had never been celebrated in this way by his father and, in this country, was never even mentioned by him. Margaret was uneasy when she heard her father making plans for these two, the nephews he referred to as his heirs, Peter Clokie and baby John McGuffie. Had he been sensitive to her at all, he would have noticed her silences while he happily chatted to her about his schemes to endow Peter and John. He might have then realised that she would, indeed, be uncomfortable with his passing over the existence of his own son in their favour. Further, he might have had some thought for her position, as his acknowledged daughter. He made no mention of provision for her future in his planning. She tried to quell feelings of resentment that rose in loyalty to James and in concern for her own situation. She was not always successful.

★

She slowly, very gradually, made the acquaintance of some of the other inhabitants of Wigtown. It was the kitten that introduced her to her neighbours over the wall. Mrs. Simson, the proud wife of the customs collector, was not inclined to encourage social contact with a mere merchant and his young lady, especially a young lady whose origins were somewhat dubious, but her second daughter's pet kitten knew nothing of social embargoes. It particularly favoured the stroking ability of Miss McGuffie's soft hand, the occasional treat of titbits it received from Miss McGuffie's kitchen, and the knowledge that while it played in Miss McGuffie's garden there would be no Elizabeth Simson to pull its tail.

Whenever Margaret McGuffie heard young Margaret Simson calling out pleadingly, 'Ginger, Ginger, where are you?' She would lift the sleeping kitten from her lap and hand it over the low dividing wall into the young searcher's welcoming arms. Eventually, young Margaret Simson began to come directly to the exchanging place to call, 'Miss McGuffie, do you have Ginger?' and conversation, starting with kitten matters and moving on to other, equally absorbing subjects, grew longer and longer between the young girl and the older, dark-eyed young woman from Barbados.

Sometimes Elizabeth, the third daughter of the house, would run indoors and call out, 'Mother, Margaret is talking to that lady again,' and then wait, peeking from behind a curtain at the window to watch as Margaret Simson was marched back into the house and lectured firmly against wasting time in casual conversation with strangers. The kitten would scamper into the house behind its young mistress, and Elizabeth would run to catch its tail.

Despite such interruptions, Margaret Simson told Margaret McGuffie, over a period of months and in broken-off instalments, about her family, her mother, her father the customs collector, the hugely confusing tribe of children, the servants, and all the pets of the Simson establishment. Miss McGuffie wondered where they all slept, for the house was smaller than her own and hers would have been overflowing with such a multitude of people and pets occupying it.

★

The Barbadian newcomer had noticed, in her glimpses of the members of the family next door, in the faces of her staff and the people of the town, and in the appearance of her father's family, that they all looked something alike in the way that siblings resemble each other, like trees of the same leaf, flowers of the same bloom, or stones cut from the same block. There were certain variations in sizes and shapes amongst their facial features, in eyes and noses, cheeks and chins, but only to a degree. She realised that in Barbados there had been African people of many different tribes as well as English, Scottish, Dutch and Jewish people, all with distinctly different facial features, physiques, postures and, most obviously, skin and hair colourings and textures. In Liverpool, there had been people from all over the world, and the variety of human appearances had been almost infinite. Not here: these people had all belonged to each other from forever.

One day she searched her own reflection in the looking glass more carefully and thoughtfully than she had ever done. She noted the planes of her face, the shape of her nose, the texture of her hair, the fullness of her lips, the colour of her skin, and the depth of the black of the eyes looking back at her; she was not one of them.

★

Cecelia wrote to her – a long letter full of the doings of the Wilsons and the Vartys. The coming of the new railway station to Lime Street would be the making of their fortunes, it seemed. Thomas Varty was overjoyed with the prospect of a bit of a fortune coming to help turn his dreams into reality.

Cecelia told Margaret of developments in Liverpool, of works of art she had seen, and of her hopes of one day travelling to London. She was particularly determined to visit art galleries there and to view for herself the new Parliament buildings, designed by the famous architects Messrs. Barry and Pugin. According to Cecelia, these men were at the vanguard of a new movement in architectural tastes, a movement the whole nation appeared to wish to emulate in building styles. 'Thomas may dream only of Stagstones these days, Margaret, but let us together dream of a trip to London to see the wonderful sights there.' Her letter ended with the sad news of the death of Thomas Wilkinson of Yanwoth. Margaret had spent only a brief time in the presence of the man, but she felt a sense of loss when she read that he was gone from the world, a sadness that she would never have the privilege of seeing him again, and a sorrow for a world now poorer without him.

CHAPTER TWENTY-SIX

1837–1838

The King died and his nation mourned him respectfully, but only briefly. The sound of dutiful sorrow barely hid the whispers of eager curiosity and anticipation. The girl Victoria was coming to reign. Wigtown, the tiny country town on the edge of the Solway, mourned a death that struck more deeply into its peoples' hearts. News came that the custom collector's son James Simson, a lad of the same age as the princess who was coming to her throne, had died in India. The people of Wigtown had never seen their king, but they all knew James.

Margaret McGuffie heard sounds of weeping coming from the garden of her neighbours.

She went to the place where she shared the kitten and frequent conversations over the wall with Margaret Simson, and she saw the young girl huddled on the ground, sheltered against the boundary, sobbing distractedly. She called gently to her friend.

'Oh, Miss McGuffie, my brother has died. I'll miss him so much!' She cried bitterly into her hands and tears ran between her fingers. Margaret handed across her handkerchief and stood still, just waiting for the storm's passing. 'We've lost babies and old people from the family, but not people like James. I cannot believe that he is gone ...' She choked and blew her nose. 'We can't even bury him here. Where will his body lie? He is so far away from us.' She wailed, 'I cannot bear it; it hurts so terribly!'

Margaret McGuffie stroked the ginger cat; it had come to the wall to stand between its two Margarets, ignorant of the meaning of the sounds of human sadness. It rumbled its purrs, smiled its contentment, and arched its back as it padded and pirouetted on the stones. When the younger Margaret was calmer, the older said quietly, 'I do know what you are feeling.'

'Do you?' asked her friend. The sorrower looked up and carefully searched the eyes of her sympathetic confidante.

'Oh, yes!' She told the girl of her grandmother's death under the baobab tree and of how she had only learned of it later, how she had never found the grave. She told of her mother dying in the terrible storm and how three children had laid her in a mass grave with no blessing over her. She even told Margaret Simson of the recent news of the death of Thomas Wilkinson, now laid to rest in an unmarked grave because of his Quaker beliefs. 'They are all gone from my life, but they are not really gone,' said Margaret McGuffie thoughtfully. 'If we believe that they are with God, then they are just waiting for us. James is safe, Margaret; he has just gone on somewhere ahead of you.' It was strange how, as she spoke words to comfort the distressed child, they comforted her own heart. Faith shared took deeper root.

Later, when Margaret Simson slipped back into her house, more at peace than when she had fled from it, she did not betray the secret of the source of her comfort. She had been told that strangers from foreign places had little or only flawed knowledge of religion, were not true Christians, and that all their beliefs were suspect. 'Heathens', they were called, even when they attended church with everyone else. Her brother James had died among such 'heathens', and Margaret Simson hoped that they had been like her friend in the next garden.

★

James McGuffie and his wife Jane produced a second child, a daughter named Mary, in the year of Queen Victoria's accession to the throne. In that same year, William McGuffie, of Mochrum, the eldest son, died, and John McGuffie of Barbados Villa became the head of the family. He was now support and mentor to a family of sisters, brother, nieces and nephews. He had inherited from William some property in Port William and in the developing hamlet beside the Bladnoch River. He began to spend more time travelling to Port William on family business there and, at the same time, he was becoming more involved than ever in the politics of Wigtown burgh.

Margaret was increasingly, left alone in the large house. She found company and diversion in the home of her Uncle James and Aunt Jane, the house over their draper's shop. In that busy, noisy place, she helped to keep the babies occupied and entertained, much as she had done for the Whitfields in Barbados. She enjoyed working, again, with children. She often returned to her own fine house with her clothes stained by little, grubby fingers, spotted by crumbs and milk, and creased from having held damp, little, sleeping bodies in her lap as she rocked them.

One day she had slipped back into her room unseen by any of the servants. She had overheard the maid, obviously unaware of her presence in the house, complaining to the housekeeper. 'It's no' a fit thing for a proper lady, Mrs Grey. Her claes're proper mucky. Ah'm fair affronted, fer folk'll be thinkin' we're no' da'en wur job.'

'It's not your fault, Annie,' said Mrs Grey, iron in her voice. 'She's foreign, that's what she it. They don't care about cleanliness as we do. People understand that you have a difficult time, I'm sure.'

'She's more'n foreign. I reckon she's anither type a 'th'gether, if ye ken whit ah mean, Mrs Grey. They black e'en 're no like broon e'en, no way! They're pure black! I reckon th'on yin's a n*****!'

115

'Annie!' Mrs Grey was astonished at the girl's bold outburst. She had wondered the same, but would have never dared to articulate her opinions. She laughed a shrill, unpleasant laugh.

When she first come to Wigtown, Margaret McGuffie had struggled to understand the speech of the local people. Now she wished that she could return to those days of oblivion. She felt heat flushing her face and her eyes flooded with angry tears. In the instant of hearing their words she had understood so much. She stood in the window of her room and looked out across the Simsons' woodland garden. She suddenly remembered how voices almost always called her young friend away while they spoke together. She also recalled how the street of the town grew quieter, emptier, whenever she passed along it. People in shops, chatting in an animated fashion, always fell silent when she entered. Children, she realised, were pulled into doorways often by unseen hands as she approached, and curtains were mysteriously drawn as she passed windows. No one sat near her and her father in their accustomed pew in the church. She had seen backs turned on their carriage lately, as it had travelled the length of the street. No one in her house, on the street, in a shop, or in any home she had visited, had actually been less than polite to her face, but the words she had just heard in her own house, like the tearing of an obscuring veil, had revealed to her that, in spite of the well-maintained facade of civility and service she encountered in all her dealings with people, she was despised.

She quietly changed her gown and tidied her hair. She carefully checked her appearance in her mirror. When she left the room, Annie and Mrs Grey were on the stairs. She swept past them without a look or a word. She went outside to sit on her garden seat for the rest of the afternoon.

Margaret McGuffie was never the same again. She became a watchful and reserved person. She did not speak as freely to people in public places, and she appeared to have adopted a haughty manner. She became cold, even imperious, in her dealings with her servants.

She eventually persuaded her father that the services of the increasingly sullen Mrs. Grey were no longer necessary. She took over the management of the household and shortly afterwards replaced Annie with a maid of more timid temperament. She was skilful and intelligent in her organisation. Surfaces were better polished, linens were snowy white and crisply starched, and the cooking was improved. She herself became known for her impeccable appearance. There was never a hair out of place or a crease in a gown. Tiny cousins were clucked at from across the room, but sticky fingers were not allowed near her. Queen Victoria was no more regal or superior in her manner than was Margaret McGuffie. Only Margaret Simson saw no change in her. For young Margaret, the neighbour girl, there was always a sympathetic ear, a sweetness of disposition, and the former tenderness of heart now firmly stowed out of sight to all others.

Margaret McGuffie's first Scottish summer had been comprised of long days filled with extraordinary light. At its ending, the leaves on trees and hedges had mostly turned from green to brown or gold, and had then been blown away in swirling, biting winds. After this, it seemed that light vanished almost altogether from the skies. A pale sun briefly nodded above the horizon each day, barely high enough to illumine the grey, sodden winter world, and then dipped out of sight again. She endured a dreary succession of cold, wet months huddled in front of fires, burning candles beyond number for light.

She had never known such seasons. The year in Barbados was all summer; the cobbled streets and bright lamps of Liverpool disguised the wet ground and dark times of winter. Wigtown, though, was a place where seasons were very evident, where the weather affected life, and none of its inhabitants were more keenly aware of this fact than the young, cold Barbadian. She learned to dread the bare, dark winters, as one year folded into another and then another. When the skies grew dark and cold, she wanted nothing more than to be able to creep into the depths of the coverings of her warm bed and to sleep until spring brought light again. She longed all through the winters for the return of warmth, of light, and of green foliage into the dark landscape.

In her fourth Scottish winter, terror came with the hated season. Just days into the doorway of a new year, a hurricane blasted Galloway. One Sunday night, Margaret lay huddled in the mound of blankets covering her bed. She was just drifting into sleep. Her tiny fireplace, still glowing with the evening's coals under a banking of dross, began to hiss and spit, and she lifted her head to look for the origin of the strange sound. Water was splattering down the chimney and she could hear it lashing at her window behind the heavy wooden shutters. She lifted their iron bar from its bracket and swung open the shuttering for a view just as a howling noise, like an invading animal or an angry ghost, roared into the chimney. She peered out into the night. Light from a kitchen lamp shining out of the room below hers cast a dull glow out into the storm, and she could see grotesque shadows – tree branches gesturing as if in a wild panic.

Inside the house she heard the sounds of opening and closing doors, and the clumping of footsteps in the attic and on the stairs. She slipped into a warm robe and went out onto the landing where she called, in an exaggerated whisper, 'Who's there? What is happening?'

Her father appeared, coming towards her up the stairs, a glass of water in his hand. 'It's all right, Margaret; just a storm brewing. John and I have been checking that the shutters are all closed.' John Muir, the son of the neighbouring farmer, was the house servant, and it would have been his footsteps she had heard in the attic. If he had been outside clamping the heavy wooden storm shutters against the windows, she realised, he must be soaking wet from the rain.

She returned to her room and climbed into her bed, pulling the bedclothes tightly over her head. She wriggled into the warm space she had left. She did not hear, from under her blankets, the sound of the wind changing its direction, beginning its assault from the west, right against her window.

A flying branch torn from a tree smashed the glass of her window; its force hurled the thick wooden internal shutters apart, and sent one crashing into the wall. She leapt from her bed, screaming at the pitch of her voice, and ran out from her storm-blasted, howling room into the hall. She dropped, cowering, against her father's door and screamed like some demented thing. He flung his door open, and she fell into his room, the piercing sound of her cries never diminishing though he gathered her into his arms. The terrified servants clustered about her in alarm.

In desperation, John McGuffie roared at her with a roar louder than her screaming or the wind. 'Margaret! Stop that!' She whimpered, her eyes tightly shut, and he signalled a maid to help lift her into his own bed. 'There is less noise on this side of the house,' he said. 'I shall sit up with her and sleep later, if I can, in the front guest room.'

'It'll no be aired, Mr McGuffie,' the efficient maid protested.

'Never mind that,' he snapped, and looked back at his cringing, moaning daughter. 'Please warm some milk and bring it up for Miss McGuffie.' Left alone with Margaret, he watched her with curiosity. She was not hurt. She was not a fearful type of person, normally. Why was she so traumatised by a broken window, a howling wind? She whimpered again and moved restlessly; her eyes were still tightly closed.

'No, no!' she whispered and, more loudly, 'No! No! Please!' She shoved the warm blankets away from her. 'Mama,' she whined in a piteous voice. He touched one of her hands and she started up, wildly, then looked at him with an expression of horror on her face. He rubbed the hand, then her other hand, and he murmured her name quietly until the fear left her eyes and she seemed to recognise him.

The maid knocked and brought in the milk. He held it carefully to her lips until, sip by sip, she had drunk it. She sank back onto the pillows and, though she seemed calmer, tears began to run from her eyes, faster and faster, until the torrent of her weeping seemed to rival the pouring of the rain outside the window and her sobs became more distressing than the howl of the wind.

He sat with her all night, and during its long hours he learned the story of the Barbados hurricane six years before. In gulps of sound and wrenching broken phrases, she told him from a memory revived in distressing detail by the crashing of the shutter, the breaking of the glass and the howling of the wind. When she finally slept, he continued sitting beside her, staring at the puffy face, the soft hair, the small fine hand resting on the coverlet still clutching a soaked handkerchief. He should have been thinking that night of the damage done to his property and to the town itself. Instead, he returned in his thoughts to his past and to his memories of the beautiful Mary Ann, of proud Minna, of mischievous Caroline, and of shy James. There were memories of plantations in the sun, of the faces of slave people, of the smell of leather in Stenhouse's saddle shop. The pictures assailed him, and they came now overlaid by newly planted mental images of an assault upon his child, of his love lying bloodied in a doorway, of an unmarked grave. He could not sleep, but he wept and, as the cook crept downstairs past his door in the dark hours of early morning, she heard the man's groaning above the sound of the wind that still roared around the house.

★

John McGuffie was deeply affected by the night of the storm. Before that wintry blast he had been kind, even mildly indulgent towards his daughter and he had become proud of her skill as a hostess on the occasions that he had brought business associates or friends in to dine but he had ignored her beyond that, and had felt that he was a rather generous man in allowing her a place in his life. Sometimes, especially when he had enjoyed a good port, he had gone so far as to congratulate himself for the liberality of spirit which had prompted him to own her at all. Many a man wouldn't have, he would reason. After the storm, though, he became her faultless benefactor and her fierce protector, her champion with all his heart. She had been wounded at times when he had ignored slights against her. Now he noticed them more quickly than she did, sometimes saw them where she did not, and he was always incensed by them. He began to cut acquaintances who made light remarks about her, or who did not treat her with due courtesy. This alarmed her, for she did not want him to court unpopularity for her sake. She began to exaggerate to him any instance where kindness had been shown to her in order to counter his moods. Then he became so ridiculously grateful to people who had only been civil to her that she felt an even greater embarrassment.

He gave her a riding mare, a gentle but lively creature she dearly loved. He leased the large field that ran behind his garden wall and the mare was kept there with the larger coach horse and his own riding gelding. Margaret would ride southwards, whenever the day allowed, from the town and across the Bridge of Bladnoch, sometimes turning westwards to follow the winding riverside road, and other times turning east for a gallop along the lanes of the flat land of the Baldoon estate right down as far as the edge of the bay.

One day near Baldoon her riding hat blew off in a puff of wind and she sent her mare cantering in crazy pursuit of the feathered thing. She laughed until she gasped as she chased and as it danced and whirled out of reach in front of her, caught and caught again in the twirling, swirling breezes.

A young man on a fine black horse appeared from the road that led through the trees to the old castle of Baldoon, and he joined in her chase. It ended, to his consternation, with his horse's hoof planted right through the top of the spinning, tumbling hat.

Margaret looked down at the apologetic man with nothing but amusement in her eyes. 'I think your horse could take up millinery, Sir,' she laughed as she examined the ruined offering. 'I quite like a hoof-shaped hole in my head gear!' she said, and then she galloped off.

They met again, by chance at first, but soon they rode together by appointment. James Caird, the young gentleman who had taken up residence at Baldoon, had a great interest in politics and in the world of agriculture; he had intentions of introducing sugar beet production into Scotland. Miss Caird, his sister, often visited with Miss McGuffie when James called to speak with her father. He quickly became a favourite of John McGuffie who was impressed by the young man's enterprising genius, his influence, and his contacts, but even more by his open friendliness with Margaret. She, as they rode together ever more frequently, by the bay or in riverside woodland, began to dream, in a shy and reluctant way at first, of marriage and of a new position in life, even of having children of her own.

★

There was a wedding in Mochrum. Mary Johnstone became the wife of staid, serious Samuel Goodwin of Port William. Samuel had long pursued Mary, they had all known, and she had held him off until, as her mother had predicted, she was ready to settle down for good and all.

Margaret stood as witness for her cousin that day and glowed with a happiness that came from more than the sharing of Mary's joy. She felt, for the first time, that she belonged in this new world. Her father undoubtedly loved and protected her,; her cousin and extended family received her kindly, and there was an eminently suitable match upon her horizon, she felt more sure as the days went by. She was more beautiful than she had ever been, radiant, serene and content, and her father's pride in her was a visible thing as he looked at her.

★

One day soon after the wedding, as they rode beside each other, chatting together companionably, Caird told Margaret about the developments in his sugar beet plan. She described to him the sugar cane plantations and industry that had been part of her earliest memories.

'It must have been very difficult for you,' he said, his voice full of sympathy, 'to see your own people being used like animals in the hot fields. I understand they suffered some terrible treatment in the days of slavery. Our agricultural workers here have a rigorous life, to be certain, but they are clearly regarded as fellow human beings with us, not just animals to be used and then discarded. We are always trying to make conditions better for our workers. We feel a genuine regard for them ...' He went on and on, but Margaret heard little, had heard little, since his words, 'Your own people' had been uttered.

She clung to her saddle, so dizzy had she become, and wished to be home, away from the riding that only minutes before had been her chief delight. 'Your own people ...' She knew in that instant that the young gentleman, a kindly, brilliant and energetic man, had no intentions towards her other than companionship in riding.

She remembered seeing slaves working in the cane fields as she rode by with her father, so long ago. They had been, to her, another people, an alien species. Minna, her adored grandmother, had been black with their blackness, but somehow did not link her with them in her thinking. Her father was 'her kind', and his family were 'her people', but never once had the toiling, glistening ebony creatures in the sugarcane fields seemed remotely connected with her. To this James Caird, she was one of them, and, to him, 'one of them' could be a favourite friend, but would never be a wife, never the mother of his heir.

She realised then the trap that she was in. To him and all like him, she was 'one of them'. Yet, to the blacks of her island, she had been also 'one of them', only in that instance, a member of the European peoples. To no one, not even perhaps to her family of either colour, had she been or would she ever be 'one of us'. She was a breed apart.

★

There was a tea party in Wigtown. Queen Victoria was to marry her beloved, adored Prince Albert. The nation rejoiced with her in many celebrations and, in the county town of Wigtown, a large group of older spinsters, game, grey-haired and jolly ladies, gathered in the assembly room of the public buildings in the town square for the Spinsters' Tea Party. They covered their hair with wigs and powder and ribbons, and they had a very merry time. Margaret McGuffie sat at home that evening in grumpy silence while the rest of the town laughed at the delightful idea of the spinsters publicly celebrating their never-dying hopes of wedded bliss.

★

During the next year there was another great storm. Baldoon castle, weakened during the hurricane of the previous year, came crashing down when the next strong winds came. James Caird was not at home at the time. They said he was away courting his young lady.

CHAPTER TWENTY-EIGHT

1843

One year the whole world seemed to go wild with dramas and crises, one after the other, everywhere. Things boiled and exploded in realms physical, spiritual, political, economic and social. Mount Etna erupted; there was an earthquake in the West Indies; there were hurricanes blasting and returning to blast again; Liverpool caught fire. There were revolutions, wars, and massacres in Jamaica, San Domingo, South Africa, New Zealand, and Afghanistan. An expedition forged its way up the fabled Niger River in Africa, and whales swam into the waters of the Solway Firth between England and Scotland. Scotch fir trees died mysteriously, as if from a plague. A tunnel was opened under the Thames, and a canal was cut through Canada. Industry was howling that it was dying, and the nations were threatened with the imposition of an income tax. A Scotsman tried to assassinate the Prime Minister, and he killed a secretary by mistake. Publicity about that incident inspired another Scotsman to set off for London, announcing his intention to kill Queen Victoria for daring, as a woman, to usurp the God-given right of men to rule always and utterly. That winter, England lay blanketed under fourteen feet of snow.

Scotland heard what was happening elsewhere in the mad, cracking-up world, but was absorbed too much in a momentous eruption of its own to pay full attention to other places. The Church of Scotland was a proud Presbyterian body born in a national movement of reformation three hundred years before. In the seventeenth century, when it was barely less than one hundred years old, that church had endured struggles and sorrows for an entire generation. Its stout heart had won through those times, and it had, once again, been granted its own freedom of self-determination as a denomination. In the eighteenth century, it had weathered the storm and survived the sadness of a secession from its ranks nationally. Now, in the middle of another century, an even greater storm, a yet deeper division, threatened its existence. Patronage had long been a thorny issue in Scotland. The practice of land-owning heritors, charged with responsibilities to provide stipends and buildings for the churches in their communities, using their influence to interfere in the intended democratic decisions made by congregations was widespread and much resented by many of the Scottish people. Evangelicals of the national church, their consciences crying out about the need to rid themselves of secular influence upon spiritual decisions with spiritual implications, found that they could no longer dwell together in the same denominational house with moderates of the church who were willing to endure domination by patrons for the sake of the financial benefits of patronage.

There was a huge split, and the Free Church of Scotland sprang into being all over the land. Where heritors refused to grant their feued land for the building of rival sanctuaries, narrow little stone churches were built in back gardens of sympathetic freeholders or on rocky foreshores. Small, utilitarian manses, less ostentatious than those provided by generous heritors for established parish ministers, were built near the new places of worship.

Even in Wigtown, where the popular Rev. Peter Young had held spiritual sway over the town almost unchallenged for forty-four years, and where a Secession Church on the western approach to the town already provided a home for the dissidents of the former generation, there were enough anti-patronage people in the parish church to be able to form a third Presbyterian church. They built it, with a manse beside it, just past Rev. Young's manse on the road leading from the tolbooth to the harbour. The shyer, more sensitive members of the movement slipped down the back lane, at the southern edge of the High Street's back gardens, to their services. The more aggressive types walked loudly, proudly, and with very serious faces past the door of the home of their former minister, their purpose clear, their consciences making them more determined to display their integrity than making them concerned about Christian unity.

Newspapers were full of the dispute. Week after week, column upon column, page after page, arguments were examined, public meetings described opinions sought, and developments recorded. One of the issues raised was that concerning the allowing of women to vote in the choice of their ministers. Many felt that the possibility of women in the congregation affecting the outcome of the vote in any calling of a minister was an alarming one, for women had been commanded, had they not, to keep silence in churches, to be guided by their husbands, not to challenge the authority that God had given to men in the rule of the church? If they voted as equals in a secret ballot, it might be women, even unwittingly, who altered a decision that should rightfully be made by men, and they would thus be transgressing the commands of Holy Writ. Another dreadful thought was that women, in a secret ballot, might not actually vote the way their husbands or fathers instructed them to.

★

Margaret McGuffie read all these things and much more in the Free Press newspaper which arrived weekly from Stranraer. Its four pages of tightly packed print were eagerly devoured by her on the day of their arrival and then read and re-read all through the following week. She had grown lonely, and her mind revelled in the experience of feeling in communication with the world again, even if only as a spectator. In earlier years, regular newspapers from Dumfries had kept her informed in a general way, but the new paper, printed in Wigtownshire, with its lively political outlook, its closer local links, and its faithful recording of national and international news, opened a large new window in her world.

She experienced feelings of great concern and sorrow as she read graphic descriptions of the devastation caused by an earthquake in the West Indies. Antiguan scenes, vividly recounted by a reporter who told of buildings crashing, of people rushing into the streets in terror, and of destroyed churches, were very like her memory's pictures of the Barbadian hurricane, and for weeks she experienced restless days and nightmare dreams. Her father suggested that she give up reading the papers, but, instead, she gleaned the news from them with even more intensity of interest.

She became fascinated by reports from Africa. She followed stories in the paper of the explorations reaching into the previously unknown parts of that continent, and she wondered if the explorers would encounter among the Africans any children of the twin of her grandmother Minna, her own cousins in blood as much as were the McGuffies of Wigtownshire. She read of the establishment of model farms, the only safe refuge from continued forays by slave traders from America. The dispute between Britain and the United States over the continued trade, long since outlawed in Europe, raged on. Margaret hated knowing that people still endured what her grandmother had experienced, the harrowing things she had heard from Minna under the baobab tree in Bridgetown. She felt rage when she read of the interception, on the high seas, of slave ships and of the people discovered by rescuers in the stinking holds of the ships. Her rage was made greater by her impotence to do anything about it. She could not even find relief from the spirit of sadness the stories created in her by talking about it with anyone, for by merely raising the subject some attention would be called to her colour, and she could not bear that.

She read once of a reported judgement in the state of Missouri in the United States in which the judge declared that 'an accused negro slave could not be regarded as having committed forgery for, by the laws and the Constitution, a negro slave was not considered human.' An animal could not be charged with forgery.

One week a black man came to Wigtown to perform in the assembly room. With her Aunt Jane and a maid, Margaret McGuffie attended the concert. There were curious looks cast in her direction as they took their places, and some of the audience whispered to their neighbours. She tried to ignore them. The singer had a wonderful voice, and his theatrical presence mesmerised the audience. Margaret heard little of the music and took in less of the drama, for the performer was the first black person she had seen since leaving Liverpool, and she was deeply, strangely moved by him. To her, there was a jarring sense of incongruity in the appearance of such skin and such tightly curled hair, such posture and such movement, being all suited up in English style, performing to

British taste, being an object on view in this place, in Wigtown. She wept silently, as she watched, and the whole experience seemed a crazy mistake. She could not stop her hands from shaking; she did not join in the applause.

She read of the concert later in her paper, and she was shocked. The critic of the event claimed that the performer had overplayed his dramatic roles but that this was to be explained by his being 'unlike our cool-blooded countrymen ... a soul touched with fire and a child of the sun.' She was informed by the article that white people most enjoyed black people when they comically performed pieces like 'Jim Crow' and 'A Drunken Negro'. Margaret McGuffie felt shame and sadness for such words about the African Roscius, who had sung and acted with all his heart so splendidly before an apparently admiring crowd in the small country town.

In the same paper, she read of the marriage that had taken place in England between Mr James Caird of Baldoon and Miss Henryson, daughter of Captain Henryson. It was a most suitable match.

★

The railways were creeping closer. A new length of line was proposed linking Lancaster to Carlisle. The advance of the iron horse was a matter of great interest and also of great trepidation to men, like her father, who had spent their lives, their money, and invested all their hopes in the shipping trade. Someday trains might link Wigtown to the rest of the country by land, and then the water route, now so alive with traffic, so very necessary for trade between the small port and Liverpool, would be in jeopardy. Sailing ships had been swallowed up by steam; wooden vessels were being replaced by iron ones; railways were only a matter of time in a world developing and changing at a running pace.

The Galloway Steam Navigation Company, with its proud, graceful steamer the Countess of Galloway as its flagship, the company into which John McGuffie had thrown his resources locally, was already being challenged by a newcomer concern, a band of men who were trading with an iron steamship called Warrington. The newspaper printed the trumpeted boasts of one followed, the next week, by the even larger boasts of the other. What they could carry, how they could carry it, when they could carry it, how cheaply they could carry it, back and forth, on and on, week after week, the challenges were displayed in print on the front page of the paper.

The Warrington defiantly cried, 'Our first class is cheaper than another ship's steerage!'

The Countess haughtily retorted, 'Our steerage is more comfortable than another ship's first class.'

At first, they competed for different days, 'better days', for the journey. Then they dared to advertise for the same day at different hours. Finally, the inevitable duel was announced in the scheduling of a departure from Liverpool one day, the same day, at the same time, from adjoining docks. It was to be a duel.

On the day of the race, the atmosphere in Wigtown was like the electric tension of the air before the beginning of a summer storm. Business was conducted negligently, and people kept running up to south-facing windows or out to vantage points in fields or along roads so that they could scan the water's horizon. As the scheduled hour neared, John McGuffie and his associates, for the Countess, set off in a purposeful-looking march towards the harbour. Warrington supporters followed them there, but took their stance some distance from the first group on the embankment. Margaret, in a burst of loyal enthusiasm, called for all the house staff and the stable lad to follow her to the flat rooftop of Barbados Villa. The dour old gardener, who had earlier professed disinterest in 'all such nonsense,' finally could bear the suspense no longer and grumbled his way up the ladder to join the rest.

There was an excited shout from the roof when first one, and then a second, boat appeared in the distance, funnels churning desperately. John Muir was dispatched to run as fast as he could run, to tell the dockside watchers that the Countess led the chase, but only just.

As the ships, their bows running as horses, neck to neck, ploughed forward into the waters of the bay, there were shouts and roars, whistles and cheers, calls and cries, howls and shrieks from windows, roofs, knolls and trees, and from all along the embankment at the side of the river. For a sickening or thrilling moment, depending on the eyes of the beholder, it seemed that the sturdy Warrington would reach the channel's entrance first, but the graceful Countess sprinted forward and turned up the Bladnoch just before her. She sped up the winding river to the first docking while cheers rang out and flying hats filled the air.

Warrington supporters marched sullenly up the lane, back towards their abandoned businesses, but celebrations went on all day and into the night for the men of the Countess. In the most spacious room that the largest hotel could provide, a raucous, happy crowd of gentlemen wallowed in their success and John McGuffie led the cheers when he called for a toast to their hero, the expert Captain Broadfoot. No one said it aloud, but they were all thinking that the next Countess of their line must be an iron one. Wooden ships were a thing of the past and the ugly iron Warrington would beat them another time. The need for progress was not to be ignored. Before the year was out, Captain Broadfoot was appointed to the position of dockmaster in Liverpool.

★

Races between ships might be an acceptable adventure, but Wigtown's schoolmaster, Maxwell McMaster, suddenly announced publicly that his pupils were not to be entered in county scholastic competitions any longer. He wrote at length, in the paper, his disapprobation of the misguided principles which encouraged students to vie with each other, and he urged his readers to agree with him that better, more Christian virtues and values ought to motivate study than competition for prizes.

Scathing answers appeared in subsequent issues of the paper pointing out that the same master had been only too keen to set his own students against each other in competing annually for Provost McHaffie's medal on offer to the town's best scholar; it was only, it seemed, in a situation when the headmaster's pupils were to be judged against the pupils of other masters, in other schools, that he had discovered his fine scruples.

★

A greater scandal than the schoolmaster's rowing with the people came to the town's notice. Provost McHaffie's honesty in administering the town's affairs was publicly challenged by a man known for his high principles. The challenger, known for his successful work in the abstinence movement in Wigtown, a man formerly mocked for daring to found such a group now boasting three hundred members and popular local support, dared to challenge the man known as 'King' of Wigtown. Mr Cowper's public charge against Provost McHaffie was that the provost was personally profiting by town schemes by employing his own, already salaried estate workers, to do work in the town square, and then using town money to pay them. It was claimed, further, that a large number of unemployed carters in the town could have done the work for which the money had been allocated. Another complaint was that the harbour, which had been damaged by council neglect and failure to de-sludge the area properly, was being allocated yet more of the town funds for repairs. Finally, it was alleged that Provost McHaffie had been overheard boasting about how much money he had given from the town's coffers, without official permission, to an already well-to-do acquaintance for the purchase of a house that was knocked down to make the new road into the main street. Margaret read the claims made by good Mr Cowper in the newspaper, but she did not ask her father about them. He was not in the same euphoric mood as he had been on the day when the Countess had steamed home ahead of the Warrington.

★

London raised a monument to Lord Nelson and placed it in a grand square named Trafalgar. The far-off West Indian island of Barbados had done the same thing thirty years before, in the year that Margaret McGuffie was born.

CHAPTER TWENTY-NINE

1844–1850

James McGuffie, draper in Wigtown's High Street, died at his home when he was only fifty-six years old. The widow and her young children were part of the extended family to whom John McGuffie of Barbados Villa was the patriarch. The senior figure of the McGuffie family provided security, financial support, advice and counsel as the family moved from the shop premises into a smaller domestic property in Agnew Crescent. By this time Margaret was in her thirties and had become resigned to the probability of never having a family of her own. Nieces and nephews would be, for her, the next generation. People from outside the family circle viewed her as an intimate part of this blood-bound group, 'one of the McGuffies'. From inside the circle, though the family members accepted her without question, even with affection and loyalty, she was still the foreigner of the group. She might have been, to them, 'our foreigner', but she was foreign, nonetheless.

★

Communications between the island of Barbados and the McGuffies of Barbados Villa in Scotland were sporadic, usually connected with business interests. Two letters came, not long after the death of James of Wigtown, with personal news. One was a brief and formal announcement in which James Stenhouse declared to his reputed father that he had taken the name of McGuffie and had married Ellen Farley in St. Michael's Cathedral. He was working as a clerk in a Cheapside office.

The second letter, a long, rambling and gossipy one from Caroline to Margaret, brought Barbados clearly to her mind and close to her heart as she read it. James had taken his father's name for the sake of the children he hoped that Ellen would bear. Determined to be a McGuffie with style, he had applied for a special license so that the wedding could take place in the island's cathedral rather than in the local parish church. Caroline had given up taking in lodgers, letting the newly married couple have the house so long regarded as the Stenhouse home. She had taken rooms for herself above a shop where she served as shopkeeper. George Whitfield, their old friend and benefactor, their father's friend and associate, seemed to have become a changed man. After Jessie died, he had begun to travel extensively between the islands of the Caribbean region and eventually rumours had begun to circulate that he had women in other places, sons in other islands. Some said that he had two sons, one in Jamaica and one in the Bahamas, and they both bore the name Henry Wase Whitfield. It was a strange story, wrote Caroline, and seemed so at variance with all they had known of the man; the people of Barbados were slow to believe the stories, but the rumours kept coming and belief in them was beginning to grow.

Times were hard in Barbados. Emancipation had brought poverty of some degree to all classes of its inhabitants. Struggling European types complained about their worsening lot, but freed slaves were of an opinion that they were happier to be poorer and free than, as before, slaves in 'comfort'.

As the news was shared and discussed between them, Margaret was somewhat surprised and greatly relieved to find that her father did not seem to disapprove of James adopting the family name. 'I suppose a wedding gift might be appropriate?' he suggested. She applauded his generosity, and he glowed with self-satisfaction.

★

Time seemed to be picking up speed much in the manner of a mighty steam locomotive, and it hauled in its wake, with a gathering of power and pace, a train of innovations. New technological developments were being announced all the time, and their effect was evidenced increasingly in the everyday life even of country people. Invention was becoming so commonplace that it ceased to astonish or excite people; it was expected.

In Wigtown, homes were being fitted with gas lighting, and the people of the county town could sit up late at night with their newspapers, reading in the much-improved brightness about events taking place in their own part of Scotland, the whole of Britain and throughout the world. Far-away places and happenings became the subject of common street talk. With the opening of the new Houses of Parliament, the names of the talented architects of the age, Barry and Pugin, became as well known in Wigtown as they had been in London, or Liverpool.

Not only in London were there new buildings rising. Wigtown was sprouting a crop of them. The old Secession Church was being rebuilt, a foundation stone having been laid with due public ceremony. A new school was built on the road leading to the harbour, just below the recently-erected Free Church and manse. The school would operate outwith parish church control, for it was a Free Church school, and it would vie with the McMaster parish school to attract pupils.

The new school acquired the services of a bright, energetic, and patently ambitious young man from Fife, a teacher named James Husband. He was a little fellow, fierce and decisive in character, and obviously did not share the newly non-competitive approach to schooling of Master McMaster. He brooked no interference in his work, despised all 'nonsense' and was scathing of all he considered to be lesser men. He considered most men to be lesser men. He quite quickly found himself a nice young lady in Bladnoch's village, and he called at her house in a doggedly regular pattern until she accepted him. The locals were delighted and amused by the young fellow.

Poor old schoolmaster McMaster fell out of fashion when he was compared unfavourably with the new young man, and children, picking up an attitude of general disrespect from the conversation of their elders, began to openly taunt the man in the streets of the town. Three members of the Town Council took young Husband aside one day and urged him to use his obviously growing influence to halt the trend towards the public humiliation of the old master. They were stunned when he quipped, with all the confidence of a strutting bantam, 'Do your own dirty work!' and left the room. John McGuffie roared with laughter when he recounted the tale, as he had heard it, to Margaret. Soon after the incident, the much-beleaguered long-time parish schoolmaster Maxwell McMaster accepted a position in the next county.

Further down the harbour road, beyond the manse of Rev. Peter Young, past the new Free Church, manse and school, grounds were staked out and building work commenced on a new county prison. The town was growing and spreading, and the streets, like the homes, were beautifully lit with wonderful new gas lamps. The nights became like day on the streets of the proud county town.

Contemporary with the coming of advances and positive developments, good things like bright lights and new buildings, the changing times brought new troubles into existence. There were new kinds of difficulties and sadness, new forms of fearfulness in the modern age, and natural disasters began to happen as well.

Potato blights were widespread, and food ran short. People flooded into the towns and the rural parts of the county from Ireland where potatoes had been all they had had to eat. The crowding pressure of immigrants being stacked into the houses of the towns and the farm cottages as tightly as they could be stacked began to create new and unforeseen problems. Wigtown's Poor Fund coffers ran dry in providing for the destitute strangers, and there was nothing left in them for its own familiar poorer people. The initial tender sympathy shown towards the starving newcomers changed into bad feelings when increased rates were levied on the townspeople in order to replenish the poor funds. Charities finally had to volunteer to take over distributions to the needy.

The Irish immigrants were considered a poorer stock of farming people who had accepted as comfortable a basic subsistence level below that expected, even demanded, by their comparatively more prosperous Scottish counterparts. The Irish incomers began to compete with the locals for employment on farms and labouring jobs in towns. Their lesser bids were accepted and families who, for generations beyond numbering, had occupied local positions, were suddenly left without prospects for employment. The newspapers advertised the New World on the western shore of the Atlantic as the answer to these problems. Cheap passages were available for those who would venture to start afresh. People went in waves and the hearts of Wigtonians, in common with the hearts of people from throughout other such Scottish places, were broken as they stood at the dockside to bid farewell to boatload after boatload of young families, all their possessions bundled at their feet, gone never to return.

Cholera touched the area and the difficulties of blight, the sadness of a place bleeding out its young to another country, were forgotten in the panic of a possible epidemic with its accompanying terror and death. Even going to the parish church in Wigtown began to frighten people, for the building was sinking into its burial ground and a smell beyond enduring had crept into the church. Doctors wrote letters on behalf of their patients so that the Kirk Session would excuse, and not expel, members for whom attendance at public worship in such a place was deemed to be hazardous to health.

The Town Council recognised the need for the people, in a time so full of despair and alarm, to enjoy a spirit-reviving diversion, and a regatta was planned for the town. For a day, the waterway of the Bladnoch, the river that had once brought prosperity to the place, was to become a setting for fun and celebrations. On the appointed September day, Wigtown people excitedly dressed in their best clothes and trooped down, with families and friends, to watch the planned events. All the boats that could be spared from their work had been scrubbed, painted, and decked out with flags for the occasion. There were sailing races and rowing races with boats in classes ranked according to their size and crew numbers. Supporters shouted encouragement and opposers booed as ships large and boats tiny flew up and down the channel from starting line to finishing line. There were resounding cheers when the prizes were awarded to the beaming victors.

When the contests on the water were done, the populace tripped back up the road past the new prison, the new school, the new church and the old manse, into the square, where there were organised foot and sack races, putting contests with a stone, and much-hooted-at attempts to climb a greased pole. In the evening, the respectable men of the town marched off to the Commercial Inn to dine, leaving their women and children, tired and contented with the fun, to wander off to their homes for their suppers.

Margaret McGuffie stood alone on her flat roof in the afternoon, watching the races with her father's telescope. She went alone into her peaceful garden while the races and games took place in the town square. She heard the laughing, squealing, singing sounds of the town having a party. She sat alone, a simple meal of bread and cheese before her, in her dining room, for the servants had been allowed the day off to share in the enjoyment of the occasion. Her father was dining with the gentlemen. No one noticed that she was not there. She had no one to share her thoughts with that day, and none would bother to wonder what they had been.

CHAPTER THIRTY

1850–1851

Margaret McGuffie was approaching the age of forty years and she began to feel that she could bear this life no longer. When she had been young, beautiful and optimistic, she had dared, with Caroline pushing her, to come uninvited into her father's world. Her life had all stretched before her, hidden in the mists of an unknown future, but full of exciting possibilities. She had had dreams then. As year followed year, any mistiness had cleared from her vision and the only things she saw ahead were harsh realities.

The people of the lovely old Scottish country town had not rejected her; they accepted her in their way and also ignored her. Some did so because their lives were already filled to the brim. They were surrounded by family connections born of generation following generation in one place until most people had become kin to each other to some degree. These people had, not only seemingly endless family connections, but friendships rooted further back than their memories. There were no spaces left in such lives for lonely incomers to fill.

Others, who were incomers like herself, had room in their lives but did not want to include her in their circle. They were people struggling to find their own places in a world of such deeply rooted, already-established local social hierarchy, and friendship with an only reputed daughter of a retired merchant, a spinster lady with strangely black eyes and a rather spiky nature, would not enhance their precarious climb up the social ladder. They, therefore, also ignored her.

Servants did not openly defy her, nor did shopkeepers completely disregard her, but her orders were not treated as a priority. Her commands were obeyed a little less quickly than those of her father; her business was attended to with a casual air; curtsies were none too deep; faces were pulled behind her back; giggles were stifled less than efficiently.

Her father's people were kind and welcoming to her, but she remained, even after twenty years, a family curiosity. No matter how hard she tried to blend in, to think and be like them, she was not. When they gathered with McGuffies, her father reverted immediately and unconsciously to the broader accents of his childhood. The family sang songs together that she did not know, and they did not take time to teach her; they quoted poetry that she could not understand, and they did not explain; they used words, quaint little Galloway expressions, that she had never heard and, when she looked puzzled, they laughed together gleefully. She knew that they did not mean to be cruel but, every time they laughed, a deeper wedge was driven between her and the people who called themselves her family.

Her father loved her and would have given her anything, but her utter dependence upon his provision began to eat into her sense of self-respect. He loved her, but she was not to him what his nephews Peter Clokie and young John McGuffie were. He spoke much with Margaret about the futures of the young men and his plans for them. He still never spoke with her about her own future or any plans for her. He grew further distanced from her as his involvement in the boiling pot of town affairs increased. There were more and more meetings and more and more dinners at inns; she was more and more alone.

She could not return to Barbados. James and Ellen had their own family and lived in the house that had been her home. Caroline lived somewhere else and had her own work to do and made her own living independently. Margaret had no independent money with which to establish herself there, or anywhere. She had no skills, training or experience with which to seek a situation of employment.

Into her darkness came two sudden, unexpected proposals. Cecelia Wilson wrote to from Liverpool – a long, news-filled letter with descriptions of her growing family and of life in the city. 'Come to us again, friend. We have not seen you for too long, and I am sad that my children do not know you. Barton meets with your father when he comes here on business, so we know that you are well enough. Thomas Varty is still planning for his life as a country squire. He speaks of you often.'

That same day, her mood already lightened, her neighbours Margaret and Elizabeth Simson arrived at her door in the company of their haughty mother. 'Miss McGuffie,' the proud Christina Dun Simson began, 'I have come to ask for your help.' She sniffed a bit, looked a little while around the room as if expecting a rabbit to leap on her or the furniture to move of its own accord, and went on, 'Elizabeth here is to marry James McLean, the banker, at the end of the summer, and the gels have their hearts set on an adventure before she settles down at the Bank House. It's nonsense, if you ask me, but then, I suppose, there must be a little sparkle somewhere in one's life.' She frowned and smoothed her skirt over her knees. She looked at the girls, who were watching her intently, hardly breathing with suspense. 'The Great Exhibition is to be on in London, and we thought that journey there might be a not entirely unprofitable experience. They cannot travel alone, of course, and we wonder whether you might do us the service of accompanying them. You've travelled. You are old enough to be sensible. Our Margaret has always expressed her partiality to your company. Please consider it. We will leave the matter for you to discuss with, - ehm, - your father.' She was rising, already, from her chair. 'Come, girls; we have taken up enough of Miss McGuffie's time,' and they were out the door before Margaret could say a word. Young Margaret Simson glanced back and flashed her an impish grin, and they were gone.

★

At the beginning of the year, in the cold of wintertime, Margaret went to Liverpool for an extended visit with her friends. The lights came on again in her mind and in her heart. The bustle, confusion, overwhelming size of the place, the noise and sense of energy there, filled her with a renewed zest for life. She had once happily left this city, its griminess and greyness, its coldly cobbled streets and crowded feeling, but now, after years spent in the quiet sameness of a tiny town, she felt called alive again by all that she had then gladly abandoned. It was not beautiful, as the gentle rolling landscape of Galloway with its richness of greens was beautiful. It was not peaceful anywhere in Liverpool like the tranquil and secluded gardens around her home were peaceful, but it was invigorating, like a splash of cold water on her face.

Cecelia had borne two children successfully, after the loss of one. Her daughter Mary Frances was twelve years of age, and her son Barton Worsley was ten. They were dear, good children and they warmed the heart of the emotionally frozen spinster lady, their mother's special friend, with their affectionate ways and tender care of her. They never went to their beds at night without coming to receive a kiss from her. They never walked out on the streets without carefully arranging themselves, one on either side of her, each taking a hand. Cecelia laughed at them, sometimes, for their odd, serious little ways, but she adored her children and wished that Margaret would share her love for them.

The two women reminisced daily about the times they had spent together in Liverpool and about their journey to Penrith. Margaret told Cecelia all about her cousin Mary, now a staid businessman's wife with a family which included her own namesake, Margaret McGuffie Goodwin.

'If I'd had another daughter, I would have named her for you,' confided Cecelia.

'But you didn't,' laughed Margaret. 'And I won't have children of my own now to bear my own, or their father's, or my father's, or any friend's name,' she thought with sadness.

★

Thomas Varty was in his middle thirty years and had solidified, since she last saw him, into a handsome man, a strong figure, without losing the boyish quality, the joy in life, the twinkling humour that Margaret remembered of the stripling boy.

'Margaret McGuffie, queen of my heart,' he crowed, when he first saw her. He bowed low over her hand, then crushed her in an utterly improper embrace, and swung her off her feet in the whirl of a celebratory dance that brought delighted shrieks of laughter from Mary Frances and Barton Worsley.

'Uncle Thomas, do it again,' they chimed together as he deposited their quiet Miss McGuffie in a blushing heap in a chair.

'No, no, my gnomes!' He charged at them playfully, and a mock bullfight ensued with Thomas the bull dashing wildly around the room in pursuit of the two screaming children.

Margaret watched the playing, laughing trio as she struggled to repair her tousled, tumbled coiffure, but she found, as she was laughing with them, that she was struggling to keep herself from bursting into tears. It was just fun, she sternly told herself, biting her lip. Her eyes shone with the tears she would not allow, and no one noticed when she blew her nose.

In the days and weeks that followed, she began to wonder if it were, after all, not too late for her. She began to entertain, almost unwillingly, thoughts of Thomas, the once-only-a-boy Thomas and herself as a pair. She remembered Stagstones, high on the hill above the Eden valley. She remembered the mountains and lakes, and she recalled the tender blessing of the old Quaker. Something of the softness, the openness of her heart in those days began to creep back into her, but she would panic then and clamp down fiercely, turning her mind to anything and everything that would stop the flow of her imagining. She was terrified to dream. She could not bear to open up the hopes that dreaming caused again, only to find them to be as empty and unreal as they had been before, in the days when she had ridden with James Caird. She would not be made a fool of again.

And so, Thomas Varty was treated by Margaret McGuffie just as he had always been treated by her – as a boy to be shooed away. She was merciless in her light disregard of his gradually decreasing protestations of devotion. The harder she pushed him away, the more he retreated; the more he retreated, the colder she became. In her deepest heart she screamed at him, 'Don't you dare give up!' Her manners, her eyes, her words, all said, 'Go away.' He saw what he saw.

★

Cecelia still longed to visit London, as she had once planned, but her domestic situation bound her too tightly to home to make such a trip possible. Margaret and Elizabeth Simson came to Liverpool on the boat from Wigtown in the early summer, and they claimed Margaret McGuffie for their arranged trip to the capital. The entire world had been called to come together to pay tribute to the reign of Queen Victoria and the genius of her beloved Prince Albert, and the

138

three Wigtown women were a tiny part of the throng answering the summons. They found a compartment in the early morning train and were soon tucked up cosily together there, full of the excitement of their long-proposed excursion.

Elizabeth chattered incessantly, as she had since she had come off the boat the day before, about her coming marriage. 'Of course, it would have been more suitable for Margaret to have been married before me,' she nodded across the aisle towards her silent elder sister, 'but James McLean is impatient for us to be married and, as he is rather older than I am, I cannot expect him to wait until my sister finds herself a beau, can I, Miss McGuffie?'

It had quickly become obvious to the spinster chaperone that the exceedingly smug about-to-be-married younger sister could and would skilfully turn any subject of conversation into an opportunity to compare her own success with her sister's pitiable condition. Margaret McGuffie had tried to outwit her, to find a subject not turnable, but Elizabeth Simson was a mistress of stubborn single-mindedness, and she managed her trick every time. When asked for the health of people in the county town, she responded by following her description of the health or happiness of each named subject with a further description of the named person's reaction to the news of her marriage, or of their present to her, or how their son was particularly disappointed in having not claimed her hand, or how their niece was terribly broken-hearted since the wonderfully eligible Mr James McLean had expressed his preference for Miss Elizabeth Simson. When asked about the state of the town's affairs, she explained the improvements there were in the burgh since James McLean had become an influence on the scene, and how terribly sad it was that Margaret, her older sister, would not be able to find a man to equal her one-and-only marvel. When Miss McGuffie steered the subject forward to their visit to London and the Exhibition, Elizabeth launched heartily into the subject of Queen Victoria and her Albert, following which, without the slightest degree of modesty, she likened herself and James McLean to the royal pairing in terms of power, influence, wealth and true love, albeit, of course, on a Wigtown scale. At that point, Margaret McGuffie looked across to Margaret Simson and rolled her black eyes in an expression of mock horror. Margaret Simson's face went bright pink, and she quickly stifled her giggles in her lace-edged handkerchief.

Just at the last moment before the train began to move, a young gentleman entered their carriage and begged permission to claim the empty seat beside Margaret Simson. As he settled his bags, the massive iron engine began to draw their train, slowly and with great chugging noises, away and upwards, through the Lime Street tunnel towards the sky at Edgehill and then, whistling as it gathered speed, out and onwards to London.

The newcomer was seated across from the delectable Elizabeth. He looked across to Margaret McGuffie and softly, shyly, apologised for his intrusion into their company. 'The train is so full, you know,' he explained, 'with so many rushing to see the Great Exhibition. May I introduce myself? I am George Anderson.'

Margaret, in turn, introduced herself and her charges. They learned, as the train sped past the city's edges and into the countryside, that young Mr Anderson, whose origins were in Scotland, had moved to Liverpool as a child with his parents and that now he was on his way to London. He was not on a pleasure jaunt as they were, but was to be interviewed with regard to a merchant appointment in the capital city.

Margaret Simson was engrossed in the view rushing by her window, the towns and farms, the hills and rivers, the woodland and pastures of England. She sometimes gasped with excitement, sometimes squeaked out, 'Oh, look!' and sometimes sat in long periods of utterly absorbed concentration. Elizabeth, Margaret McGuffie had noted with a censor's antenna, had ceased to speak of marriage or of James McLean. She had turned her full, rapt attention onto the young man opposite her. The chaperone could almost hear the girl's thoughts, her wondering whether the title of 'wife of a London merchant' might not sound more prestigious than that of 'wife of a Wigtown banker.' Elizabeth coyly asked her new target more about himself. She was demure, the soul of gentle femininity, and perfect in her courtesies as she made reference to 'Miss McGuffie, my chaperone.'

George Anderson asked, 'What do you most look forward to seeing in the exhibition, Miss Elizabeth?'

'Oh, just everything, especially the grand people. I am sure that we will seem so dowdy in comparison with them. We haven't such up-to-date fashions in the country. We just do our best.' She patted her sleeves and touched her hair, glancing across at him demurely.

'You look very well; I am sure that London will have no finer trio of ladies than the three of you,' he assured her. A look of horror flashed across Elizabeth's face, and she looked sideways at the middle-aged, simply dressed spinster she did not consider as worthy of being placed in a category, in any category, with herself.

George Anderson turned to the window-watching Margaret beside him. 'And you, Miss Simson? What do you most look forward to seeing?'

She turned from her viewing to meet his gaze with steady eyes, answering firmly, 'The Gothic exhibit and the elephant.'

He burst out laughing, as did a surprised Elizabeth, and Margaret Simson's face went red as she turned back to her window.

Elizabeth flapped her pretty fan about and leant across to whisper, 'My sister!' as if in apology.

★

London went on forever. They had arranged rooms in a modest boarding house in Cadogan Place and they spent the first day after their arrival walking in the wonderful, exciting city that seemed to them the very centre of the entire world. The new, huge and glorious Parliament buildings made them gasp. The whole city was alight; it buzzed, it teemed with the most magnificent, elegant, curious and exotic people, merchandise, sights, sound and structures that they had ever seen.

'Oh, Miss McGuffie,' exclaimed Margaret Simson,' I love it here! I never want to leave it. I have never imagined a place to be like this.'

Elizabeth seemed rather more thoughtful than usual, and her chaperone only heard her mutter, 'Perhaps I shall stay. I expect ...'

They went the next day to Hyde Park, and they were so full of excitement that they could barely speak. They saw the Crystal Palace long before they reached it, its soaring cliffs of glass and curved domes rising above buildings and treetops, glittering in the sun. They stood and looked and gasped again, stunned by the great shining beauty of the fullest expression of the nation's pride. There were people everywhere walking, arriving in carriages, crowds of them just standing and, like themselves, just looking in wonder at the scene. Around them were exquisitely dressed ladies and gentlemen. There were rustic country creatures; there were Africans, Orientals, French people, Germans, Eastern Indians in saris and turbans, and even an American Indian in a beaded and feathered costume.

They merged with the throng entering the Palace and began then, inside the vast exhibition space, to make their way around, section by section, to see the wonders of the world. There was a huge lump of gold. There were areas devoted to the latest advances in coal mining. There was a room full of the finest carriages, where Margaret
McGuffie annoyed her wards by insisting on inspecting each and every vehicle. They went into the Gothic room where the two Margarets examined in wonder and admiration the beautiful recreation of a style evoking the grandeur of centuries long past. They exclaimed over the delicate tracery of the carved wooden arches, the richness of tapestry designs, the tiles, ceramics and heavy furnishings so unlike the pale severity of more recently fashionable styles of neo-classicism. As they examined the work together and fingered the lovely, heavy fabric hangings, Elizabeth turned, bored, and wandered off through the crowds.

They had lost her, and they decided to separate to try to find her. Margaret McGuffie, as she searched, came upon the strangest piece she had seen in the exhibition. It was a massive carved stone panel designed to feature as the top piece of an even more gigantic tombstone for a man of whom she had never heard. On one side, the carving was of Pharaoh's army down in the depths of the Red Sea bed, with the waters of God's judgement ready to crash over their terrified heads. On the other was a scene of riotous, joyous jubilation, the triumph of Moses and Miriam, occasioned by the drowning of their persecutors, the enemies of their people. Margaret could not imagine, as she gazed at the astonishingly beautiful carved scenes, that such workmanship was to be mounted over the tomb, obviously an enormous tomb, greater than that of many a king, of an unknown man. She wondered whether the vanity of the man or his family were as great as it seemed, in having commissioned such a work, or whether the architect's plans had exploded in a frenzy of his own madness. The designer, according to the accompanying plate, was Mr David Rhind, an Edinburgh architect. She wondered whether he was the architect brother of Wigtown's Sheriff Rhind, an elder in her own parish church. She rushed on to look for Elizabeth.

★

'There you are, Elizabeth! What made you disappear in such a way?' chided Margaret Simson when she caught sight of her sister who was smiling happily and chatting with a young man whose face Margaret could not see. He turned and smiled at her. 'Miss Simson, I knew I'd find you on this corner eventually.'

She looked at him with puzzlement. 'What do you mean, Mr Anderson?' He glanced up and she saw that he was standing directly beneath a huge, magnificent, bejewelled and canopied stuffed elephant. She gasped and cried out, 'Oh! Oh! How wonderful!' and he laughed with delight.

'Me? ' he asked, teasingly, 'or this thing?' and she laughed with him, while the younger sister, the about-to-be-married-to-a-country-banker Elizabeth looked on with a rising temper replacing the sense of triumph she had been experiencing just moments before.

When Margaret McGuffie found them, Margaret Simson and George Anderson were walking slowly around the elephant, pointing up and discussing its glories in an animated fashion together. Elizabeth was standing alone under a tusk, one little foot tapping petulantly, her hand flicking her fan about in little movements of impatience, her eyes snapping. 'Well, Miss McGuffie,' she spat, 'I could have been properly lost by the time you got around to finding me. I do not think Mama would approve of your losing me like that.'

George and Margaret had just come up behind her when the sound of a chaperone's retort was fired back, 'Perhaps your Mama was so delighted with your coming marriage to an older man because she knew that you have a tendency to wander!'

142

Elizabeth glared furiously at the woman but, had she looked behind her, she would have seen that the eyes of George Anderson had never been interested in her anyway. He had obviously already been won by the girl who stared out of windows and wanted to see an elephant.

CHAPTER THIRTY-ONE

1851–1852

The sisters returned to Wigtown after their adventure in London, and preparations began in earnest for the wedding to take place between Miss Elizabeth Simson, daughter of the esteemed customs collector, and Mr James McLean, prominent young banker. It was acknowledged to be the social event of the year, involving all the important interests within the royal burgh and the county because of the connections of the bride and groom: town officialdom, country gentry, banking and shipping would all be represented in the marriage of the two.

When asked about her visit to London, the slightly peevish bride-to-be was heard to comment that London had not suited her at all, that her sensitive and refined nature was not at home in the noise, the clamour, or the crowds of the city. Her chin would tilt again to its customary superior angle and she would begin to describe her preparations for a trousseau inspired by the London fashions she had been so diligently careful to observe, she never ceased to declare, while her older sister had mooned about the place being obsessed with such unimportant things as Gothic design and stuffed elephants.

The Queen had worn pink for the opening of the Great Exhibition, and Elizabeth Simson would wear pink, only pink, for her wedding. Her gown was of silk, with silver lace tucked into the plunging decolletage and used for trimming the short sleeves. A pointed bodice accentuated her tiny waist, and from it flowed tiny pleats into the fullest of skirts bedecked with pink satin ribbons. Murmured descriptions of the exquisite gown being made for Elizabeth Simson found their way, detail by detail, from the house of the weary dressmaker via her maid to the produce-purchasing wives of the town, into the eager ears of their daughters, and on into the general news-swapping discussions held on the street by gathered groups of people enjoying the warmth of long summer evenings out of doors. The very street sweepers, who could not have told what colour gown their own wives, daughters or sisters possessed, learned the details of the design of the pink creation.

Every other dressmaker of repute in the town was involved in some way, for Elizabeth Simson must also have a walking dress and a morning dress, a dress for receiving visitors to the Bank House, and a visiting dress for the ceremony of calling cards, a travelling dress, a dinner dress and, just to be safe, in case the occasion demanded, a ball gown. The dresses were suitable for the season following her wedding, but a selection of heavier dresses for the colder winter months coming was also in preparation and, being a young lady of foresight, gauzy muslins, crisp cottons and delicate silks were being considered and discussed with a view to the spring.

There were undergarments, stockings, nightgowns, dressing gowns, gloves and hats being made in houses all over the town, all for Elizabeth Simson. On the subject of her boots and dainty indoor shoes, the bride nearly drove her chosen shoemaker into a state of premature dementia, for she would insist that a proper craftsman could make her large, practical foot appear as dainty as that of her older sister without creating any discomfort from toe-pinching tightness. John McLean became the object of great sympathy in the minds of many people.

As Elizabeth energetically occupied the attention of the town, no one noticed the regularity with which letters arrived at the house in the beech wood from Liverpool steamboats, or the wonderful happiness of the 'poor spinster' sister of the bride.

★

The newly pronounced Mr and Mrs James McLean drove in a smart open carriage from the bride's home to board the Countess of Galloway for the commencement of their wedding trip. People gathered along the route to watch, the young admiring, contemporaries bestowing good wishes on their friends, and the elderly dreaming of their own past day. Among those the bridal pair passed was a group of young people, two teen-aged girls pushing baby carriages and a lad of their own age. Mary McGuffie, niece of John McGuffie and young cousin of Miss McGuffie, was giving an hour's airing to baby Grace Fraser, daughter of the harbourmaster who was her neighbour. Annie Tait, the sweet-tempered and much-loved daughter of the local postmaster, was looking after Jessie Dickson Cowper, baby granddaughter of an imperious old widow of the town, Margaret Dickson. Their friend, Gordon Fraser, was a druggist's apprentice who made a habit of knowing everyone and everything in the town, being anywhere when anything of interest was happening. His curiosity about local doings was regarded by his peers as being a strangely feminine trait in a lively-minded lad, especially when it was discovered that he also wrote poetry.

'Her husband looks awfully old,' said Mary McGuffie, when the waving couple had passed them.

'He is a nice man,' said Annie. 'I think he looks very kind.'

'Bankers are never kind,' said Gordon, sagely. 'They cannot afford to be kind.'

'That is not true, Gordon!' argued Mary. 'My mother says that John Black is the kindest man in the world, and he's a banker.'

'I think to marry an older, kind man would be better than to marry a rude young one,' teased Annie, giving Gordon a significant look.

145

'I would like to travel in the Countess after I'm married,' sighed Mary.

'Only people who have wealthy fathers or who marry bankers can do that,' asserted Gordon.

Mary's face clouded at his insensitivity. He knew that her father had died when she had been very young. Annie immediately perceived the gaffe and reminded Mary, 'Aren't you fortunate, Mary? Your uncle has so much money, and he loves you as much as any father would.'

'Your uncle will probably leave all his money to his black woman,' Gordon dug in more deeply.

'Gordon Fraser!' shrieked Mary. 'Margaret McGuffie is his daughter, and she is not black! She is my cousin.'

The owlish boy sucked in his cheeks, pursed his lips, and slowly shook his head.

Annie Tait flashed an angry glance at him, grabbed Mary's arm, and pulled her friend off back up the lane in a diplomatic retreat. As they shoved the heavy baby carriages with their soundly sleeping infants ahead of them up the hill, Mary muttered, 'He can be so horrid.'

'Don't mind him,' soothed Annie. 'Gordon just loves to think he knows more than anyone else. He makes up what he doesn't know. He always says he needs to learn peoples' stories because he is going to put them down in a book one day.'

The girls stopped pushing, laughing merrily at the thought of Gordon Fraser, the druggist's apprentice, writing a book.

★

The Great Exhibition year had been memorable for London, but it was also a great year for Liverpool. Queen Victoria stood on the balcony of the city's Town Hall and looked
down on a sea of hats stretching all the way along to the Mersey; there were more hats, she had been heard to say, on more gentlemen, than she had ever seen in one place at one time in her life. The annual Welsh Eisteddfod, with its celebration in song, poetry, costume and language of an ancient British culture, came too to fill the port city with entertainment. Among the witnesses to both events, royal and Welsh, was Margaret McGuffie, revived and happy in the company of her friends the Wilsons and the Vartys.

She delayed her return to home and duty as long as she could, but finally she said farewell to the bustle of the place and the companionship of the people, reluctantly boarded the familiar Countess of Galloway, and was carried northwards across the Solway to resume her quieter, lonelier place at home.

★

In the summer of the following year, in a day of deep and quiet happiness, Margaret Simson, eldest surviving daughter of James Simson the customs officer of Wigtown, became the wife of Liverpool merchant, about-to-become London merchant, George Anderson. The tranquility of the bride and the simplicity of her wedding day could not have been in greater contrast to the wedding of her sister Elizabeth the year before. Margaret McGuffie beamed with pleasure and pride upon her young friend and wished her happiness with all of her heart.

★

The Duke of Wellington, hero of Waterloo and late Prime Minister, died full of years in September, 1852. Augustus Pugin, famed architect and designer, leader of the Gothic revival throughout Victoria's realm, the man whose work had featured so dramatically at the Crystal Palace exhibition and who remained so much in the news with his co-creation of the new Houses of Parliament, died tragically and prematurely on the same day.

James McGuffie of Barbados, reputed only son of John McGuffie of Barbados Villa, Wigtown, in Scotland, died two days later at the age of thirty-seven years. He left a widow, a daughter, and three sons, two of whom were twins. In the same year, at its end, John Black of Wigtown lost his twenty-one-year-old son and namesake to a fever in India.

In Wigtown, there had been appropriate recognition of the death of Wellington, interest in the death of Pugin, and grief expressed over the news of the death of young John Black. No one knew anything about the death of James McGuffie of Barbados except his father and his sister, and they spoke little of it even to each other.

CHAPTER THIRTY-TWO

1852–1858

When Margaret McGuffie returned from Liverpool to Wigtown after her extended trip, she found that her father had installed a young widow from Port William in her place as housekeeper. Margaret's insistence that she, herself, again take up the reins of household management was agreed to by her father, but she was puzzled by the way he took such pains to find a little cottage in Port William for the woman upon her departure from Barbados Villa. His mood was not particularly agreeable, his patience with her less than it had seemed before she left, and at first, she assumed that he had merely resented her lengthy absence. Eventually, though, she came to realise that he had enjoyed more than a mere employer's relationship with the temporary housekeeper. Her return had forced an end to the arrangement, and it took some months before the atmosphere in the house returned to normal. Neither of them spoke of the matter.

There was much else to speak about. The large new parish church, cunningly designed to reflect the old parish church structure, was nearly completed. The older building, a sanctuary for worship for a thousand years, had been such a hallowed place that the locals were loath to move to the new site, albeit one just yards from the old. In order to make the move as little a change as possible, the very shape and design of the ancient place was copied, in careful detail, and then enlarged and made grander in the vision, by the skills, and with the wealth of the Victorian age. The old windows from the building dating back to the Reformation period of Sir Patrick Vans were carefully removed and placed in garden structures at John Black's house so that worshippers could see and pass by the old stones on their way to worship in the new. One wall of the ancient structure was to be retained as a mark of the hallowed antiquity of the former site.

A new public park was being created on the Windy Hill, a place for the people to walk and from which they could at leisure admire the beautiful scenery, with views over the town, the lush rolling countryside, the Bay of Wigtown, and further to the Galloway hills in the distance.

Conversations at the dining table between father and daughter were full of family news as well as of developments in Wigtown. There was a new baby named John McGuffie Goodwin, and Margaret Simson Anderson in London had named a baby daughter for the proud grandmother in the neighbouring house. Margaret of London had not, however, managed to produce as yet anything like the steady stream of babies arriving at the home of her younger sister in a Wigtown bank house.

John McGuffie's favourite niece, Mary McGuffie, was to marry John Fraser, a young assistant in John Black's bank. Mary was only seventeen years of age, and, to Margaret, it seemed that the young cousin was not past childhood long enough to be ready for marriage. Young Fraser was being offered a position with his bank in Port William, and the couple were to set up home there. The generosity of John McGuffie, who was to represent the bride's deceased father at the wedding, would make certain that their settling in was a comfortable one.

News came of a cholera epidemic sweeping Barbados, particularly the country areas of the island, and John McGuffie expressed concern several times over the fate of his son's widow and her children. It seemed strange to Margaret that he who had so consistently ignored the son throughout his life, never really even acknowledging him as his son, was so concerned for the grandchildren he had openly acknowledged since the son's death.

On a court day in Wigtown, most sorrowful news swept the town. John Black was dead. Depute Sheriff Macduff Rhind was so shocked by the sudden loss of his friend and esteemed colleague that he rose and cancelled the court. As with one voice, gentry and labourers, officials and tradesmen, old and young, rich and poor, men and women mourned loudly in public and deeply in private. It seemed that the very heart of the town had died. Suddenly people realised that the spotless integrity of the man, linked with the deep compassion he and his wife had consistently evidenced, had been at the core of all that was good, all that was kind, all that was tender, in the conduct of life in the burgh for a long generation. Provost McHaffie had presided publicly over the physical regeneration of the old town, making lovely its central square and surrounding garden areas, and opening up a new road into the main thoroughfare. Councillor John McGuffie had, since his return to his homeland, had inspired enterprise and heralded a new age of affluence in the area. Rev. Peter Young and the other ministers had tended their flocks and guided the people in aspects of worship. James Husband had created a vigorous new spark in the education of the young. Gordon Fraser was bringing the history of the ancient burgh to life again with his research and writings. Christian Simson and her ilk had added a sense of dignity, even aristocracy, to the social scene. Eccentric characters among the townspeople had added colour and spice to everyday life. Each and all of these had contributed to the compilation of a picture that was life in the town that lay on the quiet Solway shore, but John Black had been its good, warm, beating heart, and without him the town felt hushed and empty.

More sadness followed. The next summer, Margaret Simson Anderson came home from London with her little daughter for a visit with her family. The tiny child suddenly sickened, and she died in the arms of the broken-hearted grandmother whose name she bore.

One day John McGuffie called his daughter into the dining room. He asked her to sit at the side of the large table and he placed in front of her a document of many pages. He asked her to read it, and he left the room, closing the door behind him.

She had never thought about him dying. He had never spoken of a will. She was astonished that the long, complicated document now presented to her, obviously the result of many hours of discussion and arrangement with someone, had never been mentioned by him to her. As she read, she realised how much had been in his mind, how much had concerned his heart, and how little she knew of his inner feelings. He had spoken openly with her about business dealings. He had rambled on about Town Council politics and the participants in them. She knew about his money and heard his plans for Wigtown but, apart from his two favoured nephews and his dearest niece, she had known nothing about his cares or concerns for other individuals. She learned all that she had not known, had not thought to inquire, as, page after page, she read his heart toward them all.

The house and all that it contained were to be hers and she was to be given the largest single amount from his money. She read of the provision for her, through the stilted circumlocution of legal terminology, and saw in it his love for her. In the event that she to die without heirs of her own body, her cousin John McGuffie would inherit the property. As she would have expected, her cousins John and Peter, and her two cousins the Marys, were the major beneficiaries after herself. Though he saw them less, her father remembered all his other nephews and nieces and the widow of his brother James. He had even made provision for a certain widow living in Port William, one who was not a relation.

Among all the pages, the sweetest words to her were those she discovered written in granting the largest bequests, apart from her own, to the children of his deceased son James McGuffie of Barbados. It was the first time that her father had recorded formally that the child born James Stenhouse, so long repudiated by him and even eventually only reluctantly owned, was, in truth, his son. Mary Ann was dead and could not be glad; James himself had died, with his rightful name tacked onto him at his own insistence; his children, though, at last, were owned and legally acknowledged by the grandfather they had never seen. Margaret was grateful for the rightness of it, however belatedly it had come.

When she was done reading, she was not asked, and she did not offer, an opinion. In the months following the incident, though, they were softer and gentler in their manners with each other than they had been since her return from her wanderings.

John Fraser accepted a new post in banking in Runcorn, near Liverpool. As an advance on her legacy, and as an encouragement towards the success of their new venture, John McGuffie gave the young man a considerable sum of money to be used in the establishment of their new home in England. Soon after, Mary's brother, the namesake and pride of their uncle, the focus of many of John McGuffie's plans for the future of the family's prestige in the town, decided, counting on the money he had discovered that he had coming to him, to give up the family business in Wigtown. An angry uncle remonstrated with his nephew, but to no avail. The final straw on the heap of the uncle's disappointment was that the young John then announced his plans to try his luck in New Zealand. John McGuffie was white-faced with rage as he stormed at Margaret, 'All I have given him, even making him your heir, and he will fling it away for a dream on the other side of the world!'

Margaret looked up from her embroidery, watching her father as he strode about in circles, puffing with temper. 'Just as you did?' she asked, mildly.

'Not the same!' he bellowed, his face beginning to redden, his breath coming in shorter snorts. 'I wasn't leaving behind a secure future. I went from nothing to make something.'

'Perhaps he sees this as nothing compared with what he dreams of creating,' she remarked.

He slammed out of the room.

She remained at her work, thoughtful. Her father had said that he had made John her heir, and she suddenly realised what she had not seen in her earlier grateful reading of his will. The house was to be hers, but not ever really hers. In the terms of her father's bequest, it was only hers to live in and then, upon her death without children of her own, an impossible consideration for her now, he had designated its eventual owner to be her young cousin, her adventurous, irresponsible cousin John. If she could not choose her own heir, her home would never really be hers. She would continue to be a tenant, living in someone else's rooms. A grumbling, hurtful feeling grew inside her as she realised that her position in the future would be no more one of independence than was her status in the present.

★

A great monument to the memory of the Wigtown martyrs, the two Covenanter women named Margaret, was to be erected on the top of the Windy Hill. It would crown the town. It would mark the position of the burgh to travellers coming from any direction. It would proclaim the proud, solemn history of the place to passers-by. The monument had been discussed for years and years,

151

discussed and planned, preached about and funded. It was finally going to be built but, before the long-awaited ceremony of the laying of the foundation stone could be held, Provost McHaffie died.

There was a huge row at the Town Council meeting. McHaffie had been on the council for fifty-four years, and he had reigned there virtually as king for the last twenty-five of those years, for so long that many who had waited to succeed him had almost given up on their ambitions. McHaffie had made it clear during his last years that his successor to the title of provost was to be John McGuffie and any objections had remained unvoiced. For a startling moment, opposition reared an ugly-tempered mood in the town's affairs, for there was a refusal to accept the heir apparent. Somehow, though, the rebellion lost its nerve and died away as quickly as it had appeared. The Town Council declared, in pretence of unanimity, that its choice for Provost of Wigtown was John McGuffie, Esquire, of Barbados Villa. The new provost was designated to lay the foundation stone at the martyrs' memorial.

★

A London solicitor who had been at the forefront of the campaign to raise funds for the monument addressed a great gathered assembly on the appointed day. Dignitaries and local onlookers who had processed to the top of the lovely hill, a hill recently turned into garden grounds, watched as Provost John McGuffie laid the stone with quiet dignity. A choir led the singing of a psalm to a tune composed in honour of the courage and faith of the martyred women. Before the singing was done, the sky opened to drench the crowd who ran, soaked and splashing, down the hill into the old Seceders' church to continue with the arranged service indoors.

It was Miss Margaret McGuffie's first official outing as 'Provost's Lady.' In honour of the solemnity of the occasion, she was neatly attired in a black gown and wore a black bonnet. She had a red ribbon on her hat. The ribbon, the hat, her hair, and the dress were soaked from the sudden downpour, and she sat, shivering and wet, thoroughly, miserably chilled, through the long proceedings.

Two ladies sitting behind her began to whisper together. 'Certainly isn't the same as when Mrs. McHaffie was Provost's Lady, is it?'

'Never!' shot back her neighbour. 'She was a proper lady.'

'Bit severe, isn't she? All that black. The martyrs've been dead long since,' was whispered with a wink.

'Aye, but see th'on red ribbon? I was telt ye can aye tell folk wi' black blood in 'em, fer they must hae a touch o' colour 'bout their claes.'

'Aye?'

'Aye!'

They both jumped when Miss McGuffie, right at the front of the church, suddenly sneezed very loudly.

CHAPTER THIRTY-THREE

1859

Among his assortment of nephews, John McGuffie had openly favoured two as his male heirs. The one who bore his name, John McGuffie the draper's son, had abandoned his responsibilities and disappeared to the other side of the world. The other, lively, land-hungry and delightfully ambitious Peter Clokie of Port William, had married a local farmer's daughter and had charmed his way into popularity not commonly granted to an illegitimate son in a propriety-conscious country village.

Peter's wife had died, and the village had sympathised with him in his sorrow. He became very ill with a lung complaint, and the people of the village fussed about him, wishing him well. Suddenly, unaccountably, he decided to rise from his sick bed to marry another farmer's daughter, and everyone wondered at him. In a month, he was dead, and in too few more months his grieving new widow produced a son. He had given the boy his name just in time.

It was an unhappy season of life for the newly appointed Provost of Wigtown. Sitting on the pinnacle of his achievements, just when he should have known only happiness and triumph as all his dreams had become reality, he was full of sorrowing for young Peter, was suffering with physical complaints of his own, and faced nearly daily battles with the hostile Town Council who would not be ruled by him.

McHaffie had made the decisions for so long that they had become accustomed to appearing to agree with him. It had been habit. McHaffie may have chosen John McGuffie to carry on with his regime, and they may have, half out of habit, finally nodded their assent to McHaffie's commands, but now they wished, many of them, that they had persevered in their earlier, momentary rebellion. They discovered that, with McHaffie gone, they had ideas of their own. Some had even realised, too late, that they would have liked to have been provost themselves. Rows erupted in the council and meetings were disorderly. Some argued that the choice of provost had not been from an open field of candidates; others replied that it mattered not, for John McGuffie wasn't fit; they should just put up with their decision, however much they regretted it, and bide their time. Some grew angry; others carried on doggedly. Nothing worked any more. There were thefts in the town and a madman had gone on the rampage. Law and order were going the way council peace had gone in their once well-organised town where affairs were conducted with a firmer hand.

While the politics of Wigtown were turning sour and the noise of turbulence there was increasing, something of a different nature was stirring in the town's spiritual heart. A new assistant minister had come to work with the Free Church minister, and his ministry was having an effect in the parish. There had been reports of a revival movement in Ireland, and that news, together with the effects of the passionate preaching from a much-admired minister in another nearby town, had begun to create longings for a religious awakening in religiously minded people. A devout schoolmistress in Wigtown had given the use of her schoolroom for an independent prayer meeting. For a time, it was held there weekly, and more prayer groups had sprung up in private homes. The new assistant began to lead the prayer services in the schoolroom, and he succeeded in uniting the voices of members of all the churches in an entreaty to God to touch the town. The town known for the faith of its martyrs, the town now bereft of the great influence of the good John Black, was asking, in one voice, for blessing.

One evening a local labouring man, a man with no interest in religion but with a lot of experience of drinking, was walking along one of the back lanes of the town when he was suddenly and dramatically overcome by a sense of his need to be made right with his God. Broken and distressed, with a desperation quite out of character among the reserved Galloway people, he sought a minister to guide him to peace of heart. News of the man's sudden and dramatic conversion to faith surprised the whole town, all but the few whose custom had been of late to pray to God, with all their hearts, for just such light in their darkness. The event was reported, in every detail in the weekly newspaper.

On Sunday, churches were filled and buzzed with an air of expectancy. Each congregation was accustomed to being made aware, by dint of clever theological line-drawing in the sermons, of its own particular points of doctrinal superiority over its less-than-perfectly-Scripturally-based Christian neighbours. On this Sunday, all three branches of the Presbyterian faith in Wigtown received the stunning news that, in view of God's gracious movement in their midst, theological differences and the expounding thereof were summarily dismissed from the agenda and, in their place, Christians were to unite, using each church in turn, for weekly prayer meetings. Together the town's people of faith were to implore God to send them even more blessings. The people of the congregations, once they recovered from the sense of shock that such a thing was happening, were profoundly touched by the evidences of humility and good sense in their spiritual leaders. If God's smile were to be looked for in their sad, divided town, it must be sought by them all together with no desire, even in the deepest recesses of naturally competitive hearts, that one group might be seen to be the one that 'received', while others ' missed out on' God's special grace.

At a stroke, schism ceased, and genuine prayer began. There was a curious effect upon the town. In their private lives there were apologies, softening attitudes towards neighbours, tender reconciliations, a gentler tone prevailing. There was a quiet but sweet gravity among the people on the streets. Strangely enough, the Wigtown Town Council was unaffected, and it battered on as loudly and as angrily as before, its members in a total muddle of cross purposes.

Provost McGuffie was not pleased when his daughter began attending the large public prayer meetings. 'Why must you go to these things?' he growled at her one evening. She ignored him, continuing to fix her hat, to drape her cloak around her shoulders. 'I do not like to think of you among common loose-tongued locals spouting religious feelings to all and sundry. It's not dignified, Margaret. Council people just aren't seen at these things.'

'Perhaps,' and she turned to look at him with a glint of mischief about her, 'if they did, there would be fewer rows and better, cleaner dealings in the town's business, Father. Anyway, be at peace. I shan't pray aloud and will not plead for your soul, at least not in public!'

He spluttered, but left her alone. In truth, an increase in religion did not seem to have harmed her. She was more contented and less fractious. She spent a lot of her time reading the Bible and books of devotions, he had noted.

Since coming to Wigtown, Margaret had regularly attended the parish church. The service had been strange at first, for the Presbyterian worship was significantly different in style, if not in belief, from that of her early Episcopal upbringing in Barbados. She found it quite natural now, after long years of sitting, rather than kneeling, through prayers, but sometimes she did wish that it would be accepted as proper to kneel. She listened to the long, well-constructed sermons with profit, but sometimes she longed to hear the sound of the congregation's voice raised, together, in a proclamation of its belief. She listened to the lengthy prayers of the minister, but she would have liked to have voiced prayers aloud with those around her. She had learned the tunes of the metrical psalms, and she now recognised their metres with ease. She had gradually come to feel at home with the simple Scottish form of worship, but she just occasionally, especially on holy days in the year, yearned for the half-forgotten liturgy of her childhood years and understanding.

Rev. Peter Young, the old, old man who had been a young minister when her father had run away to the West Indies, had preached well in his prime. Now his voice, as old as he was, was cracked; his body was weak; his senses were dimmed. In his final years of life and ministry in the town, honoured as he was as the oldest serving minister in the whole of the nation's church, he still came to pronounce blessings in marriages, baptisms and public ceremonies, still said his farewells to the people for whom he had always been the minister, some significantly younger than he, at burials in the churchyard. His preaching place, though, had been filled by a succession of young assistants appointed to help him, to support the weary hands of the aged gentleman at the end of his days. Their preaching was different. They did not know the people as he had done and their love for them was not as his had been. They were keen enough to practice their skills, but the declarations of their doctrinal positions and samples of eloquence had not moved the hearts of their hearers.

Margaret McGuffie, like many others, had spiritually starved until the revival came. From the first week, her heart had opened to its light as a flower will open to the sun. She drank deeply from the sweet waters and found that she had been very thirsty for them. In the atmosphere of openly acknowledged and shared faith, in the general sense of love among the worshippers, and in the stirring of vision in their gatherings, there was no room for loneliness in the days of Wigtown's religious revival.

★

John McGuffie's health was rapidly failing. After his nephew John McGuffie had left for New Zealand and Peter Clokie had died, without Margaret's knowledge he had changed his will. He left Barbados Villa to her without qualification. His daughter was to be his heir.

CHAPTER THIRTY-FOUR

1861

At the end of 1860, Scotland observed the tercentenary of its religious reformation. In Wigtown the shops were closed on the officially appointed day of remembrance, and the people thronged to services in the three Presbyterian churches in the town. The bells that called them to their services were the same bells that had tolled on the day in May of 1685 while the two Margarets, Covenanter martyrs, were led by soldiers down the main street of the town to be drowned in the old harbour. Reformation celebration services were marked by prayers of thanksgiving for those whose courage, even unto death, had helped purchase the freedoms now cherished, the freedom to worship according to the dictates of one's conscience, and the freedom to do so without fear.

Within months, a controversial book was published saying that the story of the Wigtown martyrs was a fable, a myth, a lie, and the claims of the book spread throughout Scotland. The people of Wigtown who had so recently begun to build their own monument to the memory of the martyrs, who had experienced a joyous and unifying religious revival, and who were so lately present at crowded services in all the churches as thanks were given for blessings brought by the martyrs' courage, protested immediately and in unison. The witnesses to the drownings were dead, and the children and grandchildren to whom those events had been described by those witnesses had recently all died, but the passed-on memories were still very much alive and would not be allowed to die in the burgh where it had all happened less than two hundred years before.

John Waugh, a ninety-three-year-old clock maker in the town, repeated in his creaking voice to all who would listen the same story he had been told in his youth. His father, Alexander Waugh, who had died in 1818 at the age of ninety-one years, had heard the story of the Wigtown martyrs from his own father who had witnessed their deaths. Old John Waugh, when told of the new book and its claims, said firmly and with passion, 'Those who doubt the drowning might just as well doubt the crucifixion of our Saviour.'

A Wigtown lady of unquestioned integrity wrote a letter of protest to the local newspaper when she heard the modern claims. She told that when she had first come to live in the town, a local resident, Mr McAdam of Woodside house, had come to call on her. He had told her that his own grandfather had shown him a petition he had sent to Parliament seeking official prosecution of Grierson of Lagg for the part he had played in the deaths of the Wigtown women. The petitioner had taken the action because he had married one of the Wilsons of Glenvernoch, the family of the younger martyr Margaret Wilson of that place, and he believed that justice had not been done in Lagg's having escaped punishment for his cruel deeds. The lady who wrote the letter into the newspaper was named Margaret Wilson, and for that reason she had been told the story.

As these voices were raised in protest, the people of the town spoke together and remembered together more and more the stories they had heard from people who had in turn heard from the people who had seen it all so long before. In other places in Scotland, the man Napier's book was read and its claims were believed, but, in the town where the deed had been done, where the same bells still rang weekly to call people to worship, where the same street still ran from the dungeon to the old harbour site, where twice daily the tides ran deeply and strongly in and out of the channel of the Bladnoch River, and where silent graves inscribed by 'Old Mortality' lay in the quiet churchyard, the claims provoked only a freshening of memories and strengthened the local knowledge of what had taken place. The newly erected memorial obelisk on the beautiful Windy Hill became more significant in its witness than it had been when it was first begun.

★

The provost who had laid the foundation stone was becoming too weak to properly discharge his duties of office. His carriage brought him to several of the meetings of the Town Council, but it waited outside the door so that, when he became too breathless to speak, too ill to preside, he could abandon the session and be driven home. Others there signed his name on the roll and took his place in the top chair at the council table. Heirs presumptive began to jockey for position, their feet eager to step into his shoes. Some manoeuvred with subtlety and others plainly bullied, but none retreated at the signs of others advancing with the same intent. The meetings became even more ill-tempered affairs than they had been before.

Spring, creeping northwards with her warming, always arrived earlier in England than in Scotland. Margaret McGuffie decided that her father could not wait for the balmier air to reach him; he must sail to Liverpool and benefit from the earlier warm season there. She bundled her gasping charge onto the Countess at the harbour and hovered over him during a restless crossing.

They took rooms outside the city's sprawl in a green-gardened house overlooking the distant Mersey. She stayed there with him, day after day, observing the healing touch of the warm sun, and the relief to his spirits from having escaped the strains of the noisy, scrapping rows of council meetings at home. Gradually he improved and even seemed ready to grow well again.

Brighter and stronger, in the care of a kindly proprietress, he urged Margaret to leave him for a day in order to pay calls on friends and relations.

She travelled to nearby Runcorn to visit her young cousin Mary. The busy bank of John Fraser was in the heart of the small commercial centre of the town. All around the high street were seemingly endless rows of little brick houses. A large shipping canal, from which emanated industrial fumes and grime, separated Runcorn from the Mersey banks and the grand city of Liverpool. An enormous transporter bridge was being built to straddle the canal and to link, thus, the poor, teeming working town with its grander neighbour. Margaret found the situation of the place depressing to her spirits and discovered that the usually bright young Mary seemed pale and strained. She felt, when she left, that she was abandoning Mary.

On another day, she met with her old friend Cecelia Wilson in Liverpool, and they strolled together through the streets of the once-familiar city. Liverpool seemed to Margaret like another place altogether from the Liverpool that lived in her memory. It had been, before, a large but easily mastered city, one full of adventures and softened by the kindly spirit of its people, a city with a conscience where there had been calls for the emancipation of the slaves in discussions on street corners. Now, the vaster, sprawling, still-growing thing seemed out of control and was possessed of another spirit. It was impersonal and no one could know it as a friend. It reached beyond the horizons in every direction, even to settlements on the other side of the Mersey waters, and its buildings soared like Babel. Blatantly supporting the American Confederacy against the declared sympathy of the Queen's government, it was gaily decked with the flags of the secessionist southern states across the Atlantic. The virtues of slavery, no longer its vices, were loudly proclaimed on the street corners. Minna could not have walked in Liverpool with any safety in the new days. The city was richer and grander, but it was bolder and harder in spirit, and Margaret did not like it.

Liverpool's trade prosperity had been severely affected by the emancipation of the slaves in the British colonies, a movement for which its people had called. There had been a price to pay for their morality. Since then, trade had relied more heavily than before on the cotton plantations in America, slave-dependent cotton plantations, shipping the cheap raw materials across to supply the Lancashire mills. Without the cotton grown by slaves, the mills of the middle of England and, with them, the port of Liverpool, would be finished. In the desperation of a need to survive economically, a new morality had risen, and it cried, 'Slavery is, after all, not forbidden by the Bible; it cannot be wicked; the blacks were meant, evidently, to be enslaved; we need the cotton; long live the Confederacy!'

It would never end, Margaret thought, for setting free was not really ever a final act. After it was done, someone else would rise and call subjection back into being, the reinstitution of slavery of some kind among some people. Lincoln might win his war, and the voices of Liverpool might even again come to champion the cause of freedom for all men, but, one dark night in some unthought-of corner of the world, it would all come back again. To the earth's ending, there would always exist the possibility of a tyrant man or a tyrant nation rising to declare some kind of people, some colour of them, male or female of them, some creed of them or lack of belief in them, some language spoken by them or any other distinguishing feature borne by them or marking them, to be a people designed by God to be possessed, ruled, broken, maybe even extinguished, by the people of the tyrant's own kind. It would be mere coincidence that the tyrants would always be made richer or more powerful by their tyranny; or, not coincidence, but, seen by them, part of the divine plan.

★

Margaret returned from the city to her father's side, and she refused to leave him again. He became nearly well enough to travel and they made plans to go back to Wigtown, its own northern summer having come at last. On the Sunday evening before their Monday morning's scheduled departure, she entered his room to find that his life was over. She sat in shocked silence for some time beside the empty form. The father who had sung his way through her childhood, who had left her world to re-enter his own, the father who had later become in this land her protector, provider and, sometimes, her torment, the one whose existence had underpinned her own for thirty years in a new land, was no more, and she was truly alone.

Eventually she left the darkening room to tell the landlady the news, and she sent messengers to John Fraser in Runcorn and to the captain of the Countess, informing them of her father's death. In the late hours of a dreadful night, it was decided among them that, as it was too late to register John McGuffie's death in Liverpool that night, and as this could not be effected before the hour of the ship's sailing on the morning tide, his body must be taken immediately, regardless of failure to complete legal formalities, to the boat. The tides would not wait, and if this were not done, the funeral of the Provost of Wigtown could not take place from his own home. John Fraser and Captain McQueen arranged for the transport of the body while Margaret, with Mary's tearful help, hastily packed the bags with their belongings.

In the darkness of the night, unseen by neighbours or any passers-by, the shrouded body of John McGuffie was trundled from the house and down the road, through Liverpool's hauntingly silent streets and down to the waterway.

Long before passengers arrived at the dockside the next day, the remains of the retired merchant and shareholder of the ship's company were placed in a hastily acquired makeshift coffin and taken to his usual large cabin. The cabin door was locked, and Margaret kept her lonely vigil there beside her father for the entire journey across the Solway. None of the passengers and few of the crew were aware that the proud Countess of Galloway, as she turned into the channel of the river Bladnoch and docked at the harbour of Wigtown, was serving as a hearse for one of her owners, the Provost of the Burgh.

After the ship had been emptied and the crowds had left the quay area, Captain McQueen tapped on the door of the locked cabin and Margaret McGuffie, her eyes clouded and circled by shadowy rings, opened it to him. The town's funeral carriage stood waiting beside her own on the deserted dockside, and soon the coffin carrying John McGuffie's body was being borne up the road to Barbados Villa, the house that he had built out of his sugar-coated dreams.

★

They could not wait. Within a week, the meeting to elect his successor was convened. The Town Council first expressed its sense of loss to itself and then extended its formal sympathies to the grieving only daughter, his heiress. Someone, in a thin, wheedling voice, piped up, 'Is it not, gentlemen, inappropriate that the sentiments customarily sent on these occasions,' and the speaker paused, running a sweaty finger around the inside of the top of his carefully starched collar, 'be extended to … uhm …' and he looked around nervously until he saw knowing, encouraging looks on the faces of several of the men listening to him, '. .. uhm … illegitimate family? … Er, no slight meant towards poor Miss McGuffie, of course.'

Little mutterings and mumblings filled the air. Quietly it was decided that Mr. McLean the banker should extend the council's sympathy verbally to her, rather than the Town Council sending an official letter, and that the comment regarding the sending of sympathy, already minuted by the clerk, should not be included in the newspaper report of the provost's death. A pencil line was drawn through the words of sympathy.

'Quite right,' said one.

'A correct procedure,' nodded his neighbour.

The meeting progressed to its election for the vacancy and feathers flew as voices were raised, the table shook and even gaslights flickered. The course of Wigtown politics moved on and into a new era.

★

In Barbados Villa, the ex-provost's daughter, a forty-eight-year-old spinster lady, waited during the early period of her mourning for the customary official letter of sympathy from the Town Council. She had seen the formal, black-bordered letter that had been sent by the council to the widow of Provost McHaffie only three years before. Her letter did not come. James McLean visited her and kindly voiced the sympathies that had been expressed by them to her; she would have preferred to have received a letter. Her father had other memorials to his existence, though; there was the house that he had built and there was a simple granite obelisk in Mochrum churchyard. In faraway lands, also, there were children who bore his name.

Prince Albert died of typhoid fever that same year. The nation mourned with and for their Queen who would never outlive her sorrow. She was forty-two years of age. The people had taken to him but slowly, for he had been a foreigner. Now he was regarded as almost a saint, and the wonderful Crystal Palace in London was seen as a monument to his genius. The Wigtown Town Council sent a letter to Queen Victoria, black-bordered and beautifully inscribed, in which it extended, on behalf of the people of the county town, their sincere sympathies to the Sovereign upon the new of her, and their own, incalculable loss.

CHAPTER THIRTY-FIVE

1862–1866

Barbados Villa was no longer described as 'John McGuffie's house' or 'the provost's villa'. It was referred to as 'the dark lady's house'. Its owner, it was whispered on good authority, was worth five thousand pounds but, for all her money, the whisperers hissed, she couldn't keep her staff.

It was a time of change again, and Wigtown was astir. Once more there were new things, new buildings, new adventures. An impressive, wider stone bridge was being built over the Bladnoch River by the distillery. A great, handsome edifice was rising in Wigtown's square in the place formerly occupied by the assembly rooms and, before that, by the ancient tolbooth. Adding to this site the space until recently occupied by a substantial family home, wonderful new County Buildings were being erected to dominate the square in the heart of the administrative centre of the shire. Made in French style of red sandstone, the arms of other ancient burghs in the area would adorn the building whose tall clock tower rise above the old martyrs' cell. The shire itself, some six miles to the north of the town at Newton Stewart, was linked by railway to the rest of Britain since the opening of the line from Dumfries to Portpatrick.

★

Summer's swallows left their nests and winter's geese appeared to fill the skies, then the tidal inks, at the beginning of another cold season. Catching the mood for change from the world around her, Miss McGuffie decided to make alterations of her own. She moved from the small western-facing bedroom in the house into the suite of three rooms at the front of the first floor. Within the rooms she formed a bedroom, a dressing room and a library. From a comfortable chair beside the large south-facing window of her reading room, she could look down on people passing by the house on the road leading to the harbour. Across the Muirs' field of Maidland Farm, she could see travellers leaving the town on the road to Bladnoch bridge.

Her life was lonely. On most days, her only company was her group of sour-faced servants and the glimpses, at a distance, of the travellers along the roads beyond her garden walls. The town had reverted to the reserve of its pre-revival days and the new isolation brought back dark clouds of depression for Margaret McGuffie. She lived through a long, dark winter of solitude; she saw the skies lighten and the days lengthen, the winter geese flying south and the beautiful swallows returning for the summer, before she decided, a year after her father's death, that she would leave the place, at least for a time.

Her solicitor was summoned, and, at her request, bills were drawn up to advertise the house for a let as from Martinmas in November. Ebenezer Stott Black, the solicitor, was kind and helpful in his arrangement making on her behalf. He mentioned, as he left her, that he perhaps knew of someone looking for just such a property. Several days after the bills were circulated, Sheriff Rhind arrived unannounced on her doorstep with a young girl in tow. Margaret McGuffie received her unexpected guests in the drawing room. The Depute Sheriff, indicating the child, began, 'Miss McGuffie, may I present my niece, Miss Marion Alice Rhind?'

The girl was already performing a deep curtsy, arms lifting her skirts in an extravagant sweep, when her name was announced and she halted, midway into her dipping, to hiss at her uncle, 'Nimin, Uncle MacDuff!' before continuing her respectful descent.

The dignified man seemed entirely accustomed to being reprimanded by small children, for he beamed upon her and corrected himself, 'Oh! So entirely sorry! Forgot! Excuse me, Miss McGuffie, my niece Miss Nimin Rhind.'

'You need not curtsy to me, Miss Rhind,' Margaret said, flashing a rare smile.

'Oh, but yes, I do,' argued the curly-topped and bright-eyed Nimin. 'I have made myself a rule to curtsy always very fully whenever I meet the occupants of castles, just in case they are particularly important persons, and you do have the most curious looking little castle beside your house. Is it a Georgian house? There's something not quite regular about its style, though it seems Georgian. It looks like a castle in the hallway, and I've never seen a Georgian house with a castle in its hall or beside it. Of course, one isn't always sure when it is advisable to curtsy, but I'd rather curtsy and be wrong than not curtsy and have been wrong, wouldn't you, Miss McGuffie? In any case, right or wrong, castles just seem to provoke me to curtsy!'

MacDuff was fairly choking with suppressed laughter as the tangled string of words came tumbling from the eager child, and Margaret McGuffie was enthralled by the outburst. 'Perhaps,' she offered, when the child finally paused for breath, 'you ought to be curtsying to my coach instead of to me, since it is the occupant of the castle.'

Nimin roared with laughter, and she did a pirouette while she clapped her hands in delight. 'Oh, Miss McGuffie, what a hilarious idea!'

Eventually, MacDuff Rhind managed to explain that Nimin's father, the architect, Mr. David Rhind, was about to commence work on a commission to design courthouses for Dumfries and Kirkcudbright, and that his large family wished to take a let on a property in the area for a time. They toured the house together, Nimin bouncing from room to room with excitement, bubbling with questions.

After they left her, Margaret did not go to her usual solitary retreat, but spent time in her garden before retiring to her light-filled drawing room to compose a long letter to Cecelia Wilson. She thought, later, how much more tolerable life in this lovely place would be if she had, from time to time, the pleasure of company such as the lively, sparkling Nimin child had been, or even pleasant and compliant servants.

★

A week later, a note arrived in the hand of the Depute Sheriff Rhind informing Margaret that the David Rhind family had accepted the offer of a let of Machermore Castle near Newton Stewart. 'You will not be surprised to learn that my niece, Miss Nimin, has not stopped dancing since her father agreed to allow her to live in a real castle. She has asked me to join her name with mine in thanking you for so kindly receiving us when we descended upon you without warning, and she requests that you visit the family in their new residence soon. She hopes that your coach will not be offended if you, and not it, are received in the castle at Machermore.'

Margaret smiled and mused with pleasure on the invitation. The next day she sent a note to her solicitor, instructing him to proceed no further with arrangements to let her house. 'I have decided to remain here for the time being,' she wrote.

★

People all over the world were shocked as the news gradually spread to every corner of every country that President Abraham Lincoln of the United States of America had died at the hand of an assassin. Shot while attending the theatre, the eloquent giant who had risen from poverty and obscurity to lead a war against secession in his country and to proclaim emancipation to the slaves of his nation, had been killed by an unknown actor named John Wilkes Booth. At the reading of that name, something stirred deep within the memory of Margaret McGuffie. She finally remembered. Her father had returned from a journey to and from Liverpool with entertaining stories, silly stories, about a strange Liverpool actor who was going to seek his fortune in America. She remembered, as a child, laughing merrily whenever her father did his funny imitation of the man, sweeping off his hat, rolling into a deep bow, and proclaiming, 'Julius Brutus Booth, at your service.' The name had been, so long ago, a family joke, used in family fun.

Rev. Peter Young, Wigtown's parish minister for sixty-five years, the Father of the Church of Scotland, slipped from time into eternity and a huge, beautiful triple window of deeply-coloured stained glass in his memory was placed in the eastern transept of the large new church.

A message came from Runcorn to say that Mary McGuffie Fraser, aged only thirty years, had died. Her mother Jane had died just the year before Margaret's father. The only surviving member of the draper's family was the adventurer son lost somewhere, piling up debts somewhere, in New Zealand. Margaret began to feel that a tide was slipping away from beneath her, receding and leaving her like an abandoned piece of driftwood on the high-water mark of a beach.

CHAPTER THIRTY-SIX

1867–1869

Cecelia Wilson proposed to make a journey from Liverpool to Penrith, and she summoned Margaret McGuffie to meet her there. The McGuffie carriage had been sold and replaced by a smaller, neater, deeply upholstered dark green brougham, and it was in her new coach that Margaret was driven to meet her train at the Newton Stewart station for her first trip into England overland. England always seemed near. On any clear day she could see its northern mountains across the Solway water and previously she had always crossed to it by boat.

The journey was across terrain not often seen by travellers until the coming of the railway, for the track cut deeply inland from the shore. Starting out in a long curve to cross the broad estuary of the river Cree, the train chugged up the slope of the far side of Wigtown's Bay and then disappeared into the wild winter landscape of the empty Galloway hills and moorlands. It flew alongside a great, louring, grey rock face, crept cautiously over a cathedral-high viaduct, and then seemed to travel at galloping pace, stopping only at a few local stations, into the town of Dumfries. Margaret changed trains there and, after a short journey skimming the inner reach of the Solway Firth, she changed for the last time at Carlisle station. In mere minutes she was arriving in Penrith, emerging through the door and moving across a steam-shrouded platform into the welcoming embrace of her friend. Thomas Varty was there, beaming at her as he always did, and organising the transport of the luggage and the women to the rooms they had taken in Penrith. He left them there with their firm promise to visit Stagstones by foot the next day unless there was rain, in which case his carriage would call for them.

They shared a cosy parlour's fireside in the long, dark evening and they told each other, as hour succeeded hour, all there was to tell since they had last been together. Barton worked on, Margaret learned, unwilling to follow Thomas Varty into a well-earned retirement. He had always assumed that his son, a lad so gifted in the woodworking part of their carriage production business, would follow him into the coach works. Young Barton Worsley Wilson had surprised them all by announcing his decision one day to enter the church, and nothing now would distract him from his deep and solemn studies, his attendance at services, his concern about matters of the soul. Mary Frances quietly supported her brother, waiting on his every need, hearing and confirming his every expressed thought. She had no plans, no desires, she said, for a home and a name of her own. Her father's work, her mother's home and her brother's calling absorbed her life and fulfilled her completely. Cecelia just shrugged. 'I am proud of them. They are good children. They haven't an ounce of personal ambition between them,' and she grinned impishly across at her friend, 'unlike their father. One would wonder where they came from, if one didn't know!' The friends chuckled quietly together, comfortable in their shared intimacy and humour.

Margaret told Cecelia of her life in Wigtown during the time since the death of her father. She told her of the town's general silence with regard to her presence, signified first by the absence of an official letter of condolence from the Town Council. She told Cecelia of the moody, sometimes quite openly defiant servants. She described the view from her library window, the loveliness of her gardens, and of her delight in the challenge of wisely investing the money her father had left her, the legacy that must provide for her future years.

Very late, just as they were rising to go to their rooms, Cecelia said very quietly, almost as an afterthought, 'Oh, Margaret, I must tell you: Thomas has said that you should know that he has at last found someone who will marry him. Her name is Lucy Nicholson. She is very much younger than Thomas, being not yet twenty years of age, but they adore each other. She is distantly related to Barton. Isn't that a strange thing? It is late; I'll tell you more tomorrow.'

She had been fussing about with lamps and curtains, the cushions and the fire, as she had spoken, keeping her face averted from her friend. When she finally turned to look at her, Cecelia saw that Margaret was still sitting, silently, in her chair. She smiled, gave her hand to her, pulled her to her feet, placed a candle in her hand, and guided her to the bedroom door. She pecked her gently on the cheek and said softly, 'Good night, Margaret, dear,' and went to her own room.

Margaret McGuffie slipped into her warmed bed and lay, utterly composed, all alone in the darkness. Suddenly, unbidden, a tear rolled from beneath a tightly closed lid and then another, until a stream of them wet her face and threatened to soak her pillow. She was afraid to get up to search for her handkerchief, or to blow her nose, or to make any sound in her crying, in case someone in the house might hear her. Just as the stifled sobbing could be contained no more, the world outside her window exploded with a deafening blast, a blaze of light, and the sounds of utter bedlam from all over Penrith.

A wagon load of gunpowder had been involved in a collision on the railway line just south of Yanwoth Bridge. A driver and fireman were killed, and the fire raged on for three days. It was said that every pane of glass in Yanwoth was shattered, and for the people of Penrith there was no other topic of conversation for a week. Everyone was shocked by the blasting, burning disaster and no one but Cecelia took note of the slight puffiness of the face of her subdued guest.

★

The two women walked through a long avenue of magnificent trees overlooking the brooding ruins of Brougham Castle and then turned at Carleton village to climb straight up on a footpath leading to the eastern side of Beacon Fell. There, high up above the town, the path became the lane that ran to Stagstones. They turned into the gated entrance and walked on through the woodland, just as Margaret remembered it, until they came to Stagstones house. Thomas was transforming the old house into a grander, more modern home. He emerged from the building works, covered in dust and lime, to greet them both with his usual boyish enthusiasm and affectionate hugs. He took them for a tour around the site, showing them the spacious new rooms, new fireplaces, and stacks of marble tiling waiting to be made into attractive mosaic flooring. They scrambled about over the place with him looking, listening, admiring and questioning. When a crisis with the work called for his consultation, they took their leave of him, promising to return for their promised tea another day. Margaret and Cecelia were chatting together about all of Thomas's plans when they saw two people approaching them along the woodland lane – a tall, slender man with a lovely younger woman at his side. She had silky golden curls and carried a basket of fruit on her arm.

The couple recognised Cecelia and stopped to speak with them. Margaret looked into the deep grey eyes of the man, and she was swept back more than forty years in her memory to a rolling lawn under a tropical sun, to a massive silk cotton tree with horrible spikes on its trunk, to her hand reaching up to touch, and to those same grey eyes reproving, the head shaking, a guardian hand preventing her. 'John Nicholson,' she said quietly, with wonder in her voice.

He returned her look without sign of recognition. Even after Cecelia's polite introduction and Margaret's explanation, he could not remember. Margaret was benumbed by the coincidence. Lucy Nicholson, the beautiful golden-haired girl with the serene grey eyes of her father was the girl Thomas Varty was to marry, the young woman who would preside as mistress over the house of Thomas's dreams, who would bear him children. This Lucy was the daughter of John Nicholson of Barbados. She was, then, the granddaughter of the good, the revered, Rev. Mark Nicholson of Codrington College, the place where priests were made. Lucy was the great niece of the man named Reynold Alleyne Elcock, the plantation owner of Barbados who had been murdered by his slave because he had been kind and generous in the making of his will. Lucy's father had been born in the great stone house on the island that Margaret remembered as looking so like her own house in Scotland.

★

Margaret McGuffie was glad, so glad, so pleased, so thrilled for Thomas, and she loved Lucy. Everyone loved Lucy. Everyone would always love Lucy and Thomas. It was a perfect match. Thomas was descended from the most worthy and pious man of Penrith, the man who had worshipped in the church where stones by the entrance paid tribute to his holy life, the man who had brought John Wesley to Penrith to preach and provided the place of worship used by his followers, the man who had defied social conventions by worshipping there as faithfully with the poor as he did in the large church with the rich. Lucy was descended from a family just as generous and true in its piety and theology, but a family also brilliant in scholarship. There was, between the two families, such a heritage of spiritual strength, of genuine goodness, of intelligence, of artistic talent, and of physical beauty, that the very angels in heaven must have burst into song when Thomas had first gazed into Lucy's grey eyes. It was all as it should be, as it was meant to be.

Margaret McGuffie did not remain long in Penrith, but returned by the steaming, puffing, whistling trains to Galloway to get on with her life, her own independent and very solitary life.

★

Shortly after her return, a card of invitation arrived at Barbados Villa bidding Miss McGuffie to take afternoon tea with Miss Nimin Rhind at Machermore Castle.

The dark green brougham made its way again along the road to Newton Stewart. It clattered, this time, down the steep street that ran through the town, across the Cree Bridge, and then turned south to follow the river's course into a plantation of magnificent trees and flowering shrubs that hid the ancient castle of Machermore from the world.

The quaint woman-child Nimin had summoned her guest for a day when, her parents and siblings having taken the train to Dumfries, she would reign alone in her castle home. She stood primly on the steps with her servants and calmly directed them to open Miss McGuffie's carriage door. As the older woman alighted, Nimin turned to the empty brougham, the coach that lived in a castle, and honoured it with a deep, respectful curtsy. Then, with her ringing musical laugh, she motioned for it to be taken away into the stable yard. She greeted her visitor as an old friend. 'Oh, Miss McGuffie, I am so glad that you could come. Is this castle not truly all that I could have wished for? It is quite Gothic, and I adore the seclusion. We will see the grounds after tea. You must come again when Papa is here, for he can tell you about the architectural details of this place in a way that no one else can, and I am sure that you must be dying to know about every turret and every beam of the building. Did you know that Robert the Bruce was here, and one of the Wigtown Margarets was imprisoned here? I keep hoping to see a ghost. There must be one somewhere! It is so exciting!'

They walked through magnificent rooms, they took tea on a little table in a window overlooking formal garden and lawns bursting with crocuses, they strolled along paths and walked down to the still, brown waters of the river. Margaret was submerged, the whole time, in the sound of the tumbling torrent of words and the whirling of ideas that raced through the head and out of the mouth of young Nimin Rhind.

★

A younger sister of the Rhind family, one Margaret had never met, died very suddenly just after her visit to Machermore, and the family's mourning period meant that, for a time, there was silence between the castle and Barbados Villa. David Rhind had lost his first wife when he was a young man, and a number of children had died already during the period of his second marriage. He had learned to mourn deeply but quickly, and his family followed suit. Before the summer passed, Margaret was invited again to call at Machermore and, for months thereafter, she travelled to them and they to her as acquaintanceship and friendship grew.

One day at Machermore, Nimin showed Margaret sketches from a folder of her father's past commissions. There was among them the picture of a huge tombstone with the Biblical scene of the triumph of Moses and Miriam at the Red Sea crossing carved on it in beautiful detail. Margaret examined the picture closely. 'I have seen this!' she exclaimed excitedly. She looked up at David Rhind as he sat opposite her chair observing her study of his work.

'Which?' he asked.

'The tombstone with Moses carved on it! It was at the Great Exhibition in the Crystal Palace. I remember it very well. Of course! I thought of MacDuff when I saw the name of the architect!' She looked up at the artist. 'How wonderful! It was yours.'

David Rhind blushed a little, leaned forward, and tapped his pipe into the grate. 'Wonderful to be remembered for a tombstone, Miss McGuffie?'

She went on through the folder eagerly, astounded at the magnificence of his buildings, the handsome designs, the intricacy of their embellishments. As her interest grew, so did his willingness to explain his intentions to her and to point out details she had not noticed. She was in awe of his talent when she saw the sketches of Daniel Stewart's Hospital in Edinburgh, and was greatly impressed to learn that the building was based on a design he had submitted for the Houses of Parliament competition. She learned that his very closest friend of many years was the renowned Sir Charles Barry, the very man who had won that commission and whose dramatic Parliament buildings she, herself, had seen and admired. He told her that he had studied with the father of the even more famous Augustus Pugin, the leader of the Gothic revival moment whose exhibition had featured so prominently in the Great Exhibition and whose tastes inspired the architectural style now seen in buildings being erected across the nation.

She looked with him at sketches of fine houses, castles, banks, courthouses, insurance company offices, churches, public memorials and, again, at the picture of the massive tombstone with its beautiful carvings. Margaret began to understand, not only the importance of David Rhind's work in Scotland, but the origins of the lively, amazing mind and personality of her young friend Nimin.

The Rhinds' visits to Margaret in Wigtown were as educational for her as her visits to the castle, for the gifted architect took delight in the architectural features of the home her father had built. She pointed out to him the Caribbean influences in the house, features like the long windows with hurricane shutters, the parapet roof, the triple-gated entrance and circular drive, the colonial-pillared porch entrance, and even the little jalousie on an interior wall beneath the curving stone staircase.

Under his influence, she began to think of modernising touches that could be made in her home, details that would soften and enrich the classic simplicity of the design of the earlier period. In place of the large plain glass staircase window, she installed a coloured one, vivid stained glass red and blue side panels framing light-coloured green panes that deepened to an emerald hue under the light of a gas stairlight in the evenings. More stained-glass work was designed for the panels of the inner front door, and the outer entryway was re-laid with coloured tiles. Because of his interest, she began to see more in the details of the house she had so taken for granted for over thirty years. As she did so, her appreciation for the beauty of the home her father had built became much deeper.

When work on Kirkcudbright's courthouse was done, the Rhinds left Machermore with promises to return. They took with them her promises to visit them in Edinburgh or London. She had been enriched by them, and she settled with greater contentment and pride into her own place, her own life, than she had done before Nimin had arrived on her doorstep.

★

One evening she sat alone under the shade of a plane tree in the southeast corner of her garden. She was there to catch light from the late summer sun and to enjoy the peace of her beautifully planted grounds. A trio of young women walked slowly past her front gates. She could hear their voices as they came along the other side of the wall, but she could not see them from where she sat, and they were unaware of her presence.

They stopped walking when they reached her eastern boundary and flopped down on the grass, their backs leaning against her wall. They looked out over the lovely scene stretching away below them. They watched the sheep and cattle that were grazing on pastureland and the more distant tidal flats, the soft blue of the winding river channel contrasting with the deeper blue of the bay, and cloud shadows drifting along the gentle slopes of the hills across the water. A small boat lay in the harbour anchorage, and another was chugging steadily towards the river channel's entrance.

'My father said that the shipping will die out when the railway comes into the shire,' said the voice belonging to young Grace Fraser, daughter of the harbourmaster from John McGuffie's days.

'I like to watch the boats,' said Jane Fulton. 'The bay won't be the same if they aren't comin' in and out and goin' up and doon the river.'

'Who cares?' challenged the sharp, pert voice of the girl Margaret McGuffie recognised as Jessie Dickson Cowper. 'We must look out for ourselves, not the folk of old times. I hope we get a railway here and we can go straight to London on the train. Oh! London!'

'When are you moving there, then, Jessie?' asked Jane Fulton, her voice full of sarcasm.

'Listen you, Jane,' Jessie shot back, 'I have plans and you just see if I don't. I'll live in the biggest house in this town and I'll go to London whenever I like!'

Grace turned and prodded the braggart, 'Who, Jessie? The Blacks wouldn't have you if one were available; you're too wild.'

'Wild? Me? Never!' Jessie pouted. 'Who said anything about Blacks, anyway? Blacks! Might as well be n★★★★★s with a name like that! Speaking of n★★★★★s,' and she turned, looking at the house that rose over the wall behind her.

'Jessie!' the others shrieked, in unison.

'That's horrible of you! I'm off,' said Jane, and she left.

Grace rebuked the girl whose tongue wagged out at the retreating form of their slightly older companion. 'Why do you say things like that, Jessie? You can seem so nice and then you have to say such rude things. You don't really mean them, do you?'

'I mean what I mean when I mean it,' said Jessie, archly. 'I will live in the biggest house, and I will go to London whenever I like. I do not appreciate it when people mock what I say, Grace Fraser, and I think that, most probably, the woman who lives in that house is a stupid, uneducated, lazy n★★★★★ who would live in a shack made out of wooden sticks if the man she called her father hadn't left her enough money to allow her to give herself airs. My grandmother has more lady quality in one little finger than that black creature from a jungle has in her whole dark body, and black people should go back to where they came from.!'

★

The next Sunday in church, Margaret McGuffie saw Jessie Dickson Couper sitting near the front in the family pew she shared with her grandmother, her mother and her captain father. She could see that the girl sang her hymns clearly and with the sweetest of expressions on her young, upturned face, that she bowed her head more fully and a little longer than anyone else for the prayers, that she read intently from her own Bible as the tall young minister, Rev. James Cullen, read the day's lesson from the lectern, and that she once was seen to wipe a little tear from her eye at a particularly impassioned moment as he preached.

As the congregation left the church, she saw that Rev. Cullen was drinking in words of appreciation from young Jessie as they stood together for a moment in the doorway, and that the eyes of the handsome bachelor followed the pretty girl while she walked demurely down the path. Margaret, waiting in the queue to pass through the same doorway, became aware of the presence of someone beside her. Grace Fraser's eyes were fixed on her face and, when their glances met, Grace smiled at her sweetly, saying, 'Your garden is looking very nice just now, Miss McGuffie.' Margaret looked deeply, but she saw no guile in the eyes of the one looking so steadily into her own, and her heart accepted the apology.

After the parishioners had gone, James Cullen and his spinster sister Hannah made their way together up the lane behind the glebe to the spacious new manse built for him on the edge of the town. 'Miss Couper seems to be increasing in her devotion to spiritual things,' he said quietly to his housekeeper sister.

She laughed and said pointedly, 'She has been since the manse was completed. She has designs on you and your abode. Watch out!'

'Don't be ridiculous, Hannah,' he said curtly. 'I am far too old for such a young and pretty thing. And, anyway, I'm far too staid for her taste.'

'Mind my warning, James,' said his sister, primly, hurt by his unusual sharpness with her. 'Men can be terribly blind.'

CHAPTER THIRTY-SEVEN

1871–1875

The subject of the relationship developing between Rev. Cullen and the young lady was the talk of the town. He had begun to call regularly at the home of the ship owner Captain Garlies Couper and his wife Catherine at the time of the death of Mrs. Couper's elderly mother. Their lovely daughter Jessie had been distraught after her proud grandmother's death, and the parents had appealed to the tender-hearted pastor to comfort her. The grieving girl had pleaded, with helpless tears and gentle sighs, for his patience with her until her courage and faith were renewed. He had plunged into the pretty trap headfirst and was swept along by the powerful currents of her sweetly determined ways.

Jessie saw him to the door whenever he left the house, and she always stood close to him in the precious solitude of the hallway, speaking so quietly that he would have to bend low, his cheeks often brushing her silken hair in his attempt to catch her words. Many a person passing the Couper's' door on the main street during an evening's stroll had seen him slip out, he face visible at the closing crack of the door, and they had all nodded to each other in the knowing way of a small town, passing the news on to others who had already heard that the minister was courting young Miss Couper.

When he had gone, Jessie would check her face and her hair in the hall mirror, smile with contentment, and flounce back in to join her family. 'James, get off my chair!' she would bellow at her youngest brother.

Her mother would ask, 'How is it going, my dear?'

She would reply, coldly, 'Very well, but I must work out a plan to get him to send his sister home. That old Hannah and her hooks are holding him back from a proper proposal, Ma. He won't want to put her out. She must go!' Jessie had already hinted to James Cullen that his spinster sister must miss her native Fife, that she must be weary of her work occasionally and miss her family and friends. His relaying of her concerns to Hannah had, indeed, impressed his sister. They had caused her to raise her eyebrows, to chuckle, and to be very determined that she would not leave her brother's house, even for one whole day. Protect him, she would!

★

The shipping trade had always been a dangerous one. Ships dashed on rocks, ran aground on mud banks, slipped mysteriously away beneath the waves on the high seas never to be seen again and, sometimes, most dramatically, caught fire. Ships had burned in Wigtown Bay and even up the Bladnoch River, but two locally owned boats blazing away to charred hulks in the river channel within six months of each other rattled the nerves of even the most optimistic members of Wigtown's merchant shipping society.

Then coaches began to have accidents. Two collided trying to pass each other in a mad dash race on a road near Wigtown. The coach drivers were fined for dangerous driving. On the day of the hiring fair in Minnigaff, a crowded coach full of passengers returning to the burgh came to grief right on the main street of Wigtown after its horses had bolted and its wheel had struck a paving stone. Four of the passengers had been riding inside and eleven clinging, terrified, to the top of the runaway coach. The coach turned over with a terrible crash and bodies were flung everywhere. One man was trapped under a large wheel and others were pinned beneath the upturned coach.

Margaret McGuffie was on the street with her newly employed cook Jane Fulton when it happened. Annie Tait Henry was standing near her. She was the sweet-faced young daughter of the postmaster, now already the widow of an older man, an affable merchant who had recently drunk himself to death. While others stood in stunned silence, Annie reacted immediately, calling to a young man passing on horseback to ride for the doctor. 'Go as quickly as you can, for I saw him just moments ago riding down the Crescent towards Bladnoch! Ride, boy; go!' She turned to her aunt, the town's postmistress, 'Run down to the telegraph office, Aunt Grace! We will need more assistance here. Send for the Newton doctor.'

Margaret McGuffie got down on her knees in the street and began to cradle on her lap the broken head of the man who was lying under the wheel while Jane Fulton pulled at the wheel, with others who had gathered, in an attempt to release him.

Other people came racing and began to free injured passengers lying underneath the coach, carefully rolling the broken shell away from an unconscious man lying bleeding on the street. Two druggists came running to see what they could do and one of them, after seeing what had happened, ran retching into the greenery of the nearby gardens. Women hauled their children inside their houses, closing their curtains. Some men slunk away, white-faced, hoping they hadn't been seen.

When the most grievously injured man had been carried into the nearby coaching inn and his family sent for, and when then the other unconscious victims had been lifted on blankets to join him in the makeshift hospital, people began silently to clear the street of its shattered and bloody debris. Jane Fulton had been sent to bring the family of another unconscious victim to the inn, and Margaret McGuffie knelt alone and forgotten, bemused, in shock on the street.

Annie Tait's gentle voice and touch roused her from her stupor. 'Miss McGuffie, come. Let me see you home. You did so well, so kindly, comforting that poor man.' Annie's eyes filled with tears as she looked into the dazed face of the stranger woman, the foreigner she remembered as a shadowy figure in the days of her childhood. She had almost forgotten that Margaret McGuffie still existed, so much a recluse had the woman become. She remembered that her friend Mary McGuffie, who had died so young in Runcorn, had been this woman's cousin. She was touched, for the first time, by a sense of curiosity and some warmth of compassion for the lonely woman who had no relations in the town and about whom she knew so little.

Margaret McGuffie took Annie Tait's offered arm and rose to her feet slowly. She looked down at her brown satin walking dress with its marks of blood and of the very brains of the injured man. Annie brushed gently at the skirt with her own handkerchief and then willed the stunned older woman to look at her face again. 'Come,' she urged.

Jessie Dickson Couper stood near the post office door surveying the scene of the disaster. 'Well, Mrs. Henry, what do you have here?' she quipped as the two women approached her across the square.

Annie looked up at the girl's cold eyes and shook her head. 'If you cannot help, Jessie, you ought to go home.'

'This is more entertaining,' said Jessie, brutally. 'Of course, proper ladies don't kneel in the street, but then, I suppose, such behaviour is not uncommon among black people and drunkards, is it, Mrs. Henry?'

She had not seen, but the minister, who had only just learned of the incident, had approached, and he was virtually at her elbow when her taunt rang out. He passed her without a word to reach the other side of Margaret McGuffie and he ignored Jessie Couper as he helped the young widow to guide the shocked woman down the street towards her home.

★

Rev. James Cullen was seen no more at the door of Jessie Dickson Couper, and a year later she sued him for breach of promise. She trembled, sighed and pouted before the judge as she told the sad tale of how the older man had misled her, had won her heart and professed his love, had spoken of marriage. She told of their going to the door together alone whenever he called, a practice only allowed by her parents because they had recognised the minister as her beau. She recounted the story of a trip to London on the train when he had held her hand and accompanied her to a matinee at the theatre. She demanded one thousand pounds in damages for his refusal to fulfil his alleged promises to her. She was twenty-one years of age and considered her prospects now ruined by him; she wept

178

touchingly. He was forty-two years of age and still a bachelor. The case came to nothing as the court waited for a witness to return from abroad. The Garlies Couper family moved to Dorking in Surrey.

The bachelor minister of the Parish Church married Mrs. Annie Tait Henry, widow of a spirit merchant and drunkard, daughter of the precentor for the United Presbyterian Church. The town cheered him for his wise choice and sweet, gentle Annie became the mistress of the large and elegant manse on the hill. The minister's sister Hannah waited until Jessie Dickson Cowper had moved south and the wedding of her brother to Annie had been celebrated. Then she warmly kissed her dear new sister, wished her much happiness, and moved home to Fife. Within five years of the minister's marriage, four children were born in the manse, two little boys and two little girls.

CHAPTER THIRTY-EIGHT

1875–1888

Nothing stayed the same forever, but changes always seemed to take place in certain short periods of time, to be followed by settled periods until the next wave of changes came. It was yet another period of change in the county town of Wigtown. Old things and familiar ways, perhaps the last of them to have survived earlier times of change, either came crashing down or faded out of existence. In their place, new things came into being and were soon accepted as everyday life, as if they had always been.

Crows had filled the tops of the tall trees of Wigtown's central square for generations. The trees had been planted on ground grown rich from having served, in centuries past, as the town's common midden. Young trees, nourished in this soil, had quickly grown to be huge, flourishing crowns of luxuriant foliage. The trees were beautiful and had made the town they adorned a particularly beautiful place, but they had finally become so massive that they were crowding out the popular space in the centre of the town square used as a bowling green. Further, the crow population whose nests adorned the tops of the trees, had grown so greatly that the constant noise and nuisance they created were being increasingly deplored by the citizenry of the burgh. Town Council meetings had officially debated the twin matters of the trees and the crows, and the drinkers in the inns had unofficially debated the matters of the trees and the crows, for decades. It was said by the anti-crow factions that people could not sleep in their beds or converse on the streets for the continual, raucous cawing of the birds. Others, pro-crow people, countered that the birds had as much a right to live in peace in their trees as some of the less savoury characters of the town had to expect their presence to be tolerated by their more respectable neighbours. Some wanted the crows to be left alone. Others wanted the crows to be shot but the trees to remain. Yet others wanted the trees cut down and the crows gone forever. some cared nothing for crows, trees, or bowling greens, but enjoyed listening to the arguing.

The arguments stopped for a time while the railway moved towards the town. The line had been cut, dug and blasted from Newton Stewart and, early in March of 1875, the town simply closed down for the day while its people moved en masse to the station to await the coming of the first locomotives into Wigtown. The train was referred to as 'the civiliser', and, as it moved along the new line, people cheered the coming of greater progress into the remote country area. Its whistle announced its approach to the old county town and the people roared, in answer to the greeting, waving their handkerchiefs in the air as the train drew up at the new platform. Just as Captain Broadfoot had been applauded years before when he brought the Countess of Galloway in triumph to dock at the harbour, cheers rang out for the designer of the new railway, the clever Mr. Wheatley, when the long-awaited engine pulled into the station at the top of the lane that ran to the harbour.

A month later there were passenger services, four a day, between Wigtown and Newton Stewart, and so many of the local people wanted to make the twenty-minute journey that extra coaches had to be added to the early train.

During the four decades of her occupancy of Barbados Villa, Margaret McGuffie had watched ships sailing up and down in the waters of the bay, in and out of the harbour, the loading of cargo including livestock, the coming and going of passengers by boat, all the busy activity of shipping trade at the peak of its prosperity. She had witnessed from her home the dramatic incidents connected with that way of life: accidents and fires, capsizings and the running aground of vessels. Now she stood on the flat roof of the house to witness the birth of a new era. With Jane Fulton and Grace Fraser, her two servants, she watched the crowds gathering, listened to the first call of the whistle, saw the steam in clouds puffing up from the deep cutting, and heard the cheers as the first locomotive drew into the station that lay below her house.

She had seen this day coming for some years. Sorry though she was at the death knell the coming of trains most surely caused to ring for the familiar world of shipping trade in Wigtown, she knew that her father, had he lived until this time, would have grasped the opportunities opening up as the old ways were dying. She invested heavily in railway stock.

★

Mr. McClure built a large new house to the east of Barbados Villa, and Margaret McGuffie grumbled loudly, incessantly, about its blocking of her previously unrivalled view of the harbour and the bay. She declared the new house to be a monstrosity; it was far too big and perfectly ugly in a grand, Victorian many-chimneyed way. 'No taste,' she would mutter as she viewed it rising above her garden wall or surveyed its bulk from her windows. She planted hedges along the eastern wall to block out her view of it. If she could not see past the house to the harbour, she certainly would not look at the house.

One day while she worked in her private walled garden behind the house, she stood up to stretch her aching back and saw, to her horror, that someone in the McClelland's house, a field away behind her, was watching her from a first-floor window. She had not noticed before that the house, built before her own or the Simsons' house next to her, had a view from its upper windows into what she regarded as the privacy of her secluded garden. She went indoors.

Later, at dusk, she returned to the garden for a more careful look and discovered there that, not only the McClellands' Orchardton House, but also the row of houses along Fairacre Place, afforded views into her garden from upper windows. She ordered Jane Fulton to request that a bricklayer of repute in the town call at the house immediately. During the next week, upon her instructions, the man removed the stone slabs from the top of her high back garden wall, added four bricks to the height of it, checked that the boundary was now of a sufficient height to block all eyes in any attempt to see into her private world, and re-laid the flat stones along the top of the new bricks. She was well satisfied with the result and returned to work in her garden.

★

Margaret McGuffie's cousin and first friend in Britain, Mary Johnstone Goodwin, had died. To the family generation of cousins' children, she was the only remaining member of the 'older generation' of the family. She did not visit them often, but they sometimes called to see her. She was their elderly, interesting, quite foreign spinster aunt. Another visitor from near Port William to her home, a more frequent visitor than her young relations, was Hugh Wright of Alticry, a friend of her father. The uncle of Hugh Wright, from whom he had inherited his property, had been a man of great integrity and kindness. She gradually had allowed Hugh Wright to become her chief adviser for he always exhibited concern for her welfare and about her business interests, and because she believed that he was a man of integrity like his uncle before him. He continued faithfully to visit and to advise her, because he believed that she was a wealthy spinster woman with no direct heirs.

Cecelia Wilson wrote to her with pride in the news of her son's appointment to the parish of Lazonby, near Penrith. Penrith was too far away for her, now, to visit.

John Simson, the elderly customs collector and father of her friend Margaret Anderson, her nearest neighbour for over forty years, died. Two years later his wife followed him to the grave.

Jane Fulton, one of the best cooks and most helpful servants she had employed, annoyed Margaret McGuffie intensely by announcing her intention to leave service and to marry, at the age of thirty-two years, Mr. William McGowan, a local painter and decorator. Just before the marriage took place, Margaret McGuffie called her departing servant to her, and, having presented her with a wedding gift, the old woman gruffly told the bride-to-be that if she produced a daughter and named her Margaret McGuffie, the child would be remembered in her will.

Grace Fraser, the daughter of the former harbourmaster, remained in the service of Miss McGuffie after her friend's marriage. She was more than dutiful towards her mistress and became, in time, her trusted companion and confidante. Grace was threatened with a variety of punishments, both human and divine, if she dared to think of marriage or of any other excuse to leave her employer's service. Grace only laughed.

★

Two Wigtown spinsters, sisters who had lived during their childhood near the courthouse, had moved to Agnew Crescent with their mother after their father's death and, having lost their mother, had finally settled in a douce house known as Hope Cottage up a tiny lane off the Crescent. Miss Mary Boyd and Miss Jane Boyd, daughters of an Irish army captain and his English wife, did not speak in the accents of the Irish, the English, or the locals, but spoke in a singsong, bird-like chatter all their own.

Since their removal to Hope Cottage, they had established the habit of strolling together every afternoon to the now often deserted harbour. As they passed the garden of Barbados Villa going down the hill, one of them would always twitter over the wall or up to a window, 'Good day, Miss McGuffie,' and, as they walked back up again later, the other would twitter, 'Good evening, Miss McGuffie.'

One Monday Margaret McGuffie ventured to invite the sisters to stop for tea with her the next day, and that became part of the pattern of Tuesdays of each week, but only on Tuesdays. On a different day, she walked out to their little tucked-away perch of a house in the mornings to take coffee with them, always, but only, on Fridays. It was the first time in her fifty years of residence in the town that she was regularly expected as a guest and friend in a house other than one of her own family members, and she loved to pay her weekly call on the Misses Boyd.

★

In the year that David Rhind died, Margaret McGuffie summoned her solicitor to the house and prepared her will. Because her surviving family were mostly in Port William, she nominated her cousin's son, namesake to her father, and her kindly friend from Alticry, along with the minister of Mochrum parish and her solicitor, Ebenezer Stott Black, to be her trustees.

She had decided after the traumatic coach accident in the town over ten years previously that she wished to leave a sum of money in the form of two specific bequests, one for Wigtown and one for her father's home parish of

183

Mochrum, to be used for the medical treatment of poor people at the Royal Infirmary in Edinburgh. In that terrible accident, one man, the man whose head she had held in her lap, had died. Others had been severely injured and were left with extensive disabilities made worse by the fact that, because they were poor, they could not afford to seek further treatment in the large hospital that could have helped them. She had remembered how the slaves on the island of Barbados, before their emancipation, had been entitled to receive the very best of medical and surgical care at their owner's expense. It had seemed strange to her that, though slaves on a tiny colony island had been seen as entitled to medical care, free people in the greatest nation on earth could be left to suffer or die just because there was no one to pay for their care. She planned that the McGuffie bequests would provide for such cases in the future, and the administration of her bequests was placed, as was customary, in the hands of the minister and session of the respective parishes to this end.

As she listed to the solicitor the names of those she wished to receive personal legacies from her estate, she was stirred by the memories the exercise provoked. She remembered Caroline, her half-sister, still living in Barbados. She thought of the widow of her brother and of their grown family, those complete strangers who shared her name and her blood. She thought of the Wilsons and the Vartys from Liverpool and Penrith, and of the children they had produced, and of how Thomas and Lucy had named their fourth daughter Margaret in her honour. She thought of her neighbour in earlier times, Margaret Simson Anderson and of her later acquaintance, Nimin Rhind, the daughter of the brilliant architect. She included all these, together with her newest friends, the quaintly chirping Misses Boyd, in her will.

As she gave instructions for legacies, she remembered the cousin whom her father had intended to be her heir, the man who was to have followed her into the loaned-for-a-lifetime house that was her home, the man who was still far off across the world trying to find his fortune and was always said to be almost drowning in debt somewhere in New Zealand.

She remembered the loyal, kind Grace Fraser and even the cook, Jane Fulton, who had abandoned her to become Mrs. McGowan. She left a small legacy to her second servant, the one whose name she had difficulty remembering, but only if the girl were still in her employment when she died.

She had made the most of what she had been given and she had survived long past many of her contemporaries. She had lived longer than those who had viewed her as a stranger right to the ends of their lives, and she was still regarded as a stranger by those whose births she could remember. Her life had been a lonely one but, as she remembered and placed in writing the record of friendships and family relationships that had survived to this time, she was grateful that all along the solitary pathway of many decades, there had shone little beams of friendly light, never very brightly, but just enough to keep her from losing her way in the darkness.

★

A year after the making of her will, there was an argument in the parish Kirk Session meeting, an argument that leaked out and into the town where it was then continued in discussions on the street. An educational bequest under the church's administrative control had been asked for money to pay fees for poorer children in the town. Although this, in fact, had been part of the designated purpose of the trust at its inception, the money had usually been used instead to provide prizes for scholars who had done well at school, whether they had been poor or not. The session had decided that this practice should be named as the established purpose of the trust fund for, they argued, the money should not be used to fund any children just because they were poor, for the poor children might not do well at school at all. When she heard news of the session's decision on the issue, Miss McGuffie of Barbados Villa summoned her solicitor and altered her will, cancelling the provision in it for the McGuffie Bequests.

Sheriff MacDuff Rhind died only one year after his retirement and, in that same year, word came from Penrith of the death of Dr. John Nicholson. Grace Fraser's mother died. It seemed to Margaret McGuffie that everyone that she had known was dying.

CHAPTER THIRTY-NINE

1891–1896

When she was almost eighty years of age, Margaret McGuffie received a visit from her dear friend and former neighbour, the London lady Mrs Margaret Simson Anderson. If they had passed each other in the street, there would have been no recognition between them but, as they sat together in long conversation, the accumulated years rolled away, they even remembered the kitten that they had shared between them over their mutual garden wall.

Another visitor was a little girl, dressed prettily in a pink-sprigged frock, and led to the door by her mother Mrs Jane Fulton McGowan. The former cook had brought her daughter, little Margaret McGuffie McGowan, to take tea with Miss McGuffie. The little child shyly reached out her hand to receive an offered apple from the old lady who wore a rustling dress and had exceedingly black eyes. She lisped softly, 'Thank you.'

The old lady held onto the fruit, a fierce expression gathering on her face, and corrected the child. 'Say, 'Thank you, Madam.'

The little girl ducked behind her mother's chair and refused to come out. The old lady muttered darkly, 'I'll cut you out of my will.'

★

Lucy Varty died at Stagstones, and Cecelia Wilson wrote from Penrith that Thomas was inconsolable. He was planning to commission a beautiful fountain for the grounds of the castle ruin in the town, and to dedicate it to the memory of his beloved wife.

Nimin Rhind died in Edinburgh while staying with her cousins, and Margaret McGuffie began to feel that a scythe had moved through ripening fields, missing her in its ruthless but strangely erratic sweep. She still breathed on while the young and the beautiful, the deeply loved and the wonderfully lively, were taken. She was old and tired from the burden of too many years, and she would have gone in their place without complaint.

★

One night there was a great storm that blew down mature trees, brought slates crashing off roofs, and smashed ships on rocks. Grace Fraser was wakened during the storm by the terrified screaming of her mistress. The house was undamaged and there seemed to be no rational cause for the hysteria, but the old woman clung to her servant's arm and refused to be left alone until morning light brought calm to the world.

Margaret McGuffie's speech became peculiar. Instead of summoning Grace with the bell, she would roam through the house croaking, 'Is you dere?' She would call out, 'Bring candles, quick, quick!' or accuse, 'You is slow, slow, girl.' Sometimes she called Grace 'Caroline'', and the servant knew no one of that name. In her sleep, the old lady would shout, 'Papa!' Once, as she dozed in a garden chair in the sun, she was heard to whimper, 'Mama.' She went missing, and Grace found her sitting, blankly, on the ground at the foot of the large beech tree in the courtyard by the back door.

She suffered a stroke and, eleven days later, another with right-sided paralysis. She did not speak again, but her yellowed, deep black eyes followed the ever-faithful Grace while she ministered to the old lady's needs for four more days. Margaret McGuffie died in the house that her father had built on 8th July, 1896. She was almost eighty-four years of age.

Her solicitor, in the absence of any close family in the town, registered her death. He was the grandson and the namesake of the kindly John Black, so long revered in Wigtown. Young John Black, coming to the blank space in the form into which should be entered the birth status of the deceased, the space in which was commonly written the carried-for-life brand 'illegitimate', left the space blank. In all other legal documents referring to her existence, Margaret McGuffie had borne the title 'the reputed daughter of John McGuffie'. She had claimed no more than this title throughout her whole life. By this last, best, act of kindness, one never granted before to her by anyone else, Margaret McGuffie was allowed to rest in her death beside her father, her name, as his daughter, carved on the same granite obelisk that marked the grave of the respectable John McGuffie, Provost of Wigtown.

★

In the year that Margaret McGuffie died, the people of Britain were absorbed in their reading of newspaper reports about a terrible massacre of British men in the depths of savage Africa. In retaliation for the killings, British troops blasted and burned the city of the Benin kingdom, killing its people and expelling its king, the Oba, forever, from his ancient kingdom.

CHAPTER FORTY

1896–1897

A talented new solicitor, a Stranraer man, brought his large family with him to take up the practice of his profession in the county town of Wigtown. The family wished to purchase a house suitable for people of quality, and they took up residence temporarily in Bladnoch village while they waited for such a house to become available. When news of the death of Miss McGuffie was whispered through the town, the solicitor moved quickly to secure for himself the property already admired by himself and his wife. Within months the family were in possession of Barbados Villa.

'Much more the thing,' said local admirers of the bright new presence established in the house that had for so long seemed a gloomy place.

'Proper types for a house like that,' was the satisfied local opinion.

The new owners changed the name of the villa immediately to the name of a Scottish village, a village that looked out over the Irish Sea and had a ruined castle beside it. No one spoke much about the colonial origins of the house anymore. When they did, they argued over whether the builder had made his money from slaves, or tea, or even maybe from sugar plantations. 'Everyone made their money from sugar in those days,' said knowing voices.

The old black lady who had lived there was quickly forgotten in the dawning of a new century, the ultimate century of a millennium, perhaps the dawning of a new age. The people who had known Margaret McGuffie were mostly dead. Even their children were dead before very long. In much less than the new century's passing, no one remembered anyone who had spoken to anyone who had ever seen her. Nearly one hundred years after her death, one Wigtown lady vaguely recalled that her aunt, an aunt named Peggy, whose formal names had been Margaret McGuffie, had been taken to see a gruff old lady in the big house when she had been a very small child. Aunt Peggy said that she had been a dark lady.

Another old man of the town, a man whose family had for generations lived in Bladnoch village, remembered to tell someone, just before he died, that as a child he had been threatened, 'If you are a bad boy, the black lady will get you!'

AFTERWORD

FACT OR FICTION?

Although the opinions, motives and emotions of the characters of The House
That Sugar Built are largely a work of fiction, very many of the details of this
book are based on fact. For the curious, who might wish to investigate the
historical background, or the lives of individual people described within it, I
append the following points based on facts recovered from geographical and
historical study, memoirs of contemporaries, descriptions by descendants,
newspaper reports, and personal observation:

AFRICA
Chapters 1–3:
The general description of the slave trade from Western Africa to the Caribbean;
the Oba of Benin; the unexplained apparently Christian shrines found in Benin;
the compulsory deaths of twin children and banishment of their mothers by some
tribal groups; the responsibility of African grandmothers to pass on tribal lore to
children of the family

BARBADOS
Chapter 4:
The development of Maxwell's new town of Port William in Mochrum parish,
Wigtownshire, and Maxwell connection with the West Indies

Chapter 5:
The baobab tree in Bridgetown

Chapter 6:
Nelson's visit to Bridgetown during the threat of a Caribbean invasion by
Napoleon; Nelson's memorial service; the birth of Caroline Stenhouse

Chapter 7:
The place called Maxwell coast in Barbados

Chapter 8:
George Whitfield, successful dry goods merchant, and Scottish coach painter John
McAra

Chapter 9:
John McGuffie, Mochrum born, saddler by trade, eventually proprietor of dry goods business in Egginton Green, Bridgetown; Nelson's statue and Trafalgar Square; the birth of Margaret McGuffie

Chapter 10:
The birth of James Stenhouse, later James McGuffie; concern expressed publicly about the implications of the emancipation of slaves; war with America

Chapter 11:
Waterloo and the pact to outlaw slave trading; rumours of slave registration in Barbados and the subsequent revolt (Bussa's rebellion) as described

Chapter 12:
The reputation of Rev. Mark Nicholson, Principal of Codrington College and details as recorded of his family; son, John Nicholson, born in Barbados in 1808 (buried in Penrith); the avenue of palms and the silk cotton tree in the grounds of Codrington

Chapter 13:
Samuel Hall Lord's famous castellated plantation house at Long Bay and the house's popular designation as 'Sam Lord's castle'; the admired house of Highgate in Bridgetown; burgh reform movement in Britain; Princes Dock, Liverpool; the emigration of Julius Brutus Booth to America; the murder of Reynold Alleyne Elcock; the marriage between George Whitfield and Miss Jessie Duguid

Chapter 14:
Bridgetown's parish church made a cathedral; the restoration of St. Ann's Garrison; baby Whitfield born; John McAra's explosion and fire; changes in attitude toward the moral base for slavery; the purchase of land at Egginton's Green for public buildings; John McGuffie's return to Liverpool and assigning of authority in business matters to George Whitfield and John McAra

Chapter 15:
The hurricane with its details: 1,700 dead in one day; the official proclamations

Chapter 16:
George Whitfield's care of his young apprentices; news events as listed

Chapter 17:
The devastation of Barbados and its eventual rebuilding

Chapter 18:
James Stenhouse as clerk; Jessie Duguid Whitfield's death en route for Liverpool

Chapter 19:
The building of Barbados Villa; the Galloway hurricane and its destruction; details of John Simson's house and of the McGuffie family

Chapter 21:
The Varty and Wilson coach building business in Lime Street, Liverpool; family details and connections with Penrith; artistry of Thomas Varty and Cecelia Wilson; everything about Thomas Wilkinson

Chapter 22:
The formation of and agitation by unions with the subsequent forced Australian passages; new poor laws with unprecedented pressure on provision for the needy; destruction of Houses of Parliament by fire; award of commission for rebuilding to Charles Barry and Augustus Pugin; emancipation of the slaves in the British Empire; details of the Varty family history in Penrith

Chapter 23:
Description of Barbados Villa

Chapter 24:
Provost McHaffie's work to improve the appearance of Wigtown's square; details of the character and reputation of John and Susan Black; the story of the Wigtown martyrs, its known witnesses, and the description of graves in the old churchyard

Chapter 25:
Personal details in the lives of the McGuffie and Simson families; 'fortunes' made by the Varty and Wilson families because of Lime Street Station; the Gothic revival in architecture led by Augustus Pugin

Chapter 26:
Accession to the throne by Queen Victoria; death of James Simson and McGuffie family events

Chapter 27:
Galloway hurricanes; residence of James Caird at Baldoon; his sugar beet interests, friendship with John McGuffie, and the presence of his sister with him; his

marriage to Miss Henryson; McGuffie family events; the spinsters' tea party in Wigtown in celebration of the royal marriage

Chapter 28:
Historical events as listed, especially the Great Disruption within the Church of Scotland and its impact on the nation; establishment of the Wigtownshire Free Press and the articles printed in it; the African's performance in Wigtown and the critique as described; the development of rivalry between the two Wigtown ships; the race to Wigtown from Liverpool; McMaster's campaign against school competition and the subsequent disputes; Mr. Cowper's charge against Provost McHaffie; London's construction of Trafalgar Square with its Nelson's Column

Chapter 29:
McGuffie family details; the marriage of James Stenhouse in the name of McGuffie in Bridgetown's cathedral; incident with Mr. Husband regarding the tormenting of the parish schoolmaster; changes in Wigtown; potato famine and Irish immigration, with the subsequent difficulties; cholera; the Wigtown Regatta

Chapter 30:
Personal details of the McGuffie and Wilson families; the description of exhibits in the Empire Exhibition at the Crystal Palace in 1851; absence of Margaret McGuffie from Barbados Villa during 1851 census

Chapter 31:
The marriages of the Simson daughters; Queen Victoria's visit to Liverpool; deaths of Wellington and Pugin; deaths of James Stenhouse McGuffie in Barbados and John Black in India

Chapter 32:
Cholera in Barbados; death of John Black in Wigtown and the cancellation of the court; death of the child of Margaret Simson Anderson; John McGuffie's will and its details; removal to Runcorn by John and Mary Fraser; abandonment of family business by young John McGuffie and departure to New Zealand; John McGuffie of Barbados Villa named Wigtown's provost after the death of Provost McHaffie; council disputes; creation of the Windy Hill Monument and the building of the new parish church

Chapter 33:
Religious revival in Wigtown as described an its effect on the town

Chapter 34:

Widely-observed celebrations in honour of the Tercentenary of the Reformation; publication of Napier's book mocking the story of the Wigtown martyrs, and the local response as recorded in newpapers and books; the death of Provost John McGuffie in Liverpool, return of his body on 'Countess of Galloway' steamer and burial in Mochrum parish churchyard; support in Liverpool for the Confederacy in America during the Civil War; the deletion of sympathies in the Town Council record book; the death of Prince Albert and national mourning

Chapter 35:
The inheritance, the will having been changed as described; new county buildings in Wigtown; the railway opened at Newton Stewart; Barbados Villa offered for let; the death of Abraham Lincoln; the death of Rev. Peter Young, sixty-five years parish minister; windows installed in the new church in his honour; the death of Mary McGuffie Fraser in Runcorn

Chapter 36:
Thomas Varty's enlargement of Stagstones; the Penrith explosion; John Nicholson of Barbados at Penrith; marriage of his daughter Lucy to Thomas Varty; David Rhind as architect of public buildings in Kirkcudbright and Dumfries; details of his works; his residence at Machermore and his daughter's friendship with Margaret McGuffie

Chapter 37:
Coach crashes as detailed (except for the fictional involvement of the characters of the novel); suit for breach of promise brought against Rev. Cullen; marriage of Rev. Cullen to widow Annie Tait Henry Cullen

Chapter 38:
The saga of the crows; the coming of the railway to Wigtown; the buildng of the new house beside Barbados Villa; the raising of the height of the back garden wall; personal details in the lives of the servants, friends, neighbours and relatives of Margaret McGuffie; the details of her will and the intention to form McGuffie Bequests; the Ross Bequest argument; the deletion of the McGuffie Bequests from the will

Chapter 39:
The visit of the child; the storm; the deaths of Lucy Varty and Nimin Rhind; Margaret McGuffie's stroke and her death; the kindness of young John Black, Solicitor

Chapter 40:

The sale of the house; the change of its name; the stories that developed; the forgetting, almost entirely, of Margaret McGuffie

A final curious fact: In Barbados, if you wish to describe a man who is rich, who puts on an impressive show and who is, perhaps, not quite straight, you can do so by saying, 'He's a Big McGuffie!' No one seems to know why or when the expression originated. There are no McGuffies in Barbados.

ACKNOWLEDGEMENTS

If it had not been for a comment by the late Miss Hill of Port William, this story might have never come to light. My sincere and grateful thanks are due to her and to all the people who helped and guided me over the years this work took to research. There are too many to mention each one, but there are some whom I must name.

AFRICA AND SLAVERY:
Anthony Adeloye, Librarian at the Nigerian High Commission in London; the late Mrs. Gibson of Minnigaff, formerly of Africa; my friends and true counsellors Fleur Menzies of Kenya and Rosemary Argente of Malawi. Also, Lorna Argente, Michael Curtis and Diana Mavroleon for insights and inspiration they provided, even unwittingly.

BARBADOS:
Mr David Williams of the Lazaretto, Bridgetown, whose patience and guidance in the work of discovering important records and whose advice on the work was deeply appreciated. Also, Gabriella Springer, Mrs Betty Shannon, Professor Henry Fraser, Dr. Anthony Phillips, and Mr Ronnie Hughes.

LIVERPOOL:
Iris, Mount Pleasant, for a clue, and the staff of various libraries and record offices for their help; Liz Howard of Runcorn.

PENRITH:
Dr. Connie Christie who opened the door to many discoveries; the Kitsons of Stagstones; the Grahams of Yanwoth; Eden Graham of Penrith; the Rector and Mr Mounsey at Lazonby; Mrs Corner of Penrith for family knowledge.

WIGTOWN AND AREA:
The Editor of The Wigtownshire Free Press, Mr Andrew Neil and his kindly staff; Mr and Mrs I. Brown of The Galloway Gazette; Mrs Marilyn Neil of Wigtown Library; the staff of Register House, Edinburgh; the people of Wigtown and surrounding area, especially Mr Bobby Thompson, Mrs N. Coid, Mr Peter Makepeace, Mrs Elma Parlane, Mrs J. Simpson, Mr John Stewart, Mrs Kerr of Bank House, Mrs R. Reid, and Rev J.C. Render.

Some who gave valued help and information in the early days of my 'gathering' are now gone, and are missed: Miss Gwyneth Roberts, granddaughter of Mrs Elizabeth McLean; Mrs Jean McGregor; Mrs Winnie Anderson, whose love of

Wigtown was legendary; Mrs Barbara Hunter, whose interest in people was genuine; Mr. James Birchman, without whose work so much detail and so many connections would have been untraceable.

SPECIALIST KNOWLEDGE:
Mr Ian Gow, RCAHMS, Edinburgh (details of the life and work of David Rhind); John Thompson, Jimmy Watson and Kenny McCulloch of Scot Mid carriage works in Edinburgh; the Victoria and Albert Museum, London, for the information gleaned from the Pugin exhibition; Dr Colin Steven, Dr. Grace Steven, and my husband Dr. Forrest Brewster for medical details.

PERSONAL ADVISERS:
My neighbour and friend Mrs I. Millar, a former occupant of the house and my link with its past history – for all her kindness and for being there; Mrs Elizabeth Whitley for encouragement and a particular thought; my friend Mrs Margaret McGuffie for her constant encouragement and interest in the project; Dr Grace Steven for her patient consideration of the earliest forms of the work and her valued advice in all things; Ina Munro for her thoughtful reading of the final text; my friend Sandra McDowall, who carries Wigtown in her heart and provides sustaining moral support; my husband and family who have been neglected while I walked, searched, thought and wrote, and who always seem to be forgiving.

Sincere thanks, with hearty applause, must be given to Jayne Baldwin of Second Sands for her vision and steady work in production of this edition. I am very grateful to her. Thanks also is due to Gillian Carruthers of Dark Skys Pages for her careful work with the text and format for this publication.

There is a deep sense of gratitude to Graham and Fay Cowan for their continued inspiration and dedication to a task only they could have performed as brilliantly as they did.

AND FINALLY …
I remember with respect and affection the late Jackie Weinberg of Africa and Northumberland, a man greatly loved by all privileged to know him. In one sentence, Jackie showed me that, though I would have never believed it, I had a racist heart. He died tragically before I could tell him how his words had changed me. The sentence was, 'You see, Donna, to you I am one of them, but to them I am one of you.'